Jude gazed at Leah, his throat tight with emotion. "I'm sorry about all of this, sweetheart. I had no idea the girls were treating you so badly."

Leah's shrug was lopsided. "I should've spoken up sooner. I just didn't know how."

Jude nodded. "I know the feeling. I don't know how any of this blew up in our faces—and I don't know how we're going to patch our family back together now that Adeline and Alice have ripped such a hole in it."

Leah smiled. She already looked weary, and she still had to get through a tough day with the kids. "We'll have to trust that God knows the answers, and have the patience to recognize them—to grab on to them—when He brings us the help we need."

How could she speak with such simple confidence, after the way his girls had scorned her? Jude grasped her hand and kissed it. "You're right, Leah. Let's hope God provides some *gut* ideas sooner rather than later," he murmured. "*Denki* for your faith, and for sticking with me. I love you."

Don't miss any of Charlotte Hubbard's Amish romances:

Seasons of the Heart series

Summer of Secrets
Autumn Winds
Winter of Wishes
An Amish Country Christmas
Breath of Spring
Harvest of Blessings
The Christmas Cradle
An Amish Christmas Quilt

Promise Lodge series

Promise Lodge
Christmas at Promise Lodge
Weddings at Promise Lodge

Simple Gifts series

A Simple Vow
A Simple Wish

Mother's Day books

A Mother's Love

A Mother's Gift

CHARLOTTE HUBBARD

KENSINGTON BOOKS
http://www.kensingtonbooks.com

KENSINGTON BOOKS are published by

Kensington Publishing Corp.
119 West 40th Street
New York, NY 10018

All Kensington titles, imprints, and distributed lines are available at special quantity discounts for bulk purchases for sales promotion, premiums, fund-raising, educational, or institutional use.

Special book excerpts or customized printings can also be created to fit specific needs. For details, write or phone the office of the Kensington Sales Manager: Kensington Publishing Corp., 119 West 40th Street, New York, NY 10018. Attn. Sales Department. Phone: 1-800-221-2647.

Kensington and the K logo Reg. U.S. Pat. & TM Off.

BOUTIQUE Reg. U.S. Pat. & TM Off.

eISBN-13: 978-1-4967-1219-6
eISBN-10: 1-4967-1219-6
First Kensington Electronic Edition: April 2018

ISBN-13: 978-1-4967-1218-9
ISBN-10: 1-4967-1218-8
First Kensington Trade Paperback Printing: April 2018

10 9 8 7 6 5 4 3 2 1

Printed in the United States of America

In loving memory of Ioma Hubbard,
my wonderful mother-in-law.
We miss you.

Acknowledgments

Heartfelt thanks to Alicia Condon for your editorial in-stinct and insight, which improved this book so much! Many thanks to my agent, Evan Marshall, for your career guidance and friendship! Most of all I thank God for words and ideas I couldn't have come up with on my own.

Train up a child in the way he should go:
and when he is old, he will not depart from it.

—Proverbs 22:6

Chapter 1

As Lenore Otto sat on the bed with Leah, wistfully watching the dusk of late November fill her daughter's room, her heart was torn. The two of them had shared this evening ritual of talking and praying since Lenore's husband, Raymond, had died last year. It had always brought her a comforting sense of peace, along with the certainty that she and her daughter would move forward with the plans God had for them. After all the cleaning they'd done and the preparations they'd made to host Leah's wedding festivities the next day, she was ready to relax—but she needed to speak the words that weighed so heavily on her heart.

Tomorrow, when Leah got married, their lives would follow separate paths. Lenore knew she would be fine remaining on the small farm alone, making and selling her specialty quilts. She supposed some of her qualms about her daughter's marriage plagued every mother. . . .

Lord, I wish I could believe my Leah's reaching toward happiness rather than heartache.

Before God's still, small voice could respond to Lenore, Leah let out an ecstatic sigh. "Oh, Mama, it's a dream come true," she whispered. "Starting tomorrow, when I marry Jude, my life will finally be the way I've always wanted it. My waiting is over!"

Not for the first time, Lenore sighed inwardly at her daughter's fantasy. As she returned Leah's hug, savoring these precious moments in the room where her little girl had matured into a woman of twenty-eight, she didn't have it in her to shatter Leah's dreams. No mother wanted her daughter to forever remain a *maidel,* yet during these final hours before the wedding, Lenore thought she should try once again to point out the realities of marrying Jude Shetler. Jude was a fine, upstanding man any parent would be pleased to welcome as a son-in-law, but as a widower he carried a certain amount of . . . baggage.

"Leah, your life will change in ways you can't anticipate when you marry," Lenore began softly. She rested her head against the headboard, grasping her daughter's hand. "When you move into a man's home—"

"Oh, Mama, you've already told me what to expect in the bedroom," Leah interrupted with a nervous giggle. "It's not as though I haven't seen the cows and the horses mating."

Lenore closed her eyes, praying for words that would gently pierce the balloon of maidenly naïveté in which Leah seemed to live. "There's more to marriage than mating," she whispered earnestly. "You'll be moving into a home where Jude and his kids have established their routine. We've both heard the rumors about how Alice and Adeline might be behaving inappropriately during their *rumspringa*—"

"They're sixteen, and they're very pretty," Leah quickly pointed out. "Twins are inclined to get into double trouble as part of their nature at that age. *I* certainly found mischief during my running-around years."

Lenore sighed again. She wished Raymond were here to help her with this difficult discussion. "Sweetheart, I doubt you were ever out of your *dat*'s or my sight for more than an hour at a time. The pranks you used to pull at sale barns when you were helping Dat with the livestock were nothing compared to the way I've heard the Shetler twins run the roads with English boys in their cars."

"I rode in a few cars—and pickups—you didn't know about," Leah shot back. "It's not as though I spent my time hanging around with *girls* at the auction barns, you know."

Squeezing Leah's fingers so she'd focus on the matters at hand, Lenore held her daughter's gaze in the dimness. "I probably should've insisted that you learn to cook and sew and keep house instead of tending the animals with your *dat*," she said with a sigh. "But you were a tremendous help to him—and you were the only child God blessed us with. More than anything, I've wanted you to spend your life doing what makes you happy."

"And I *am* happy, Mama!" Leah said blissfully. "I make a *gut* income selling my dressed chickens and ducks, my goat's milk, and raising crossbred cows—the same way Dat did. If I hadn't spent so much time in the sale barns around Jude, he would never have come to know me—or love me."

Lenore paused, searching for another conversational path. She had no doubt that her daughter's love for Jude was sincere, and that Jude loved Leah, too, but it took more than shared affection to make a marriage work and to keep a household running smoothly.

"And Mama, if your quilts don't sell—or if you want to stop working so hard on them," Leah said tenderly, "you know I'll help you out with money so you can stay here at home. I know how much you and Dat have always loved this place."

Tears sprang to Lenore's eyes. Once again, her daughter spoke with utmost sincerity, unaware that Jude might have different ideas about Leah's income—or that he might insist she give up raising and selling her chickens, ducks, and goats. He might also be reluctant for his wife to raise cattle, which required so much time and energy, even if he admired Leah's way with those animals.

"*Denki* for thinking of me, dear, but we're talking about you now," Lenore insisted gently. "I'm concerned because Jude's *mamm*, Margaret, also lives with Jude and the twins—not to mention Stevie, who seems rather immature for five. Margaret will have her way of doing things, because she took charge after Frieda died. And with Stevie still missing his *mamm*, you'll have a lot of little-boy emotions to deal with as you prepare him to start school next year. Most new brides only have a husband to get used to until the babies start coming."

"*Jah*, but with Margaret running the household and tending the three kids—especially Stevie—their routine can remain uninterrupted," Leah pointed out. "That will give Jude and me time to adjust to being husband and wife, and it'll mean that meals are put on the table and the laundry and cleaning will still get done. From what I know of Margaret, she'll have instructed Alice and Adeline about doing their part in the process, too."

From what I know of Margaret, Lenore thought sadly, *she'll be snipping at you every chance she gets, calling you a slacker—or worse—because you're not assuming the traditional role of an Amish wife.*

Lenore stared at the far wall, sensing whatever she said would go unheard. "Just be ready for your plans to be changed, Leah," she warned gently. "Spending most of your time with Jude at auctions, or in the barnyard tending your animals, might not work out the way you've imagined. Margaret will be a woman with a plan, too, you know."

Leah rested her head against the wooden headboard, closing her eyes. "I'll cross that bridge when—or if—I get to it, Mama. Tomorrow's my big day, and I know it'll be just perfect because Jude's sharing it with me. The light in his eyes when he looks at me is all I need to see to believe he'll love me forever and ever."

Lenore looked out the window at the half moon, which shone brilliantly in the night sky. *Bless your heart, Leah, I wonder if you still believe the moon's made of green cheese, as Dat and I teased you about when you were a child,* she thought with a sinking heart. *We probably should have done a lot of things differently as we were raising you . . . but it's too late to change your way of looking at the world.*

"I wish you all the best as you start your new life, Leah," she said softly. With a final squeeze to her daughter's hand, Lenore rose from the bed. "You'll always be in my thoughts and prayers—and I'll always love you. *Gut* night and sleep tight."

"You can sleep for me, Mama. I'm too excited to close my eyes."

Lenore paused in the doorway of the unlit room for a last glance at her giddy daughter. *Bless her, Lord, and hold her in Your hand,* she prayed. *At this point, only You can keep Leah's happiness from turning into a disaster.*

Jeremiah Shetler leaned his elbows on his kitchen table, gazing earnestly at his younger brother—who, at thirty-three, was surely old enough to know better about what he was getting into. "Last chance to see reason, Jude," he stated bluntly. "If you go through with this wedding tomorrow, you'll be signing on for a lifetime of sorrow and regret."

Jude's dark eyes flashed with resentment. "Sounds more like my marriage to Frieda—God rest her soul," he added quickly. "Why can't you let me find my happiness with a woman who won't keep secrets? A woman who adores me and makes me laugh?"

"Leah's a nice girl, *jah,*" Jeremiah said with a shake of his head, "but she's clueless about such basic activities as putting a *gut* meal on the table—"

"Why are you telling me this?" Jude demanded.

Jeremiah exhaled forcefully. He'd never understood what

Jude saw in Leah. He could only assume that his widowed brother was so desperate for affection and companionship that he was willing to settle for a woman who'd never progressed beyond being the tomboy daughter of Raymond and Lenore Otto, a girl who hadn't been taught much about a wife's responsibilities.

"Have you ever eaten a meal Leah cooked?" he challenged. "Vernon Gingerich has told me that anytime he's visited the Otto home, Lenore's been bustling around in the kitchen and Leah's been in the front room chatting with him and her *dat*. And at our family dinners these past months, Leah's cleaned up the dishes, but I've not seen any signs that she knows how to operate a stove."

"Lenore does the cooking when Vernon visits because he's her bishop, and she enjoys cooking for a man now that Raymond's gone," Jude explained impatiently. He raked his hand through his disheveled dark waves, glancing downward with an anguished sigh. "Come on, man. You know how it is to lose a wife—and you don't even have kids to look after. Doesn't the loneliness—the need for adult conversation—eat you alive at times?"

Jeremiah looked away, his heart pierced by the blatant reminder of Priscilla's absence. After three years of living without her, he did indeed know how the silence of nights alone clawed at a man's heart like a relentless beast. But he needed to pursue his present purpose before Jude made the biggest mistake of his life. "All right, so think about how Mamm will react to having Leah around," he said, crossing his arms. "She's told me she's not in favor of this marriage, and you know she'll shred Leah like pulled pork when she doesn't assume such wifely duties as sewing clothes for your kids, or cooking, or cleaning, or—"

"I've already told Mamm that she can retain her place as the head of housekeeping—so things will be done the way she wants them," Jude shot back. "It's not as though Leah won't contribute to putting food on the table by raising it, and by—"

"Do you think Mamm's going to stand for that?" Jeremiah challenged in disbelief. "And do you think it's fair to Leah to put her mother-in-law in charge of her new home? *Really?*"

Jude's sigh lingered in the darkening kitchen, but Jeremiah didn't light any lamps. He wanted nothing to distract his brother from giving more logical, realistic answers to such basic questions.

"All right, so Mamm's muttered a few choice words about Leah's tendency toward jobs that men usually do," Jude finally said. "I've known Leah for years—which is more than I could say when I married Frieda—and she's a patient, kind, optimistic sort of woman. Don't you often preach about that passage from Corinthians that says love is patient and kind? Which is, sorry to say, not a fitting description of our mother."

"But Mamm stepped in to help you and your kids after Frieda passed," Jeremiah pointed out. "Think what your life would've been like these past five months without her presence. She's expressed her concern that you've rushed your courtship of Leah—"

Jude chuckled humorlessly. "Mamm told me flat-out that no matter how many years I courted Leah, I couldn't turn a sow's ear into a silk purse," he muttered. "I *know* Leah's more at home in a barn than in a kitchen, but I'm crazy for her, Jeremiah. She gets along with Alice and Adeline, and she understands that Stevie's shy—"

"Your twins concern me even more than Mamm, when it comes to welcoming Leah into your home," Jeremiah said firmly. "If the rumors are true about them chasing after English boys, you and Leah will need to be *very* vigilant about what Adeline and Alice are up to in the name of *rumspringa*."

Jude's lips flickered. "The girls need a woman younger than Mamm to keep track of them—yet another reason Leah's presence will be a blessing," he insisted doggedly. "They miss their mother. They'll be a handful no matter whom I marry."

Jude stood up, appearing older than his age. "I know you have your objections, Jeremiah, but I'm counting on your support, because you're one of the most positive, forward-thinking men I know," he said softly, holding Jeremiah's gaze. "And frankly, love and optimism and—and *laughter*—have been missing from my life for more years than I care to count. Please try to understand that I'm going after some happiness with Leah. Is it a sin to love someone because she makes me happy?"

Jeremiah swallowed hard. His tough talk hadn't changed Jude's opinion of Leah one iota. "As your bishop, I can say I've performed weddings for couples who had less love and laughter in their souls than you and Leah do," he admitted softly. "But as your brother, I wish you'd at least postpone the ceremony—give yourselves more time to decide how you'll handle the issues I've mentioned."

Jude gripped the back of the wooden chair he'd just vacated, gazing intently at Jeremiah in the dimness. "What you and Mamm are really saying is that Leah must change—a *lot*—before you believe she'll make a *gut* wife and stepmother," he said in a voice edged with resentment. "I'll say it again, Jeremiah: I love Leah just the way she is. The traits you and our mother find undesirable—unsuitable—are the things I adore most about her. Leah is a woman of faith who dares to be herself, rather than trying to fit the mold of Old Order expectations."

"And by the same token, it's our communal conformity to Old Order ways that keeps any of us from calling undue attention to ourselves, or earning a reputation for being prideful—not that I believe Leah works with livestock to attract attention or to set herself above anyone else." Sighing, Jeremiah rose and offered Jude his hand. "Nobody wants your marriage to succeed more than I do," he said softly. "I'll see you in Cedar Creek bright and early tomorrow morning."

Jude gripped his fingers. "Mark my words, Jeremiah. This is one of those conversations we'll look back on years from now and chuckle about, after Leah and I are established and deliriously happy," he said with a boyish smile.

"I hope you're right. I'll *pray* you're right," Jeremiah added purposefully.

After his brother had closed the door behind him, the silence of the house weighed heavily on Jeremiah. Once again, he felt acutely aware of Priscilla's absence, just as he knew that tomorrow's wedding would be an occasion for the men in his Morning Star church district to tease him about when *he* planned to court and marry somebody. As the bishop, he was expected to follow the pattern of the families in his congregation—to find another wife and to raise children.

For reasons only God knew, He hadn't granted Jeremiah and Priscilla any kids during their eighteen years of marriage, and Jeremiah secretly wondered if he could find it in his heart to marry a widow who already had a family. He knew of a few Amish women around Morning Star and Cedar Creek who fit that description—as well as a few who'd remained *maidels* because no man had felt compelled to court them. When Jeremiah saw their earnest faces in his mind, he still didn't feel ready to replace his dear Priscilla. Who would ever measure up to the love of his life?

"I'll say this for you, Leah," he murmured, "you have guts enough—faith enough—to take on Jude's three kids, even if I suspect you have no idea what you're getting yourself into."

Jeremiah shook his head when he realized he was talking to himself again. Living alone in so much silence did funny things to a man's mind.

Without lighting a lamp, he made his way upstairs to his bedroom, thinking about what positive points he might make during his sermon before he led Jude and Leah in their vows. He hoped God would whisper encouraging words in his ear— words that would support the newlyweds and persuade folks in the congregation to believe the best about them.

I'm asking for a lot, Lord, Jeremiah thought as he climbed into bed. *But I believe You have a plan and You're working it out even as we humans doubt You.*

Chapter 2

After Bishop Vernon preached the wedding sermon, Leah rose from the front pew bench on the women's side, praying she wouldn't trip over her stiff high-top bridal shoes as she joined Jude in front of Bishop Jeremiah. Beneath the calf-length teal dress and white apron Mama had sewn for her wedding day, Leah's legs were shaking and her mouth felt so dry, she wasn't sure she'd be able to repeat her vows. She knew every person who sat in the front room of her lifelong home, which had been enlarged by removing a couple of interior partitions, yet being the center of their attention made her feel so nervous that she might as well have been naked. More than once during the church service that had preceded the wedding, Leah had realized that showing contrary livestock in a crowded auction barn was much easier than standing before these family members and friends to make the biggest promise of her lifetime—second only to the vow she'd made to God when she'd joined the Old Order Amish church.

Yet when Jude smiled at her, Leah forgot to be afraid.

He'd trimmed the black beard that framed his handsome face, and he'd gotten his hair cut, too. Beneath his dark brows, his warm brown eyes sparkled as she slipped her hand into the crook of his elbow. Leah felt his strength seeping into her as she held his muscled arm, and she suddenly believed she could fly to the moon if it were required—and if Jude flew with her. Leah realized then that her thoughts were wandering and that folks would be laughing at her behind their hands if she didn't focus on the words Bishop Jeremiah was saying.

"Jude and Leah, your time of courtship and exploring each other's personalities and intentions has led you to this moment of truth—this sacrament from which there will be no retraction or retreat, once you've taken your marriage vows," the bishop intoned gently. His dark eyes, very similar to Jude's but set in a slightly older face, held each of their gazes. "You have completed your time of premarital instruction, and it behooves me to ask you one final time if you're certain you wish to move forward into this marriage. If so, say 'I am.' "

Leah swallowed hard. Was Jude's brother giving them one last chance to back out of a marriage about which he and some other folks had expressed doubts? Or did every bishop ask this question before beginning the ceremony, and she hadn't noticed it at the weddings she'd attended?

Answer the question—before Jude thinks you don't love him!

"I—I am," Leah stammered at the same moment Jude replied.

"I most certainly am," he said firmly. Jude smiled at Leah again, and her heart fluttered with nervous joy.

Bishop Jeremiah nodded before gazing at the men seated at his left and then at the women who sat facing them. "If anyone here knows of any reason why this man and this woman should not be united in holy matrimony, speak now or forever hold your peace," he said in his sonorous voice.

Leah felt her pulse pound in her ears four times as she waited for someone—Mama maybe, or Margaret—to protest their union. On the front bench, her side-sitters, Adeline and Alice, looked around as though to spot any potential naysayers. Leah wished the twins would meet her gaze and smile—or at least look at their *dat*—but they seemed more interested in peering at the young men on the other side of the room.

"Hearing no response," the bishop continued smoothly, "I will remind you all that once Jude and Leah marry, you'll have no reason—no right—to speak ill of their marriage or to question the strength of the bond that binds them as husband and wife, because their union will have been sanctified by God Himself. What God is joining, let no man—or woman—put asunder."

The room got so quiet, Leah wondered if every person present could hear her thundering heartbeat. Overwhelmed by the solemnity of the moment and the way the bishop seemed to be pointing up the potential for their marriage to fail, she focused intently on Jeremiah as she carefully repeated the vows he led her in. She would not cave in to the doubts of those around her—

But maybe they know better than you do. Why on earth would a wonderful, handsome man like Jude choose you when he could have any woman he wanted for a wife?

"—till death do us part," Leah repeated loudly, before her twinge of doubt could spoil all her hopes and dreams.

Jude placed his hand over hers, to reassure her—or perhaps because she was squeezing his arm too tightly.

Leah relaxed her grip and sucked in air to keep from passing out. She had said her vows, and somehow she hadn't messed up the words and made a total fool of herself. Or at least she didn't think she'd misspoken—her thoughts were spinning so tightly, she could only trust the encouraging nods from the congregation that showed no sign she'd made a mistake.

As Jude repeated the same words after Bishop Jeremiah, she marveled at his confidence. His resonant baritone voice filled the room with each age-old phrase, leaving no doubt about his sincerity or his deep, unshakable love for her. By the time he'd completed his part of the ceremony, Leah felt amazed—overwhelmingly gratified—that such a steadfast man was promising to love and cherish her forever. She'd adored Jude since her early teen years, but as Bishop Jeremiah pronounced them husband and wife, Leah thrummed with so much joy that for the first time in her life she felt utterly, stunningly *beautiful.*

"I love you so much, Leah," Jude whispered. "December first will forever be my favorite day of the year." He lifted her chin and then held her close, pressing his warm lips into hers.

Leah wanted to savor their first kiss as a married couple— the first time Jude had kissed her in public—yet she was acutely aware that several people were watching them. When she broke away sooner than she wanted to, the question in Jude's eyes stabbed at her heart. *Not married even a minute, and already you've disappointed him—*

"I—I love you, too, Jude," Leah murmured, putting on a tremulous smile. "Just nervous, with all these people watching."

"I present to you Mr. and Mrs. Judah Shetler!" Bishop Jeremiah announced grandly. He began to clap, and soon the room was filled with applause. When Leah turned with Jude to face the crowd, she was glad her new husband had his arm around her to support her. Her legs still felt as wobbly as a newborn calf's, and the speculative expressions she noted on some of the ladies' faces gave her pause.

Do they really believe I'm the wrong woman for Jude? Do they think I'm the wrong woman for any man?

Leah was grateful for the business of signing the marriage certificate, and for the congratulatory remarks her Cedar Creek neighbors were calling out to her and Jude. After she'd stepped over to the oak sideboard to write her name, she handed the pen to Jude, who signed with a flourish.

"Next!" Jude said as he gave the pen to one of his daughters—Leah wasn't sure which one, because the twins appeared identical from the top of their fresh white *kapps* to their dark aqua cape dresses and white aprons to their black church shoes.

"*Denki* for being my side-sitters today," Leah said as the two sisters signed. "It means a lot to have you girls stand with me as family—"

"*Jah*, sure thing," one of the twins said with a shrug.

"Whatever," the other girl remarked in an identical off-hand tone. The two of them quickly disappeared into the crowd of chatting guests.

Jude shook his head as he handed the pen to Gabe Flaud, a longtime friend who'd stood up with him. "I'm so glad my girls have a new *mamm*," he said with a big smile for Leah. "This couldn't-care-less phase they're going through is testing my patience."

Gabe chuckled. "I've got teenage sisters who have the same attitude at times," he said. "My mother's remedy for that is giving them more barn chores until they beg her to just do housework again."

Leah laughed along with the men, unable to imagine Alice and Adeline going to the barn unless they were hitching a horse to their buggy to leave Jude's farm for a while. She would need to establish a way to handle the twins' aloofness, but she was determined to enjoy her wedding day—which seemed to be speeding by—rather than fretting over teenage behavior while her family and friends were gathered to help her celebrate. Her mother's bright smile raised her spirits immediately.

"Oh, Leah, I'm so happy for you and Jude," Mama said as she wrapped her arms around both of them. "I wish you health and happiness and all of God's blessings as you begin your life together."

"Hear, hear," a man behind them said. When Leah turned toward his rich, low voice, she was enfolded in Bishop Vernon Gingerich's embrace as he heartily shook hands with Jude. Vernon was well acquainted with Jude because he often bought Black Angus heifers and calves at area auctions. "It's a particular pleasure to see you two become a couple," he said, his blue eyes twinkling as he smiled at both of them. "I know Raymond's smiling down from heaven because two like-minded souls he always loved have now become one."

The mention of her *dat*'s name made tears spring to Leah's eyes because he hadn't lived long enough to see her married. She saw Mama's smile falter as well—but only for a moment.

"Raymond always admired Jude's ability to coax higher prices from the crowds at livestock auctions, and to sell a lot of animals in a short time," Mama put in with a nod.

Jude chuckled. "He thought I was a fast talker, eh?" he teased, winking at Leah.

Bishop Vernon laughed. "You're the finest auctioneer in these parts, Jude. I have no idea how you can chant so fast— and for as many hours as a sale requires—but I suspect some folks in my congregation wish I could speak that quickly, to shorten my sermons."

As the folks around them laughed at Bishop Vernon's joke, Leah's heart lightened. She gazed at Jude, and it finally hit her that the hopes and dreams of most of her lifetime had come true on this much-anticipated day.

"This is the day which the Lord hath made. We will rejoice and be glad in it!"

Leah smiled. Bishop Vernon often began his preaching by exclaiming that verse from Psalm 118, and it inspired her to rise above the doubts that had been niggling at her like naughty little girls gossiping during church. She had married Jude because she believed in him, after all. Leah had utmost faith in his ability to provide for her and to weave the separate members of his household into a tightly bound family as warm and secure as one of Mama's beautiful quilts, or one of the rag rugs Margaret had made for the Shetler home.

She saw her mother-in-law step away from the friends who'd clustered around her at the end of the wedding. Margaret Shetler stood taller than most women, and because her face rarely showed emotion, she was a hard person to read— a bit intimidating and stern, no matter what the occasion, it seemed to Leah. But Leah smiled at her as she approached, wiggling her fingers at Stevie, who was clutching his *mammi*'s hand as he shuffled along beside her, sucking his thumb. The little boy appeared so overwhelmed by the crowd and the day's activities, Leah couldn't help feeling sorry for him.

"Stevie, you were so well behaved during the long service and the wedding this morning," Leah said as she leaned down to smooth his glossy brown hair. "I'm proud of you."

Stevie flinched and immediately pressed his face into his *dat*'s trousers.

Jude lifted him to one shoulder, hugging him. "You were as quiet as a mouse," he agreed, smiling at his son. "Your new *mamm* loves you, Stevie. There's no need to be afraid of her."

When the boy buried his face in Jude's black vest and white shirt collar, Margaret's eyebrow arched. "We have a ways to go before he can believe that," she stated. She gazed intently at Leah, as though seeing all the way into her heart and finding it lacking. "After I take the twins and Stevie to spend a few days at Jeremiah's while you newlyweds settle in, they'll return home, but I've decided to take up residence in Jeremiah's *dawdi haus* again. I don't want to be the intruding mother-in-law, you see."

Leah forgot how to breathe. Panic immobilized her as she recalled her assumptions that Margaret would handle the cooking and the housekeeping and—

"You're welcome to stay with us, Mamm," Jude insisted above the rush of Leah's desperate thoughts. "You've been a lifeline in our time of need, and I couldn't have kept body and soul together after Frieda's death, had you not stepped in."

"Let me know if I can be of assistance, but I'll go back to living with your lonely brother," Margaret replied without missing a beat. Her smile had a sarcastic edge to it. "Too many *cooks* spoil the broth."

"And every blended family deserves a chance to find its new routines," Mama put in quickly as she tucked her arm around Leah's waist. "I'm only a few miles away, so I can lend a hand, too. But I believe that Jude, Leah, and the girls will find their way together—and they'll help Stevie get past the loss of his mother as well."

Leah silently blessed her mother for supporting her, but Margaret's sarcastic tone had stung anyway. *Too many cooks . . . could she have said anything more cruel?*

"With help from God and our families, we'll make our way forward." Jude set his son on the floor again and reached for Leah's hand. "Right now, I'd like to greet the folks who've come a distance to spend our special day with us. Most of the older men are heading to the barn, to stay out of the way of the women and the table setters."

"I need to help the ladies who've agreed to set up for the meal," Mama said with a purposeful look toward Margaret. "And I want to peek into the wedding wagon to see how the food's coming along. Jude, you'll never know how much I appreciate your renting that wagon so we don't have to borrow every plate and cup and spoon for miles around—most of the cooking is being done there, too!"

"Happy to help," Jude replied. "Jeremiah rented a wedding wagon as his gift to us when Frieda and I married, and it was a godsend. Right, Mamm?"

"It seemed too progressive—felt like the lazy way out—to a traditional Amish *mamm,*" Margaret replied with a tight smile. "But it really did save us and our neighbors a lot of time and effort."

Leah reveled in the feel of Jude's large hand enfolding hers as he led her through the kitchen toward the mudroom door to fetch their coats. The younger men were carrying the pew benches out to the bench wagon to make room for the wedding meal's tables and chairs, and the older fellows were migrating toward the barn, where lawn chairs and card tables were set up on the freshly swept floor. As Leah slipped into her winter coat, she joined Jude in thanking their helpers, nodding as he introduced her to a few aunts who'd come from eastern Missouri. When they finally stepped outside, Leah breathed a lot easier.

"We couldn't have picked a nicer day," she remarked as she followed Jude around to the side of the house—instead of toward the wedding wagon, where she'd intended to go. "For December, it's very warm and—"

"And I couldn't have picked a more beautiful, loving bride," Jude interrupted before he pressed her against the wooden wall. "Kiss me for real this time, Leah. Nobody can see us now."

Leah's breath left her as Jude kissed her, gently at first and then with increasing fervor. Of their own accord, her arms twined around his neck as he deepened the kiss and left her no doubt as to how much he loved her . . . craved her. Once again, she felt special, beautiful, transported to a fairy-tale place where she could believe that nothing would interfere with the unique, forever love she and Jude already shared.

Jude finally eased away to catch his breath. "Oh, Leah," he whispered near her ear, "I wish all these people were on their way home—and I wish Mamm and the kids were already at Jeremiah's—so we could be alone."

Leah's heart danced. "Don't wish away even a minute of our wedding day, Jude," she admonished him with a chuckle. "We only get one of them."

Jude cupped her face in his hand, gazing at her as though he couldn't stop. "You're a wise woman, Leah. I hope that once you've shared my bed, however, you'll be eager to wish other people would go away, too. I promise you we'll make time to be alone so the kids won't interrupt the special bond we'll share."

She inhaled quickly, overwhelmed by the intensity of her husband's words and the expression on his ruggedly handsome face. Why had she ever allowed her doubts to overshadow his all-encompassing love for her?

"Hey there, you lovebirds!" one of the men called out from the pew wagon. "You two gonna spend the day all by yourselves, or visit with your guests?"

"*Jah,* you'll have plenty of time for that kissy-face stuff tonight!" another fellow teased as he carried another pew bench.

"That would be my younger cousin Harvey and his brother, Pete," Jude explained as he eased away from Leah. He turned to wave his hand high in the air. "You guys are just jealous—and still single!" he added brightly. "If you're lucky, you'll get caught kissing your brides while you still have your teeth. I hope I live long enough to see that day."

Leah laughed as Jude grabbed her hand. Not far from the mudroom and kitchen doors, the wedding wagon appeared as busy as a beehive with neighbors who were carrying out long tables and pulling carts loaded with crates of the dinner plates and utensils that were stored in the wagon's built-in cabinets. Heavenly aromas of chicken, cooked onions, and celery made Leah's stomach rumble, because she'd been too excited to eat more than a piece of toast for breakfast.

"I'd like to say a word to my cooks and helpers," she said, squeezing Jude's hand. "How about if I join you in the barn to meet your far-flung uncles in a few minutes?"

Jude smiled knowingly. "If you find any dinner rolls or slices of pie that're up for grabs, don't forget your hungry husband."

Leah laughed. "I'll see what I can do—and I'll ask if we can eat a little earlier than two o'clock. I'm starved half out of my mind."

"Uh-huh. Welcome to my world, sweet Leah."

Her insides tightened with the realization that food wasn't the only thing Jude was hungry for. Would this giddy sense of anticipation keep her tingling through the coming months and years with her husband? Leah wiggled her fingers at him and turned toward the big, blocky wedding wagon. Enterprising Amish neighbors Elmer and Clara Eicher had built and stocked the huge horse-drawn vehicle to meet a need in the area's Plain communities. Their original wagon was rented out so often, they'd constructed a second one, which Leah was approaching. It featured two large stoves with ovens and a huge commercial refrigerator—along with a generator to run these appliances, and enough tableware and linens to serve a thousand people. The Eichers also provided portable toilets, which sat discreetly beside the barn.

About three hundred folks had joined them for this big day, and they would be eating in shifts because of limited table space in the house, so Leah and her mother had been immensely relieved when Jude had rented the wedding wagon. Her heart swelled when she saw that Alice and Adeline were pushing and pulling one of the carts, which was piled with white tablecloths. Mama's nearest neighbor, Elva Yoder, was walking alongside the twins, clasping a case of silverware between her sturdy hands.

"Congratulations on getting a new *mamm!*" Elva said to the girls as her face lit up with a smile. "There's nobody nicer than Leah—"

"I only have one mother, and it'll never be Leah," the twin pulling the wagon snapped.

Her sister scowled from the cart's other end. "My mother's rolling in her grave," she said curtly. "Why Dat wants a wife who smells like a goat and has duck poop on her shoes is beyond me."

Leah stopped short, feeling as appalled by the twins' remarks as poor Elva did, judging from her wide-eyed expression. For a moment, Leah wanted to rush up and contradict the girls' assessment of her—or ask Jude to intercede before such sentiments soured the entire day for their guests.

But Leah nipped her lip and decided not to blow this incident out of proportion. It stood to reason that Adeline and Alice would be upset about *any* woman who came into their home as their father's new wife. They would need some time to adjust to such a major change. Once they all had a chance to settle in together, they'd be a *family,* however—bound by the ties God Himself had sanctioned at the wedding. At sixteen, the twins were old enough to understand and accept that.

Leah believed that Jude wouldn't tolerate his daughters' disrespectful attitudes for a minute, and that he'd devise ways to encourage them to behave the way he expected. She also had faith that Stevie would stop crying for his *mamm* once he realized Leah loved him and would be spending her days with him. She knew from watching Stevie at the occasional sales where he accompanied his *dat* that the boy loved animals as much as she did. She would encourage him to become her helper as she tended the chickens, ducks, goats, and cattle that Jude was going to transport to his place within the next few days.

Setting aside her concerns about Jude's children, Leah stepped into the wedding wagon—but not very far, because the compact, overheated work area was already full of neighbor ladies. "*Denki* so much to all of you for your help on my big day!" Leah called out above their chatter.

"Happy to help!" Jerusalem Gingerich replied with a wave. As Bishop Vernon's second wife, she'd talked to Leah about how her life would be different after she married a man who'd survived a previous mate—with womanly insight Bishops Jeremiah and Vernon didn't have. A mischievous smile lit Jerusalem's face as she snatched a few cookies from a tray another neighbor lady was filling. "If anybody needs a snack, I'm guessing it's the bride. How're you holding up, Leah?"

"Much better now that the ceremony's behind us," Leah admitted as she accepted the cookies. "And *jah,* the toast I had for breakfast is long gone."

"We'll be ready to serve around one-fifteen, I'm guessing," Elva's sister, Bernice, put in. "We made the chicken and stuffing casserole yesterday, and enough of the hot dishes are ready for the first sitting. We're just waiting for the tables to get set up."

"I'll let Jude know," Leah said as she turned toward the door. "We wouldn't want him to be so caught up in gossiping with the men in the barn that he's late to his own wedding dinner."

Laughter followed her out the door of the wedding wagon

as she stepped to the ground with the cookies cradled in her hands. As she crossed to the barn, Leah gave thanks for the bright December sunshine and the way the coppery-brown leaves on the pin oak trees shimmered in the breeze. It struck her then that she was making one of her final trips to the barn she'd known all her life, and that after Jude helped her move her livestock to his place, only Flo, Mama's buggy mare, would remain here.

Was it her imagination, or did the barn need a coat of paint and perhaps a new roof? Most days Leah didn't pay much attention to the buildings, but in the midday sun on her last day at the Otto farm, she became aware that Mama might be facing some extensive maintenance in the near future—repairs Leah should've seen to after Dat had passed away.

No time like the present, while you've got a bunch of men in the barn.

When Leah stepped through the open barn door, the conversation stopped. Probably a dozen older men, including Bishop Vernon, sat companionably around a portable wood-burning fire pit as Jude circulated among them. Her new husband smiled brightly at her. "Do I see cookies, Leah?" he teased as he started toward her.

"*Jah*—and I'll share them," she added quickly, her gaze taking in the men, "but I've just noticed some work that'll need doing on this barn. I'm hoping you fellows can help Mama out with whatever painting and roofing you think needs—"

"Day late and a dollar short!" cried one of the guests she didn't know.

"*Jah*, you've gotta be faster to ask for help," the man beside him chimed in.

Leah blinked. Why were all these men gazing at her as though she were the punch line of a joke she'd missed out on? Four or five of them didn't live near Morning Star, but surely the local men wouldn't refuse to at least *look* at the barn—and even if they weren't able to do the work themselves, they could recommend someone.

"But—but I'd be happy to pay," Leah stammered, wondering why so many little thorns seemed to be popping up on her wedding day. To make matters worse, Jude was chuckling as he reached her side and plucked a peanut butter cookie from her hands.

Bishop Vernon rose from his chair, his blue eyes twinkling. "What they mean to say, dear Leah, is that your husband asked us, not two minutes ago, about making the repairs you've just mentioned—as well as a few others around the place," he said kindly. "We've got you and Lenore covered. A crew of us will be here on Saturday morning."

Leah's mouth dropped open. "I—well, *denki*," she mumbled. "I had no idea—"

"*Jah,* that Jude, he's full of surprises," teased the first man who'd spoken. "I'm his uncle, Tobias Shetler, from Bowling Green, by the way. We met earlier this morning, but you were looking a little distracted by new-bride anxiety."

"And I'm Tobias's older brother, Nate," the man beside him said with a little wave. "As time goes by, you'll see that Jude's usually one step ahead of everyone else, when it comes to getting things done. Maybe that's why he can talk so fast and fancy at his auctions."

Good-natured laughter filled the cleared area of the barn. When Leah gazed into Jude's sparkling dark eyes, she fell in love with him all over again. She brushed a cookie crumb from his ebony beard, aware of the little spark she ignited when she touched him. "You're a blessing, Jude," she said softly. "Just for you, I got our dinner moved up to one-fifteen."

"You're a miracle worker, Leah, and I'll love you forever," he said, bussing her temple with a loud kiss.

"Hey, save that for later!" one of the men called out.

"*Jah*, get a room, why don't you?" another one teased.

Leah laughed, greeting each of the men in Jude's family

who'd come from a distance. It was so easy to share in their banter, even if she suspected she would confuse Tobias with his twin brother, Thomas, and forget the other men's names minutes after Jude finished introducing them.

The remainder of the day floated by in a haze of happiness. Leah felt like a queen as she sat on the *eck*—a raised dais in the corner of the front room, where the wedding party ate. Happy faces filled the house as folks feasted on a traditional "roast" casserole made of chicken and stuffing, creamed celery, mashed potatoes, glazed carrots, and an assortment of pies the local ladies had provided. Although Alice and Adeline excused themselves after they finished eating, Leah and Jude remained at the table with Gabe to chat with folks who came to express their congratulations. After the first shift's dishes were cleared and the tables had been reset, they enjoyed the company of the second shift of guests as well.

Later in the afternoon, as she and Jude cut their tiered white wedding cake, the applause and congratulatory remarks again made her feel like a very special woman. It was nearly five o'clock before the out-of-town guests said their good-byes and started for the homes where they were lodging. Margaret made her way to the *eck* as well, gripping Stevie's hand as he walked in her shadow.

"Our suitcases are packed and waiting in the buggy, so we'll be on our way to Jeremiah's," she said crisply. "I'll clear the rest of my clothes from the closet when I bring the kids back on Monday morning."

Leah's heart lurched again at the thought of having to manage the household, but she kept a smile on her face. "You're welcome to stay as long as you want," she said, echoing Jude's earlier sentiments.

"I'm sure you'd like that," Margaret said tersely. "But sooner or later we all must grow up and accept responsibility."

Jude's brow furrowed. "Mamm, you've got no call to speak to Leah as though she's shirked her duties or—"

"May God's blessings fill your life, son. You'll need all of them you can get." With that, Margaret turned and started for the door with Stevie in tow.

Before Leah could respond, Jude hugged her close. "Never mind what she's said," he whispered, kissing her cheek. "If she's going to be so cranky, it's best that she'll be living at Jeremiah's, anyway. I'm going to suggest to him that Mamm needs a medical checkup, to see if there's a physical imbalance causing her to behave this way. It's nothing *you've* done, Leah, so don't go blaming yourself."

As she gazed into her husband's eyes, Leah chose to believe he was right. It would certainly be more peaceful in her new home if she and Margaret weren't constantly at odds—and if her efforts at becoming a cook and a housekeeper wouldn't be found lacking day in and day out. "It'll be nice to have the house to ourselves for these next few days," she whispered.

"It'll be sheer heaven," Jude promised with a smile.

Chapter 3

For Leah, her wedding night alone with Jude surpassed all the birthdays and other highlights of her lifetime rolled together. For the first time ever, a man was focused solely on her, and on pleasing her in ways she'd never dared to dream about. Mama had left casseroles and other food in the refrigerator, along with a pie, so she didn't have to cook—and even though she and Jude spent Friday helping her mother clean up after the wedding, it was work that soothed her soul. The three of them washed and put away the tables, and stacked the cartons of clean plates and other tableware carefully in the wedding wagon's storage compartments.

While Leah and her mother washed and hung the long white tablecloths, Jude began transporting the ducks and chickens to the large pens he'd built on his farm behind an outbuilding he'd emptied for her use.

"Jude's a happy man," Mama remarked with a lift of her eyebrow. "And how are you doing, Leah?"

Leah felt herself aglow with the smile on her face. "He's such a wonderful husband, so kind and caring," she gushed. "It feels a little odd to share a bed with someone—and to have to think about where the towels, the paper goods, and the dishes are kept in his house. But that would be true no matter whom I'd married."

"Every bride goes through that adjustment when she moves

to a different home—especially if another wife lived there first," Mama agreed as she tossed the end of a damp white tablecloth to Leah.

They folded the long piece of fabric in half lengthwise, draped it over the clothesline with wooden clothespins, and quickly cranked the pulley handle before the fabric could drag on the ground. Each time they shifted a tablecloth away from the porch post where the clothesline was bolted, it went toward the other end of the line, attached to the barn— which placed empty clothesline in front of them for the next tablecloth. On such a cool, breezy day the laundry made a sound like flapping wings.

"I hope you two will discuss the adjustment that'll come on Monday morning when Stevie and the twins return," Mama said softly. "Sorry to say it, but when I overheard some of the unkind remarks Margaret was making, I was just as glad she plans to live with Bishop Jeremiah again."

Leah sighed. She and Jude had been so immersed in each other, they'd barely mentioned his kids—and the topics they had discussed seemed far too intimate to share with her mother. "I keep believing it'll all work out, Mama," she insisted. "God understands my weaknesses, and He'll provide me the words and the ideas for bringing the five of us together as a family. Jude has already shown me how to make coffee and scramble eggs."

Mama pressed her lips together as if to challenge Leah's thoughts, but she kept her doubts to herself.

The three of them enjoyed some wedding leftovers for lunch before Jude transported Leah's goats to their new home. Leah smiled at the way Jude and Mama teased each other at the table, and she was grateful that her mother packaged the rest of the chicken and dressing "roast" and the remainder of the wedding cake for them to take home as well. "I'll never eat all that food by myself," Mama remarked wistfully.

Leah felt a pang of remorse that her mother would be living alone, yet she knew Mama would devote herself to making even more of the uniquely beautiful quilts that provided her an income. While Jude loaded her thirteen cows and calves into his livestock trailer, Leah felt at a loss for words—she was saying good-bye as much to a way of life as to her sole remaining parent.

"Mama, if you need anything—"

"By the sound of it, Jude has already arranged for a crew of carpenters to put a roof on the barn tomorrow and paint it on Monday," Mama interrupted before Leah could get teary-eyed. "I won't have the slightest chance of getting lonely any-time soon—and I have three quilts to complete in time for Christmas. Don't you go feeling sorry for me, Leah."

Leah immersed herself in the warmth of her mother's hug.

"And by the same token, if you need anything—be it ad-vice or recipes or help with keeping those kids in clothes, I'll feel mighty bad if you don't let me know about it." Mama let out a sigh that ruffled the hair near Leah's ear. "If it's any consolation, my first year as a new wife was terrifying be-cause your *dat*'s family was mostly men and boys who tended toward the gruff side while the women were like meek little mice."

Leah's eyes widened. She'd never heard a hint that her mother's early years with Dat had been frightening. "But you made a life for yourself," she pointed out. "You made it work out."

"I made a lot of adjustments to my expectations," Mama clarified. "And I prayed. A lot. A marriage is a work in progress, like a crazy quilt top you keep adding to and em-bellishing with embroidery to cover the flaws in its fabric."

"I had no idea you and Dat weren't . . . perfectly happy and meshed together," Leah whispered.

Mama chuckled softly and eased away to gaze at Leah. "Perfection is in the eye of the beholder, dear. What you see and believe is what you'll get—so believe the best about Jude and his intentions," she added quickly. "Together the two of you will deal with the trials and tribulations of an ongoing relationship. Even couples that start out fresh, without children and memories from a previous marriage, go through phases when they wonder if their initial burst of love blinded them to the realities of everyday life—or to their spouses' personality quirks."

Leah nodded, still confident she and Jude could deal with any conflicts Alice, Adeline, and Stevie created.

After Jude helped her up onto the wagon seat later that afternoon, Leah waved quickly at Mama and then turned to face the road. She would *not* cry; nor would she worry about how small and alone her mother looked as she waved from the front porch.

"Are you all right?" Jude asked after they reached the road.

"*Jah,* I'll make it."

Her husband draped an arm around her. "Can't be easy leaving home," he said gently. "I don't know what that must feel like, as we're living in the original farm home my grandparents built—which my *dat* took over when his folks moved into the *dawdi haus.* Jeremiah bought other land to build his home when he married Priscilla."

"I'll have to learn all the nooks and crannies where you've stored things, along with getting familiar with the noises the house makes when it settles in cold weather—or when rain's pounding against the roof," Leah said with a sigh.

Jude smiled boyishly. "After we get your bull settled in his new pasture later today, we'll have to make a few noises of our own," he hinted. "It's been a blessing to welcome you to my bed, Leah."

As she felt warmth creeping up under her collar, tinting her cheeks pink, Leah smiled and looked away. That part of becoming a wife was so wonderful, she decided to concentrate on making Jude happy—because surely everything else would fall into place now that they were blissfully, ecstatically one. No one and nothing could come between them. . . .

Chapter 4

Three months later, Thursday, March 2nd

Leah moaned, pressing her hands against her temples. For the third morning in a row she had a throbbing headache, and she'd awakened in the wee hours from a recurring nightmare in which Alice and Adeline had locked her out of the house, taunting her through the door with all manner of hateful names. The pounding of rain on the roof depressed her. Despite the approach of spring, March stretched before her like an endless rainstorm, cold and bleak and dreary, stripping her of the energy to fight her lethargy and depression.

But she didn't want to waken Jude with her tears. Didn't want to admit that marrying into the Shetler family had been a huge mistake.

I would rather stand barefoot in a box of shattered glass than face this day.

Despite Leah's best efforts, a sob escaped her. Her fairy-tale married life had been nothing more than a figment of her romantic imagination, and because the Amish didn't allow divorce, she saw no way out of her vow to live as Jude's wife and his children's stepmother. Mama—and even Margaret—had been right: she'd been a fool to believe that Alice, Adeline, and Stevie would come to love her and that they could all live as a happy, harmonious family.

But where can I go? If I run home to Mama, I'll eventually have to return here.

Not for the first time, Leah realized that she had no female friends to confide in. She'd spent most of her life in the world of men and sale barns and livestock, and as each day in the Shetler household wore her down, she felt smaller and weaker and more utterly alone. She turned away from Jude, clutching the pillow around her head so she could sob into it.

"Leah? What's wrong, sweetheart?" Jude fitted himself against her, wrapping his arm around her shaking body.

Leah cried harder, unable to stop. Now Jude would realize how miserable she was and he would ask her questions she didn't want to answer. He would again insist that he loved her even though those words, once so sweet, couldn't possibly save her.

"Leah," Jude whispered against her ear as he gently shifted the pillow away from her face. Once upon a time, the sound of him saying her name had thrilled her deeply, yet she'd reached such a place of desperation that she dreaded proceeding with this conversation. No matter how good her intentions—no matter how much she loved him—if she told Jude the truth, she would devastate him.

"Honey, we need to talk about this," he insisted, kissing her temple. "You've been crying a lot lately, and I can't help you if you won't tell me what's upsetting you."

Leah sniffled loudly. When Jude was home, the twins kept their unkind remarks to themselves and Stevie clung to him, so he had no idea how wretched Alice and Adeline made her feel when he was out working at sales and auctions.

"Please, Leah," Jude pleaded softly. "Turn around and talk to me. No matter what you say, I'll love you. If I've done things that upset you, I need to know about them, sweetheart."

Leah swallowed hard. The lump in her throat felt like a callus, toughened by her habit of keeping her misery and frustration to herself. Jude wanted their life to be as wonderful and fulfilling as they'd imagined it on their wedding day, yet she couldn't bring herself to burden him with the daily trials and tribulations she endured. Only a weak, pitiful, spineless wife would hide in the pantry or the bathroom to cry after her husband's children had hurt her feelings.

But Jude was persistent. Leah considered sharing the most distant of her troubles so he could comfort her and she could pretend her heart was healed. She sighed, turning slowly in his arms as she thought about airing the situations that would bring this painful conversation to its quickest end.

Jude smiled in the darkness, his beard tickling her cheek as he kissed away her tears. "I love you so much, Leah," he murmured.

She swallowed hard. "*Jah*. I—I know."

"You're the best wife a man could ever have," he continued softly.

Oh, but you have no idea, Leah thought as she took a breath to fortify herself. A few months ago, she would've been echoing his love words—but back in December, she'd been oblivious to reality and other people's warnings.

"Tell me one thing that's gone wrong," he encouraged her, speaking as gently as he did when Stevie was in tears.

Leah hid her face against Jude's warm, bare chest, wishing she could succumb to the wonder of the lovemaking that had delighted her as a new bride—mostly because it was easier than saying her painful words aloud.

Jude held her without trying to entice her. "One thing," he repeated softly.

Leah sighed. If she allowed her silent agony to continue, it would soon be time to rise for the day—and the kids would be out of bed, expecting breakfast.

"Well," she finally admitted, "at church on Sunday, I overheard Naomi and Esther Slabaugh saying how—how odd I am to be raising animals, like a man," she confessed in a pinched voice. "They talked about how dirty the house was—and it's not like this is the first time the women here in Morning Star have whispered behind my back. I—I just don't fit in here."

Jude sighed into her hair and hugged her closer. "Do you think I care what the neighbors think?" he asked, nuzzling her cheek. "Esther and Naomi are *maidel* sisters who have nothing better to do than gossip—Jeremiah has had to warn them a time or two about telling tales. Besides, how would they know what our house is like?" he queried gently. "Neither of them ever came to see Frieda, that I can recall. Have they been here to visit you?"

"Hmm. No," Leah admitted with a sigh.

Jude gently speared his fingers into her hair and let them trail over her shoulder and side. "I have no complaints about your housekeeping, honey," he said gently. "I know you work hard with the animals, and keeping track of Stevie. Nobody ever died from being attacked by dust bunnies that I know of."

Leah smiled despite her desperation. She was truly blessed to have such a supportive husband—but then, Jude's attitude had never been the problem.

"I'll have another talk with Adeline and Alice," he continued patiently. "They're perfectly capable of helping you with the cooking and laundry and—"

"But they hate me!" Leah blurted out before she could stop herself. "Every day when you leave, they call me names. Then they change into English clothes—"

"What sort of names?" Jude stiffened slightly, obviously surprised by what she'd told him.

Leah cringed. She'd let the cat out of the proverbial bag, so there would be no way to keep this insidious information to herself any longer. "Their favorite one rhymes with . . . witch," she mumbled, wishing she could shut out the tone with which the twins had muttered it. "When I informed them that a bitch is a female dog, they laughed and said it was the perfect name for me. When we're clearing the table after a meal, they whistle for me and toss bones."

Jude's body had gone rigid, and she could feel him trembling with anger. "Why haven't you told me this before, so I could—? No, wait," he whispered before exhaling harshly. "I suspect you've felt too humiliated to mention their behavior. Leah, I'm so sorry—and we're not going to let the girls get away with this. What else? Tell me everything, sweetheart."

Here, doggie, doggie. Come get your bone, you stupid mutt.

Leah tried in vain to shut out the memory of the twins' insults. Again she pressed her face against Jude's chest, hoping to draw strength from his muscular body and the steady beating of his heart. He was being so gentle and patient that she hated to spoil this precious time with him by revealing the ugly truth. But then, her silence had only made her more miserable, more sure that she should never have become a member of his family.

"I—I thought by now that Stevie would have taken to me, if only because he loves animals," Leah admitted with a hitch in her voice. "Sometimes he seems so scared when he looks at me, I've wondered if the girls have been telling him things that make him afraid to come near me. I—I hate to dump all this stuff on you, Jude, because none of it's your fault," she continued as desperation overrode her rational thought. "Maybe I should just go back home, because I certainly don't belong *here*. I—I can't take any more of this!"

Leah froze. What had possessed her to say such hurtful words—words that would offend and anger a lot of men she knew? From childhood, she'd understood that a wife was to submit to her husband's ways and to fit into the home he'd provided for her, and Jude would surely think she was ungrateful. Maybe he even believed she was lying about—or at least overstating—Alice and Adeline's rude behavior.

Leah lay absolutely still, preparing her heart for whatever Jude said or did to her next. Then, despite her fear of angering him, she burst into tears again.

Jude fought the urge to haul his daughters out of bed and demand an immediate explanation—but their denial would do nothing to console the heartbroken woman who sobbed in his arms. He wasn't surprised about Alice and Adeline's negative attitude, because he'd seen the glint of ridicule in their eyes when they'd been around Leah during his courtship—and at the wedding. He'd assumed the twins were still missing their mother, at a time when their hormones were making them a little crazy anyway, and that they would eventually grow out of this phase.

But he was stunned by the name they'd called Leah, and mortified about what his new wife had endured after he'd left the house each weekday to work at the auction barn.

"Leah, I wish you'd told me about this when Alice and Adeline first began acting out," he repeated with a sigh. "My girls pretend they're perfect angels when other folks are watching. I've suspected they were slipping away when my back—or my mother's back—was turned, but I—"

"Oh, it's become much more obvious now," Leah interrupted with a shaky laugh. "By the time you've driven to the road after breakfast, they've changed into English clothes and off they go in their buggy. When I warn them about the trouble they might find, they laugh in my face. They tell me they have no reason to pay attention to me because I'll never be their *mamm*."

Jude closed his eyes, wishing he weren't able to imagine his teenage daughters' scornful tone of voice and facial expressions as they taunted Leah. It was his job to correct such behavior—*spare the rod and spoil the child* was the Old Order mind-set when it came to dealing with disobedience, even though he'd never spanked his girls. Now they were of an age for corporal punishment to be inappropriate. . . .

"I confess that I'm at a loss when it comes to dealing with teenage girls," he admitted with a sigh. "I wish I could've nipped this nasty behavior in the bud—so we could've stood together to deal with the girls before their name-calling hurt you so badly."

Leah exhaled softly, wiping her tear-streaked face with the top of the sheet. "I . . . I should have told you these things

sooner, but I was afraid you'd think I was as spineless and incapable of being your children's *mamm* as *they* think I am,"
she said with a little sob. "Maybe I'm just not cut out to be a
mother. Maybe—"

"I don't believe that," Jude whispered as he desperately
hugged Leah closer. "Nobody's born knowing how to be a
gut parent—and unfortunately, kids don't arrive with an instruction manual. Frieda and I walked the floors and prayed
our hearts out time and again over the years, trying to raise
Stevie and the girls right. I can see now that I depended too
much upon Frieda to raise them."

He sighed loudly, feeling as inept as Leah apparently felt.
"Why have I been so clueless about Alice and Adeline's bad
attitude and how deeply they've hurt you?" he asked as she
muffled her sobs against him.

As Jude tried to comfort Leah, a harsh realization made
him suck in his breath. Long before he'd married Frieda, he
had admired Leah Otto for her competence with animals at
auctions—and for the way she'd helped her father with his
livestock, and then continued providing for her mother after
Raymond died. He'd known all along that Leah was very different from most Amish women—a proverbial square peg—
yet he'd expected her to fit neatly into the gaping hole
Frieda's death had left in his life.

*You married Leah knowing she'd had no experience with
kids and no inclination to become a traditional wife and
mother. Is it any wonder she's miserable and feeling like a
misfit?*

Jude shook his head, wishing he could turn back time.
Ever since the kids' mother had died, he'd thought only of his
own desires rather than what Leah might require if she were
to find happiness in his home. He had needed Leah more
than he'd loved her. Jeremiah had tried to point this out to
him, but he'd been too lonely and desperate to listen.

"I've done this to you, Leah," Jude said sadly. "And I
know better—I've forgotten all about the love and communi-

cation a marriage requires if a husband and wife are to truly become one."

Leah shifted. After wiping her pale blue eyes again, she eased away to look at him. "What do you mean by that, Jude? What have you done to me?" she whispered. "I've never doubted your love, not for a minute."

Too late to close the barn door after the horse has run off.

Jude was glad the darkness hid some of his anguish. He realized how difficult it had been for Leah to tell him about the twins' crude behavior, because now he'd opened an emotional door and there was no shutting it until he'd answered Leah's question. If she'd trusted him with her expression of fear—her need to leave his home because she felt like an outcast—it was only fair for him to share the circumstances surrounding his first marriage . . . the damning details he'd told no one else.

"Hear me out before you judge me, Leah," he pleaded softly. He was encouraged when she remained snuggled against him, and he hoped his revelation wouldn't drive her away. "Frieda came on to me like a house afire. I was only eighteen—flattered and delighted that a beautiful woman three years older than I wanted to marry me—and I . . . I believed it was love."

Jude paused, recalling that time when he'd believed he was so mature and ready to handle anything life threw at him. Leah, bless her, remained silent as he collected his thoughts. Frieda would've been pecking at him like a hen, demanding details and expressing opinions about situations she only assumed she knew about.

But Leah isn't Frieda. Get on with your story and trust her to give you a fair shake when she's heard it all.

Jude took comfort in running his fingers through Leah's long, soft hair. "When Frieda got sick a couple of times at our wedding, I figured she was just nervous. I didn't realize that some of our guests were speculating that I'd already had relations with her—which I had *not*."

Leah drew in a sharp breath and held it. Her gracious silence gave him the strength to keep talking.

"As a lot of newlyweds do, we lived with her parents at first," Jude continued. The story was easier to tell now that Leah had already figured out the punch line. "Her mother didn't seem a bit concerned that she was vomiting so often. When I asked Frieda if I should take her to the doctor, she admitted she was pregnant. You could have knocked me over with a feather—but I realized immediately that her baby couldn't have been mine."

"That was despicable," Leah muttered. "She knew you'd have no way to wiggle out of raising another man's child after you married her."

Jude sighed gratefully into Leah's hair. "Frieda begged me to forgive her deception, so of course I did as our faith expects us to do, without letting on to anyone about her secret. Nobody said anything about the twins arriving full-term after we'd been married only six months."

"They figured the girls were yours, conceived before you'd married," Leah muttered.

Jude held her closer, thanking God for her understanding heart. "Several years and a few miscarriages later, everyone was delighted when Stevie came along," he continued in a faraway voice. "Maybe I was too suspicious, but when I counted the months back to a time I'd been on the road with an auction company for a long while, the math didn't work out in favor of my being his father, either."

Leah gasped. "How could she do that to you? Especially after you were already raising another man's twins as your own?"

"Here again, maybe my suspicions were playing me false," Jude said with a shrug, "but Frieda didn't seem the least bit upset about my leaving to accept that job. Three other Amish auctioneers and I were gone a couple of months, helping a bunch of Plain families in Ohio sell off their farms and relocate farther west, where land was more affordable. Frieda thought such a worthwhile cause deserved a little sacrifice on her part—and my parents were living here then, so it wasn't as though I was leaving her to raise the girls alone."

Jude chided himself for stirring up the ghosts of old memories—speaking ill of his deceased wife—yet he wanted Leah to understand his emotional state. "Maybe I was partly to blame. Maybe I shouldn't have been lured away by the exceptionally *gut* pay, knowing Frieda had succumbed to temptation before we'd married," he admitted with a sigh. "Guess I'll never know how it would've worked out had I stayed in Morning Star instead of traveling those months."

"Who was Stevie's father?" Leah blurted out. "Was it the same man who'd sired the twins?"

"The kids all resemble their mother, so I have no idea—and at this point, it doesn't matter." Jude was relieved that Leah had recovered from her low mood and was being so supportive. "I didn't tell you these things to win your sympathy, sweetheart. I'm just realizing that I married Frieda in a rush of adolescent hormones, and I've married you because of a different need—without fully considering what sort of emotional support I should be providing to help you fit into my family."

"But it's not your fault that Stevie and the girls don't—"

"Hear me out," Jude said, gently pressing his finger to Leah's lips. "I love you so much, sweetheart—I've known you and admired you for years," he added, hoping his candor hadn't disappointed her. "So now I've got to find a way to turn your disillusionment and heartache around by replacing my *need* with a love you can depend upon. A love that helps *you* more than it gratifies me."

Leah kissed his cheek. "I've always loved you, Jude," she whispered. "I was only thirteen when you married Frieda, but even then, I knew nobody else would be the right husband for me—so I figured to remain a *maidel*. I didn't care if I could cook or sew, because I thought I wouldn't be leaving home. If I had it all to do over, I might've helped Mama in the kitchen more," she added with a resigned sigh.

Was that the squeak of a floorboard on the other side of the wall? Jude ignored it, determined to help Leah be a happier wife so his children couldn't drive a wedge between them—or drive Leah away.

"I love you for who you are, Leah. When I married you, I knew you'd never play me false," he said, reveling in her warmth as she wrapped her arms around him. "Starting right now, I'm going to pay more attention to Alice and Adeline's comings and goings and hold them responsible for helping you around the house. Will you believe that, sweetheart? Will you stay with me so we can work this out?"

When he felt her body relaxing against his, Jude gave thanks for Leah's willingness to try again.

"I really want our marriage to be a happy one," she stated, caressing his chest with her small, sturdy hand. "I knew it would take time and effort to become your kids' new mother, and now I'm more realistic about what that means. You're not the only one who didn't listen when folks told you we'd have a long row to hoe, adjusting to the fit of our new family."

Jude kissed her until they forgot about the kids. As they succumbed to the pleasures of being a man and a woman, a committed husband and wife who were very much in love, he knew he'd been blessed beyond belief by Leah's sweet, stalwart belief in him.

Chapter 5

Alice waved Adeline into their room and silently shut the door behind her. "Do you believe that—what he said about Mamm?" she whispered angrily.

"And that he's not really our father?" Adeline shot back. "Why was he telling *her* that, when *we're* the ones who ought to know?"

"I can't believe Mamm wouldn't have told us if Dat—or that man we've been calling Dat—wasn't really our father. Mamm told us *everything*," Alice added, crossing her arms hard across her chest. "What if it's not true? What if he's just saying that to Leah to make her feel sorry for him? Phooey! For a while there, I thought we'd be able to get rid of her. Scare her away."

"Puh! Dat's hot for her body. He'll never let her go."

"*Gut* thing it's dark, so he can't see how ugly she is."

The two of them stifled a fit of giggles as they scurried back into the double bed they'd shared since they were small girls. Their bedroom was on the north side of the house, always the coldest room in the winter, so it felt good to be back underneath the layers of quilts and blankets after their visit to the guest room, which shared a wall with the bedroom where their parents had always slept. Since Leah had arrived, Alice and Adeline had felt compelled to eavesdrop every now and again, even though they knew their curiosity was improper.

Alice grimaced in the darkness. "What if they make a baby?"

"What if Dat really isn't our father?" Adeline said without missing a beat. "Think about what that could mean for us."

"Like, maybe we could find our real father and go live with him, instead of being stuck here with *her*?" Alice savored the way her disgusted sigh lingered in the chilly air. "Now that she's ratted on us, Dat's going to be on our case *constantly*. We only threw those chicken bones at her once, for Pete's sake."

"Well, the second time it was pork chop bones," Adeline recalled with a chuckle. "But we made our point. She knows we hate her guts and we want her gone." She tucked the covers under her chin to stay warmer. "And if Dat's not our real father, well, neither of them are our parents, so that means they have no say about where we go or what we do, *jah?* I mean, we're sixteen—and we're in *rumspringa*. They can't touch us."

"Makes sense to me. But it was easier to get away when Mammi Margaret lived here," Alice put in wistfully. "She's old and clueless—"

"And she was busy with Stevie, and the cooking, and the housework. The new wife doesn't do any of that stuff, so she has too much time to spy on us from the barn and the animal pens."

"She's where she belongs out there. Just another one of the goats."

The twins pondered their situation for a few moments before Adeline grabbed the wind-up alarm clock on the nightstand beside her. "Almost five o'clock," she said. "Stevie's going to be pounding on our door—"

"I'm not getting out of bed until we have our plan in place," Alice interrupted tersely. "If we don't pack up and leave, we're going to have to put up with Dat's lecture while *she* squirms in her chair and can't look us in the eye. *Bwawk-bwawk-bwawk,*" she squawked, bending her arms and flapping them beneath the covers.

Adeline sighed. "Where would we go? None of our friends' parents would allow us to live in their homes for more than a day or two—and they'll ask a gazillion questions before they send us back here."

"Why should we be the ones to leave?" Alice challenged, mostly because it felt good to ask belligerent questions. She let out another loud sigh. "But truth be told, it's too cold to sleep out in the loft of the barn—unless Dexter and Phil are with us!" she added with a mischievous laugh.

"Forget that. We don't want them coming around here, because then Dat will know who they are," Adeline pointed out. "He'll lock us in our room until we have gray hair if he gets a look at them and sees how old they are."

"They'd take us to a motel to live, if we asked them."

"And how would we pay for that?" Adeline asked. "It would only be a matter of time before Dat or Uncle Jeremiah would come looking for—"

"Shh!" Alice clapped her hand over Adeline's mouth, listening to the footsteps in the hallway. The even, heavy tread of work boots meant it was Dat, heading downstairs to start the coffee and tend the horses. As always, the three bottom stairs squeaked beneath his weight. "If he hears us talking this way, we'll be in big trouble."

Adeline let out a mirthless chuckle. "Let's face it, if we really do leave, we'll be in even bigger—oh, here she comes."

The twins lay absolutely still as the lighter sound of sneakers came down the hallway—and when the footsteps paused in front of their bedroom door, they sucked in their breath, wide-eyed. For seemingly endless moments, Leah just stood out there.

When she finally moved on, Alice clutched Adeline's hand.

"That was close!" she whispered. "What do you think she was doing?"

"Well, we know what *we're* doing when we stand on the other side of the wall or the door, ain't so?" she remarked. "We'd better get dressed and get downstairs. Let's start cooking some hash browns and ham and eggs, with cheese sauce, for haystacks. Dat's not as likely to get on our case if we make his favorite breakfast."

"He's working that big sale over in New Haven today, *jah?*" Alice asked as she threw off the covers. "So he'll have to scoot along, rather than hanging around to keep track of us."

As Adeline's feet landed on the rag rug beside the bed, she smiled. "That's right! See there—every cloud has a silver lining, and by the time the sun's up we can be on our way out of here!"

Chapter 6

When Jude opened the mudroom door for Leah, the aromas of ham, onions, and other breakfast fixings made his stomach rumble. While they had fed the livestock and checked the twin goats that had been born during the night, they'd discussed the talk they planned to have with the twins over supper, when he returned from the large livestock auction he was working for most of the day. Jude was pleased that Leah was ready to stand with him if Alice and Adeline got sassy, and together they'd devised a list of chores he was going to present to the twins during breakfast. If the girls had enough time to taunt their stepmother and leave home to run with their friends, he'd reasoned, they needed more work around home to fill their hours.

As Leah removed her work boots and slipped into her sneakers, she winked at him. "Breakfast smells really *gut*," she called into the kitchen. "*Denki* for starting the cooking this morning, girls."

Jude noticed that Alice and Adeline were standing at the stove, stirring hash browns and scrambled eggs in skillets without looking at him or responding to Leah's compliment—*because they're in yet another of their teenage moods,* he surmised. As usual, they were dressed alike, and he became aware that their forest green cape dresses had grown snug enough to accentuate their slender waists and full breasts, to the point that their figures would draw more attention than Old Order modesty allowed.

When did they mature into women? he wondered wistfully, even as he realized it was time to insist that they sew new clothing—before Bishop Jeremiah made the same observations. Jude considered his words carefully, to avoid ruffling the girls' feathers. To Adeline and Alice, sewing was a necessary evil that ranked right up there with scrubbing floors and cleaning the bathrooms.

"How about if we all head to the Cedar Creek Mercantile tomorrow?" he asked jovially, opening his arms to Stevie. "What with spring just around the corner, I bet you girls are ready for some new clothes—"

"And I'm ready for some candy sticks, Dat!" his son exclaimed as he launched himself toward his father.

Jude caught Stevie and hefted him toward the ceiling to make him laugh. "How did I know that?" he teased, reveling in the boy's laughter. Stevie's light brown hair was mussed and needed trimming and his shirt was untucked, bunched around his twisted suspenders, yet Jude was pleased that his son had taken on the task of dressing himself.

"We're getting low on feed for the chickens and horses, too," Leah said as she took plates from the cabinet. "I'll start a list of what we need to buy."

Alice and Adeline shared a look Jude couldn't interpret, except to realize that they weren't nearly as excited about a trip to the mercantile as they'd been when they were younger. Silently the twins filled serving bowls with hash browns, fried onions and green peppers, cubed ham, and cheese sauce—the makings for haystacks, his favorite breakfast because it was filling enough to get him through a busy livestock sale until the lunch break. When everyone was seated at the table, Jude bowed his head, leading their time of silent prayer.

Lord, You know what's going on and I hope You'll give me words that will guide my daughters back to being the lov-

*able, helpful girls they were before Frieda passed. Comfort
their young hearts as You give Leah the patience to be a mother
my kids will come to love. We trust You to provide for—*

One of the twins cleared her throat much more loudly
than was necessary, ending the table grace—usurping the
privilege that was his, as the man of the house. Jude raised
his head and felt nailed by identical pairs of icy blue eyes . . .
eyes so reminiscent of Frieda's that he was momentarily
taken aback. "What's so important that you've cut short our
table grace?" he asked, carefully controlling his irritation.

Alice glowered, pointing across the table at Leah. "Why
did you tell *her* that you're not our father, yet you've never
told us?" she demanded angrily.

Jude's heart stopped. As his mind scrambled for an answer,
he realized that he had indeed heard a floorboard creak in
the wee hours. How much of his and Leah's conversation
had the girls heard?

"Why have you *lied* to us about who we really are?" Adeline
drilled him bitterly. "You didn't even love Mamm—*did* you?"

Seated at his left, Leah had gone pale, yet her eyebrows
rose resolutely. "So you *do* sneak into the guest room and listen at the wall," she remarked, crossing her arms. "You
know, my *dat* used to tell me that if I went sneaking around,
poking my nose where it didn't belong, I might learn things
that hurt my feelings—and I deserved to suffer from whatever I'd overheard."

"*Suffer?*" Alice blurted out incredulously. "Seems to me it
was our *mamm* who suffered, because Dat didn't love her.
He was just faking it, once he discovered another man had
fathered us!"

"My relationship with your mother—and with Leah—is
none of your business," Jude muttered, aware that his words
were only adding fuel to the wildfire of emotions that had
suddenly sucked all the air from the kitchen. "Seems you
heard what you wanted to hear and ignored the rest, because
I was crazy about your *mamm* when I married her—and I

thought I was the man she loved as well. The issue here is that you two were eavesdropping, and—"

"No, the *issue* is that you're not our father and she will never be our mother!" Alice snapped, again pointing at Leah.

Jude grasped his daughter's offending hand, pressing it to the tabletop beneath his.

"*Jah,*" Adeline joined in quickly, "why should we have to hang around here so you can do your *duty* by raising us?"

Jude blinked. How had his world spun completely off its axis in a matter of seconds? On the other side of Leah, Stevie's face crumpled.

"Stop bein' so mean, girls," the boy whimpered. "Dat loves us, and—"

"He's not your father, either!" Alice interrupted with a nasty laugh. "This changes everything for us, Stevie. Our lives will never be the same."

Utterly flummoxed, Jude smacked the tabletop with his hand. "That will be enough out of both of you," he said in a strained whisper. "It's one thing to be angry with me for the *private* conversation you eavesdropped on—"

"But it's another thing altogether—sheer meanness—to upset Stevie," Leah put in as she slipped her arm around the boy's shaking shoulders. "He's too young to understand what you're saying—"

"*Jah,* he's lucky," Alice whispered vehemently. "We girls know exactly what you said, Dat, and we'll never forgive you for it!"

Jude felt his control snap as he stood up, gazing sternly at his teenage daughters. Their betrayal crushed his heart, because he'd willingly raised them with all the love he possessed. It wasn't their fault that their mother had deceived him. They were furious about the secret they'd overheard, but he couldn't allow their indignation and anger to create chaos for Stevie and Leah—especially since he had to be away all day.

"Go to your room," he said in the calmest tone he could muster. "When I come home this afternoon, we'll continue this conversation after you've had a chance to consider the consequences of writing me off as your parent. We'll also address the way you've mistreated Leah with your insolence. You *knew* it was wrong to listen to us on the other side of the wall—"

"Ah, but in the Bible, it says the truth will set you free," Alice mocked as she rose stiffly from her chair.

"*Jah,* we're free, all right," Adeline chimed in as she followed her sister from the kitchen. "And *rumspringa* means we don't have to say we're sorry for what we do or say!"

Jude stared after the twins, aghast. He sat down again, fearing he might topple over if he didn't have the chair beneath him. Stevie's whimpers had become a wail, and as the little boy ran through the front room after his sisters, Jude didn't have the fortitude to go after him. "What just happened here?" he asked, feeling dazed. "I—I've sometimes wondered if they were sneaking into the guest room, but . . ."

"Time to shift the bed to the other wall," Leah suggested, shaking her head. "I'm sorry for those horrible things they said to you, Jude. They have no idea how their words have stabbed your heart. They talk tough, but where would they go if they decided to leave?"

Jude slumped, flummoxed. "I don't know, but I suspect they'll find a place that'll make us pull out our hair trying to find them. Boys tend to fess up and take their punishment, but girls are sneaky—and *my* girls are going to claw and bite like cornered wild animals now."

He gazed at the full bowls of food and the empty chairs at the table, clutching Leah's sturdy hand. "Will you be all right today? If there was any way I could skip the livestock sale—"

"I don't see that happening, what with you being the auctioneer, Jude," Leah said gently. "I'm guessing Alice and Adeline are upstairs changing into their English clothes, and they'll be out the door and down the lane not five minutes after you leave. That'll give me a chance to spend time with Stevie today, to patch up the damage his sisters have done."

Jude's heart swelled. As he gazed at his wife, who was plain even by Plain standards, he was grateful for her steadfast love and common sense—even if the girls' apparently habitual escapes upset him. "When Mamm lived here, she told me the girls behaved just fine for her," he said with a sigh. "I'm starting to think she didn't want to admit that she had so little control over them."

Leah shrugged. "At least they cooked you a nice breakfast—"

"Trying to soften me up—and then they dropped their bomb," Jude put in tersely. "I've lost my appetite, but I can't sell livestock all day on an empty stomach."

He spooned a large mound of hash browns onto his plate and handed the bowl to Leah. As he spread the fragrant fried potatoes and topped them with a layer of onions and green peppers, his thoughts raced in circles. "I should've shifted the bed to the outside wall when you first came here, Leah. Should've challenged the twins about sneaking into the adjoining room the first time I suspected they were eavesdropping, but I—" Jude gazed at Leah, his throat tight with emotion. "I'm sorry about all of this, sweetheart. I had no idea the girls were treating you so badly."

Leah's shrug was lopsided as she spooned cheese sauce over the top of her haystack. "I should've spoken up sooner. I just didn't know how."

Jude nodded. "I know the feeling. I don't know how any of this blew up in our faces—and I don't know how we're going to patch our family back together now that Adeline and Alice have ripped such a hole in it."

Leah smiled. She already looked weary, and she still had to get through a tough day with the kids. "We'll have to trust that God knows the answers, and have the patience to recognize them—to grab on to them—when He brings us the help we need."

How could she speak with such simple confidence, after the way his girls had scorned her? Jude grasped her hand and kissed it. "You're right, Leah. Let's hope God provides some *gut* ideas sooner rather than later," he said. "*Denki* for your faith, and for sticking with me. I love you."

As Leah stood at the kitchen sink washing dishes, she watched Jude drive his rig down the lane toward the road. The sounds of footsteps above her head suggested that the girls were walking back and forth on the creaky wooden floor of their bedroom. Were they packing bags to leave? Would they make good on their threat to go elsewhere because they were angry with Jude for not being their birth father?

They have no idea what they'd be getting themselves into, Lord, she prayed as she stacked rinsed plates in the dish drainer. *Alice and Adeline might believe the English world will give them a fresh start—the independence they crave— but they've led a sheltered life. Temptation and trouble lurk around every corner for Amish girls seeking to escape the rules that preserve their security.*

The sudden silence above her made Leah look toward the mudroom. Through the window, she spotted Alice and Adeline clambering down the big maple tree to the ground, as though they'd done it dozens of times. Despite the frosty morning, they were dressed only in tight jeans, sneakers, and lightweight hooded sweatshirts. They ran toward the barn without a backward glance, their long reddish-brown hair billowing loose behind them in the breeze.

At least they don't have suitcases. They don't plan to be gone long.

For a moment, Leah wanted to follow them—wanted to warn them or plead with them to reconsider their attitude toward their *dat*. They might have heard Jude's words through the wall, but they obviously hadn't caught on to the fact that their mother had been the deceptive one while their *dat* had followed the honorable course and raised another man's kids as his own.

Leah remained at the sink with her hands in the soapy dishwater, however. Alice and Adeline needed time to let off some steam, and the last person they would listen to was the stepmother who'd intruded upon their family life—the woman their *dat* had entrusted with a truth they weren't ready to hear yet felt entitled to know. A few minutes later, the girls' open buggy was heading toward the road—and their mare, Minnie, was racing down the lane as though something had spooked her.

We've all been spooked, Leah realized. *This morning's episode is all about fear.*

She pulled the stopper from the drain and dried her hands on a towel. As Leah passed through the front room, she saw the wooden trucks and trains Stevie had been playing with before breakfast, but the boy was nowhere in sight. Climbing the stairs, Leah prayed for words that would comfort the poor child who'd been so upset by his sisters' cruel words. The door to the twins' room was closed, but Leah grabbed the knob, hoping a peek inside would give her a clue about where they'd gone.

The door didn't budge.

Leah frowned. To her knowledge, none of the house's doors locked—and the knob turned in her hand. She smiled wryly. The girls had placed a heavy piece of furniture—probably their dresser—against the door so she wouldn't snoop in their absence. They figured she wouldn't have the gumption to shove the door open, and then replace the dresser and shimmy down the tree outside their window, so they wouldn't know she'd entered their bedroom.

Puh! You girls have nothing on me when it comes to climbing trees or trellises—or even ropes, Leah thought as she continued down the hall. As a girl, she'd always had the job of climbing into the apple and walnut trees to pick the highest fruit, or to shake the branches so the walnuts fell to the ground for her *dat* to pick up. She'd prided herself on being able to climb a rope hand-over-hand, too, after watching the neighbor boys do it.

Leah set aside her memories of those simple childhood pleasures, however, as she approached the room across the hall. The door was ajar, and as she heard Stevie crying, her heart went out to him.

"Mama . . . Mamaaa," he bleated like a lost lamb. He repeated the name again and again, as though his plaintive chant would bring his mother back to comfort him.

Leah stepped into the room and hesitated. Stevie was curled into a small ball on his twin bed, rocking himself as he lay facing the wall. "Stevie, I'm sorry you're so sad," she said softly. "I'm sorry your sisters were being so mean at the table."

The boy stiffened. "Mama. I want my *mamm,*" he said in a quavering voice.

Leah sighed. She'd lived here for three months, yet Jude's son had shown no sign of accepting her as his new parent. Most likely the twins had filled his imagination with scary lies about her.

But you're the adult; you have to keep trying, she reminded herself as she approached his bedside. She couldn't imagine the pain and loneliness this little boy had been dealing with since his mother had died.

Leah stopped beside the bed, but quelled her urge to stroke Stevie's mussed hair, which would probably frighten him more. "You know how we've talked about the fat mama goats getting ready to have babies?" she asked in an excited murmur. "Two of the kids were born last night! I was hoping you'd come with me to see them."

Stevie lay absolutely still for several seconds. Rather than begging for his mother again, he stuck his thumb in his mouth—but at least he seemed to be listening.

"I know how you love animals, Stevie, and I was thinking

these new kids could be yours, if you'll take care of them," Leah offered. "If you spend time around them starting today, when they're newborns, they'll get used to you—and they'll be really happy to see you every time you go to the barn."

A tiny smile flickered across his tear-splotched face.

"They'll have their *mamm* to feed them her milk for a while," Leah continued softly, "but you could be their human—you could give them water now and feed them after they're weaned. And when the other kids are born over the next few weeks, they'll want to be yours, too."

Stevie's body relaxed. "There's two babies?" he asked in a voice hoarse from crying.

Leah closed her eyes, relieved that he was talking to her. "*Jah*, and they're the cutest little goats you ever saw!" she replied, daring to step closer to the bed. "They're cream-colored, with floppy brown ears and heads, and cream stripes down their noses."

"Like the mama goat, *jah*? Like Gertie." Stevie turned to face her, his eyes alight with interest.

"*Jah*, they look just like Gertie." Leah paused, hoping she wasn't rushing the boy in her eagerness to take him to the barn. "And you know what? You resemble your mama, too, Stevie. If you look in the mirror and see her there in your face, maybe you won't miss her so much."

Stevie's brow furrowed as he considered this idea. "But I'm a boy and Mama was a girl."

Leah shrugged, deciding not to mention that the twins also bore a close resemblance to their mother. No reason to remind Stevie that his sisters had upset him with their cruel words and then left him behind. "You have brown hair like hers, and your nose and eyes and skin are a lot like hers, too. If she'd been a little boy, she'd have looked just like you."

Stevie studied her for a long moment. "How do you know about my mama?"

Leah's heart stilled. For the first time, Jude's little boy was holding a real conversation with her instead of going through the motions of dressing, eating, and other daily activities with responses that required little thought. "I used to see her at church, and at weddings and such," she replied carefully, because Frieda Plank's family had attended church in Cedar Creek—until Frieda had caught sight of Jude and began attending church in Morning Star instead. "And I've known your *dat* since I was a girl growing up in Cedar Creek. I saw him at auctions when he was just starting out as an auctioneer, when my *dat* and I took livestock to sale barns—"

"*You* went to sales? Like a *boy?*" Stevie demanded.

Was he going to judge her, or was he merely curious? Leah smiled at him full-on. She saw no point in pretending to be any different from what adults in the area had always known about her. "My *dat* didn't have any sons—I was his only child—so I was his helper with the animals at home, and when we sold them, too," she explained. "He was glad to have me along, because sometimes the goats and ducks and chickens went into the trailer—or out onto the sale barn floor—better for me than they did for Dat."

"Oh. So that's why you like animals so much." Stevie let out a single laugh. "Did you get poop on your shoes? Alice and Adeline *hate* poop, so they don't never wanna go into the barn with me and Dat. They pay me a quarter a week to clean out Minnie's stall," he added proudly.

Leah wasn't surprised to hear this, although she thought Alice and Adeline could be more generous. "If you have animals, you have poop," she replied with a shrug. "And sometimes you step in it, so you clean off your boots and go on, *jah?* You know how it is."

Stevie nodded, brightening. "When you have people, you have poop, too—but not on the floor!"

Leah's heart shimmered. Their subject matter wasn't the most inspiring, but she didn't care. Stevie was sitting up, smiling as he dangled his feet over the edge of the bed. His hair stuck up on one side and his rumpled blue shirt bunched out between his suspenders, yet the feeling of loneliness that usually hung around him like a cloud had lifted a bit. "Are we going out to see the baby goats, or would you like some breakfast first?" she asked. "You're probably pretty hungry."

"Goats first," he replied as his feet hit the floor.

Leah decided against smoothing Stevie's hair or trying to tuck in his shirt: he had accepted her for who she was, so she didn't fuss over him. They went downstairs and into the mudroom to put on their barn boots, and as Stevie skipped across the yard toward the barn, Leah sighed in relief. At least *one* conversation had gone well today.

When she caught up to the boy, he was standing outside the goat pen, gazing in awe at the pair of little goats that were suckling their mother. He glanced at Leah, delight dancing in his blue eyes, placing his finger on his lips to signal her silence. Leah nodded, mimicking his action. She was pleased that he'd known better than to enter the pen or to make a lot of noise, which would've startled the kids and perhaps inspired the mother goat to charge at him as she protected her newborns.

After several minutes, Leah walked toward the other end of the barn to muck out the large pen where the goats without kids had spent the night. When she pushed the big barn door aside on its track, the goats headed out into the morning sunshine to graze in the pasture. Leah filled the galvanized trough and tossed out a few bales of hay to supplement the sparse winter grass. When she returned to the pen, she stopped.

Stevie had grabbed his shovel with the shorter handle, and he was clearing the pen of its manure. Although he often helped Jude with the livestock chores in the evening, the boy hadn't shown any inclination to work with Leah—he had always remained on the fringe of her peripheral vision as she'd worked, watching the animals but preferring to avoid her attention or conversation. Some folks had hinted that Stevie was mentally and emotionally slow, but Leah sensed he was just shy and mourning his mother.

"*Denki* for your help, Stevie," she said as she picked up her shovel and began clearing the opposite end of the goat pen. "Many hands make light work."

Stevie's lips curved. "Matches make the lights work, too," he quipped.

Leah gaped. The boy had a quick sense of humor!

They finished mucking out the pen in companionable silence, because Leah wasn't one to make chitchat—and she didn't want to push her luck now that Stevie was feeling so much happier. Together they fed the ducks and chickens, and then Leah loaded the large pull cart with alfalfa pellets and a bag of calf feed supplement.

"How come you gotta give the calves extra feed?" Stevie asked as he walked beside her. "Aren't they still gettin' milk from their *mamms?*"

Leah considered his question. Nothing made her smile like the serene sight of the calves nursing from their mothers in the pasture she and the boy were entering. "I feed the babies extra vitamins so they'll get enough nutrition now that we're starting to wean them," she explained. "And they won't go through as much stress when we separate them from their *mamms*, so they'll graze on grass like the adult cows. I'm giving the mama cows some supplements, too, because the grass isn't as thick now that we're coming out of winter."

Stevie considered this. "Is that why Dat says we gotta seed the pastures again real soon?"

"*Jah*. The calves we're raising to sell need a *gut* diet of grass and hay so they'll grow big."

As they approached the simple calf enclosure Jude had constructed—a fence with boards at a level that allowed the calves inside but not the adult cows—Leah was pleased to see that Stevie's eyes were shining with excitement.

"Lookit!" he said eagerly. "Their ears are all perked up coz they know we're comin' with fresh feed. So how come you got a red-colored bull and some of the cows are black and the others are black with white faces and legs? Deacon Saul's cows are all black."

Gripping the wagon handle, Leah wondered how much information about reproduction and genetics a five-year-old boy needed. She decided to answer the questions he'd asked without adding a lot of details.

"Deacon Saul raises Black Angus—and so does Bishop Vernon in Cedar Creek—because they like that breed of cattle for producing beef. I think they also like the way those cattle look in a pasture," she added with a chuckle. "My *dat* began breeding red bulls, which are Herefords, with Black Angus cows because he liked the crossbred calves they make. He believed that crossbred heifers become better *mamms,* and that crossbred cattle are gentler and easier to handle— and he thought their meat tasted better, too. So my herd is a mixture of a couple of Black Angus mama cows, Patsy and Erma, and the crossbred mama, Maisie, that's black with a spotted white face like the calves are."

After a moment, Stevie smiled. "It's easier to tell your cows apart because they don't all look alike, huh?" he observed. "There's Maisie, with her two spotted calves, watchin' us. Erma and Patsy are over on the other side of the fence."

When Maisie mooed as though responding to Stevie, Leah laughed. "We have to be careful what we say," she teased, "because the cows know when we're gossiping about them."

Stevie held her gaze before his serious expression brightened with a smile. "Nuh-uh! They don't speak English. They speak in cow talk," he insisted.

"Maybe so, but *food* is a language we all understand," Leah pointed out. She grasped the handle on the gate, her pulse thrumming with the pleasure of bringing Stevie out of his shell and into her world. "You know how this works," she said softly. "We'll step inside nice and slow, and close the gate behind us. Then you can help me scoop the alfalfa pellets and supplement into the feed trough so the calves will get used to being around you."

Stevie's face lit up like Christmas. He nodded eagerly and did exactly as Leah had told him. He was too excited to talk as he used a metal scoop to fill the raised trough with the green alfalfa pellets. Leah opened the bag of supplement and walked behind Stevie, scooping the powder onto the alfalfa he'd spread. Immediately after they stepped through the gate, the four young calves walked under the board toward their feed while their mothers looked on from outside the fence.

Stevie was so excited that he gripped the board as he watched them. "They like it! Look how they're diggin' in!" he said in a husky whisper.

"They like you, too, Stevie," Leah said fondly. "And see how the other cows are sticking around rather than skittering off? They know you won't hurt them or make loud noises to scare them away."

Grinning, the boy looked around at the small herd gathered near the enclosure. "So how come those cows don't come inside? Coz they're bigger?" he asked, pointing at them.

"They're a year older," Leah explained. "Those six steers are the ones we're feeding to sell for their meat. We keep the heifers—the girls—so we can get calves from them when they're old enough."

Stevie thought about what she'd said. "So you raise these cows to make money?"

"*Jah,* just like I raise my chickens and ducks and goats. If farmers are to make a living, they have to sell most of what they raise and eat the rest."

Stevie's face brightened with expectation as he looked up at Leah. "Will I get to help with your cows, too? Like I'm helpin' with the goats now?"

Leah's heart swelled and her eyes stung with sudden tears. "That would be awesome, Stevie," she managed to whisper. "I'd love to have your help."

He beamed at her, really looking her in the eye, and for a moment Leah was speechless. As they returned to the house after they finished the animal chores, she realized that her day had taken a very positive turn, considering the way Adeline and Alice had gotten the family off to such a difficult start. After three months of Stevie's merely enduring her presence, Leah felt a first flicker of hope that she might have a real relationship with Jude's son—if she could maintain the rapport they'd established this morning.

Chapter 7

Jude was eating his noon meal at the auction barn, so Leah made a simple lunch of grilled ham and cheese sandwiches. Stevie loved home-canned peaches, so she opened a quart jar of them—and wished their supply of fruits and vegetables, which either Frieda or Margaret had canned, wasn't dwindling so quickly.

Although Leah had worked in Mama's garden all her life, and had assisted with preparing their produce for canning, she hadn't paid attention to the recipes her mother had used, or the time required for each canner load of jars, or any of the other pertinent details. Mama had been so grateful to her for taking the sterilized jars from the boiling water bath before they were filled, and then lifting the hot, heavy pressure canner from the stove burner when a batch was finished, she hadn't insisted on Leah's learning the finer points of preserving the produce that saw them through the winters.

I should ask Mama to can with me this summer, Leah thought as she bit into her gooey grilled cheese sandwich. *It makes sense for us to preserve our produce together anyway, now that she lives alone.*

When she glanced at the clock, however, thoughts about canning slipped away. Alice and Adeline had left home more than five hours earlier—which was a lot longer than they usually stayed away.

"The girls're really missin' out," Stevie said as he chewed a big bite of his sandwich. "They *love* grilled cheese sandwiches with peaches."

Leah smiled at him from across the kitchen table, a worm of worry curling in her stomach. "Where do you suppose they go?" she asked, fishing for information. "Do they have jobs that they haven't told us about?"

Stevie shrugged. "I dunno. I kinda like it when they're not around, makin' me do their chores, and tellin' me what to . . ." His expression clouded over. "Is it true that Dat's not really my *dat?*"

"Oh, honey, I'm so sorry you had to hear that," Leah blurted as her heart rose into her throat. She didn't want to lose him to the mournful mood that had so often shrouded his days—but she didn't want to lie to him, either, because then he'd have to decide whether he believed his sisters, or her and Jude.

"Sometimes a child's *dat* isn't the man who fathered him—and sometimes women raise kids another *mamm* brought into the world," Leah replied carefully. "I can think of a couple of other families in our district—Jimmy Nissley's, and Sarah Beachy's—that became blended when one of their birth parents died and the other parent remarried. So Jimmy has a new *mamm* and Sarah has a new *dat, jah?*"

Stevie nodded, yet he was still thinking about the ramifications of what his sisters had blurted out at breakfast. "So was Mama married to another man and he died, and then she married Dat? And then Mama died and Dat married you?"

Leah's stomach tightened around the sandwich she'd just eaten. If Stevie could ask such a complicated yet logical string of questions, he was far from mentally deficient. How much information was she supposed to give a five-year-old about a tangled situation—especially when Jude wasn't around? *Ask your Dat* came to mind, but it wasn't a fair response to the little boy's urgent question.

"Sometimes people make babies before they're married,"

she explained—*and they make trouble for their families when they do,* her thoughts taunted her. "If they're lucky, those babies are born into a family with a man and a woman who love them anyway. No matter what Alice and Adeline said when they were upset this morning, your *dat* has always loved you, Stevie. He loves your sisters, too—even when they spout off like teakettles and say mean things that hurt his feelings."

"He's a *gut dat,*" Stevie whispered with a hitch in his voice. "He works really hard and he plays with me even when he's busy."

"He takes *gut* care of all of us," Leah put in quickly. As she rose to gather their dishes, she came to a decision. Jude wouldn't be home for a few more hours, and the longer the girls stayed away from home, the more potential they had for finding trouble they couldn't get out of. "I think if your *dat* was here right now, he'd be getting worried about where Alice and Adeline have been since breakfast."

"He'd go lookin' for 'em," Stevie said earnestly. His eyes widened with concern. "I should saddle up my pony and ride around town—"

"How about if we ride over to Uncle Jeremiah's on Mose?" Leah interrupted him quickly. "You can visit with him and your Mammi Margaret while I look for your sisters."

"*Jah!* Uncle Jeremiah will know what to do," Stevie agreed enthusiastically. "He's the bishop, so he knows everything."

Leah smiled as she quickly rinsed their dishes and put the leftover peaches in the refrigerator. Stevie's childlike faith in his uncle confirmed her plan of action, and within fifteen minutes she was seated on her gelding with Stevie riding behind her. At four, Mose was still a spirited mount, so when he cantered along the roadside in his eagerness for exercise, Stevie laughed and wrapped his arms around Leah's waist.

Once again Leah's heart beat with excitement because the

boy was losing his fear of her. Had her mission not been so urgent, she would've gladly ridden around Morning Star and the countryside all afternoon so she could share Stevie's happiness longer. As they reached the main street of town, however, the increase in car traffic forced her to slow Mose to a walk along the shoulder. They passed the Dutch bulk store and the pizza place, across the street from the large city park.

"Look at all those kids playin'!" Stevie said wistfully. "They go to the Mennonite school, huh? I wish I could go there, come September—to play in the park every day!"

"*Jah*, they're out for recess," Leah replied. She decided not to suggest that maybe his *mammi* would bring him to the park. Why disappoint him, if Margaret was too busy for that? "But at the Amish school, you'll have a ball diamond and a place to play volleyball, as well as the swings. That'll be fun, too."

A few moments later they'd left the business district and Jeremiah's tall white house came into view. Leah guided Mose onto the long dirt lane, hoping the bishop would have some words of wisdom—or some ideas about where to look for his teenage nieces. When she halted her gelding at the side of the house by the hitching post, Stevie quickly clambered down and hurried up the steps to the front porch.

"Uncle Jeremiah!" he shouted as he ran. "We gotta find the girls! They've run away from home!"

So much for the subtle approach, Leah thought as the screen door banged behind him. After she tethered Mose, she jogged up the stairs and entered the house a few steps behind the boy, who was talking excitedly back in the kitchen. She hesitantly poked her head in the kitchen doorway, wondering if Margaret would be the one listening to Stevie's animated story.

Both Jeremiah and his mother were at the kitchen table, with coffee and a plate of fresh cinnamon rolls between them. Their questioning glances made Leah swallow hard. Did they believe she'd been negligent for allowing Alice and Adeline to leave—let alone for waiting so long to start looking for them?

Jeremiah's face creased with a smile as he motioned Leah toward the chair nearest him. He placed the plate of rolls near her after Stevie had taken one. "Stevie seems very excited today," he remarked, as though pleased that his nephew had come out from under his dark cloud of mourning. "I think he rather enjoys not having his sisters around to pick on him, *jah?*"

Leah laughed nervously, appreciating his levelheaded point of view. The rolls smelled heavenly, but she wasn't staying long enough to enjoy one. "Lately the girls have taken to dressing English and driving off in their rig, shortly after Jude leaves for work," she explained with a shake of her head. "They scooted their dresser against their bedroom door, shimmied down the tree outside their room, and ran toward the stable without telling me where they were going—and that was after breakfast. They're usually back by now, so I'm getting concerned about—"

"They certainly never did such a thing while I was living there!" Margaret said archly. "They were very respectful and prompt. If they left the farm, they told me where they were going and when they'd be back."

Leah pressed her lips together, again suspecting that Margaret had either been unaware of her granddaughters' escapades or unwilling to admit to their absences. "They didn't exactly run away," she clarified, smiling at Stevie. "They didn't have any luggage with them, so sooner or later they'll be returning for clean clothes. I brought Stevie here for a visit so I can look for them."

"I've heard the twins have been seen at various places around town," Jeremiah said calmly. "I spoke to them not long ago about the dangers of spending their time with English boys. I also suggested they start working at the bulk store or other Plain businesses, so they'd at least be earning some money—and be easier to keep track of," he added with a purposeful glance at his mother. "Wish I could give you more concrete clues about where to look for them, Leah. If you spot that buggy with the Tinker Bell decal on the back, they won't be far away."

"Tinker Bell's a fairy," Stevie said with wide eyes. He focused again on his cinnamon roll, peeling away the outer layer and pinching off a bite. "Alice and Adeline like Tink because she can fly! She likes to stir up trouble, and then flies away before she gets caught."

Leah blinked. She'd seen children's books with Tinker Bell on the cover, but her conservative parents hadn't allowed her to read them. "Have your sisters been telling you stories about Tinker Bell?" she asked carefully. Maybe, if the twins were sharing their adoration of a fictional fairy with Stevie, they were also telling him about their adventures.

"I watched a little movie about Tink on their cell phone," Stevie replied—and then he clapped his hand over his mouth. "But I'm not s'posed to tell about that, or they'll get really mad at me."

"After Frieda died, Jude allowed the girls to have a Plain cell phone, without any Internet connection on it," Jeremiah mused aloud. "While I'm not wild about our kids having such English temptations at their disposal during their *rumspringa*, I went along with his reasoning that the phone would allow the girls to get ahold of him at an auction barn faster if a problem came up when they were away from home."

"I didn't see any cell phone," Margaret muttered. She glanced at the clock on the wall, as if wishing Leah would leave so this uncomfortable conversation would end.

"But if you could watch a movie on that phone," Jeremiah continued, gazing at Stevie, "I'm thinking Adeline and Alice have gotten ahold of a fancier phone than I agreed to let them have—which means I'll be speaking with them soon about overstepping their boundaries."

The more Leah heard, the more concerned she grew. How

would Alice and Adeline pay the monthly charges for a cell phone? Or had Jude agreed to pay the fee—without realizing he was now paying for an English phone? "I'll be on my way," she said, rising from her chair. "*Denki* for your help and ideas, Jeremiah."

As he nodded, Leah could almost see the thoughts turning like the cogs of a clock in his mind. "I'll be out and about, as well," he said vaguely. "We'll need to talk with the twins when we're all together, so they'll know we adults are in agreement about enforcing their boundaries. Godspeed as you look for them, Leah."

Leah exited through the front room, feeling as relieved as Margaret probably did. She regretted that she'd not cultivated a closer relationship with her mother-in-law. It seemed apparent that Margaret disagreed with the way Leah was dealing with Jude's girls, while she'd remained oblivious to their activities. As Leah mounted Mose and headed for town, she prayed for guidance and pondered what Stevie and Jeremiah had said about the twins' phone.

Leah knew of several Amish teens who openly used cell phones when they gathered after church services. It was Alice and Adeline's sneakiness that bothered her. If she—and Margaret—had been unaware of the girls' phone, what other secrets might the twins be keeping? And if they had overstepped the bishop's boundaries concerning phones, what other rules might they be breaking while they were on the loose, possibly with English boys?

When she reached the main street of Morning Star's business district, she felt a moment of panic. Unlike her quiet hometown of Cedar Creek, the streets were lined with one English business after another, except for the Amish carriage shop and the bulk store and bakery operated by Mennonites. In most Amish settlements, folks operated their businesses on their own property, so shops were scattered along country roads rather than being part of an organized business district.

Leah wondered how she was ever going to visit every business in Morning Star this afternoon. *I could use a little help, Lord. Where would Alice and Adeline be spending so much time?*

"Let's go this way, Mose," she said after a moment. "We'll start on this side of the road and then come back on the other side, until we spot them. It's the only thing I know to do."

The gelding whickered, shaking his head as he kept to the shoulder of the busy street. Leah could feel the drivers of the cars gazing at her as though she was an oddity, riding on horseback rather than in a rig, as the other Plain folks did. Riding Mose gave her more flexibility, however—she could pass between the buildings to the parking lots behind them more easily than if she was driving a rig. As she studied the vehicles near the Laundromat, the post office, and the Goodwill store, she saw very few buggies—and why would the twins spend hours of their day at any of these places, anyway? She passed a car dealership and a hospital, which were near the end of the business district, where Main Street became the road that ran through the countryside. Should she turn back toward town?

For all I know, the girls are in a car somewhere, joyriding with boys. And maybe I've been foolish to assume they would come home for clothes, Leah thought with a sigh. She knew Jude wouldn't consider it her fault if his daughters were gallivanting around—probably to spite him—yet she felt responsible for their well-being.

A white, single-story Mennonite church sat just ahead of her. The only building between the church and a long stretch of cornfield and countryside was a pool hall. Leah shook her head, ready to cross the road and head back toward town, except a twitch at the back of her neck persuaded her to walk Mose closer to the pool hall. Neon beer signs covered its windows and several cars and pickups were parked out front. As she walked her horse around to the back of the building, past a couple of overflowing Dumpsters, she suddenly sat up straight.

A lone buggy was parked near a big self-service ice machine.

When Mose whickered and walked faster, the rig's horse perked up its ears. Leah scowled. *Please don't tell me you girls have left Minnie hitched out here all day without any water.*

The Tinker Bell sticker on the buggy made Leah nip her lip. Why on earth would Adeline and Alice come to a place where people spent their time playing pool? She wasn't all that familiar with the game, but she suspected that anyone who'd be shooting pool and drinking beer this early in the afternoon didn't have anything more constructive to do—and probably didn't have a regular job. Dat hadn't been a judgmental man, but he'd always given Leah the idea that men who frequented pool halls were shiftless and at loose ends.

You have to go inside, Leah told herself as she heard the throb of music coming from the small building. *You have to find out if the girls are in there, even if you're the last person they want to see.*

As she wrapped Mose's reins around the same post where Minnie was hitched, she wondered what she would say and do once Alice and Adeline spotted her. What if they ran off? What if they laughed at her—

Folks have snickered at you behind your back for most of your life, Leah told herself with a sigh. *At least you're not intimidated about entering an establishment that's mostly for men, after all the time you've spent in sale barns. Margaret would be ready to faint.*

Bolstered by this thought, Leah decided to go in through the back door, hoping she'd be less conspicuous. When she turned the knob, she wasn't ready for the blast of loud country music or the dim interior where the air was thick and blue with cigarette smoke. The front center of the large room was filled with pool tables where men of various ages stood with cues, playing or awaiting their turns. A bar spanned one wall, and the other walls were lined with dark tables, dimly lit by hanging glass lamps that advertised various brands of beer.

Leah shut the door and stood near it, nearly suffocated by the smoke. Her burning eyes took in a scantily clad young woman who was flirting with two of the nearby men.

"You are just *askin'* for it, when you do that to me, Natalie," one of the guys teased loudly as she plucked the cigarette from his mouth.

"Nah, Natalie's beggin' you for it," the other fellow countered with a loud laugh. "Better pour your beer on her to cool her off."

Leah sucked in her breath, hoping she didn't have to witness such an incident. A song about honky-tonk angels came over the speaker system just as she spotted two identical young women in tank tops at a back table. She bit her lip to keep from crying out.

Adeline and Alice both held cigarettes and beer mugs.

Leah's first urge was to hurry outside and ride off on Mose, back to where Plain life was quiet and predictable— but she'd come here for a reason. She had to make her point with the twins, or her search had been for nothing.

Leah kept to the wall as much as she could, hoping to reach the girls without calling attention to herself, but other folks at the tables immediately picked up on her presence.

"Say, sweetheart, you lost?" one of the young men at the bar teased her.

"If you're lookin' for the church where the guys in beards and the women in those funny little hats and long dresses go, you're in the wrong place!" his companion called out.

"You didn't come here to *save* us, did ya?" a fellow in faded, holey jeans taunted her.

Focusing on Adeline and Alice, Leah ignored the men. A squeal made her turn her head just as one of the rowdy young men yanked Natalie's lacy see-through tank top down over her shoulders. Shaken, Leah walked faster—and she knew the moment the twins spotted her. They stiffened, beer mugs poised in front of their faces, and for a desperate moment, Leah thought they were going to bolt out the front door.

"Wait!" she pleaded as she reached their table. She pressed her palms against the sticky tabletop, praying for the right words. "Please come home before your *dat* gets worried," she pleaded beneath the loud music. "I know you feel cheated by what he said this morning, but he *is* the father who's given you a home all your lives."

Alice and Adeline exchanged a doubtful glance. "What are you doing here?" one of them asked as though Leah's presence embarrassed her.

"*Jah,* how'd you find us?" the other twin demanded in a voice slurred with beer. "Why would *you* care how we feel?"

Aware that several pairs of eyes were watching her, Leah slipped into the chair nearest the girls. It wasn't the right time to chide them for seeming so familiar with this raucous place, so comfortable with their beer mugs and cigarettes—nor was it a good idea to deride them for wearing such sheer, snug tops and sparkly earrings that dangled provocatively from their ears. They'd asked her a question that demanded a sincere answer, and if she was ever to gain their trust, she had to convince them that she did care about them.

"I know you'll always miss your mother, and that I'll never replace her," Leah replied, holding their gazes. "But I want us to be a *family*. I want us all to find new ways to be happy—and that means you have things to teach me, like how to cook food you love to eat, and—"

"You can't tell . . . um, *Jude*—or the bishop—where we've been," the twin closest to Leah insisted.

"*Jah,* all bets are off if you don't promise to keep your mouth shut," her sister chimed in with a wave of her cigarette.

Nailed by two blue-eyed glares, Leah realized Alice and Adeline were testing her—expecting her to comply with their demands so they could keep coming to the pool hall without suffering any consequences.

"I'll only keep your secret if you come home with me right now," Leah shot back, holding their gazes. She bit back a retort about how they'd done enough damage to the Shetler family today—and no matter what she was promising the twins to get them out of this dangerous place, she would tell Jude about his girls' escapades in a heartbeat to keep them safe. "Please come home now, before your *dat* realizes you're gone and comes looking for you himself."

"Dat? Enter a pool hall?" the sister nearest Leah said with a snide laugh.

The other twin stubbed out her cigarette in an ashtray overflowing with butts. "Mr. Clean wouldn't have the first idea about where to find us—unless *you* tell him," she added sharply.

After a brief pause, the other girl set her beer mug down with a *thunk*. "We might as well go," she said as she plucked her hoodie from the back of her chair. "I'm tired of waiting for the guys."

"*Jah,* they should've been back a long time ago. Let's go."

Leah was so relieved that the twins were starting toward the back door, she could ignore the catcalls and derogatory whistles from some of the young men who were playing pool.

"Come back and see us again sometime, girls!" one of them teased in a falsetto voice.

"But leave your frumpy old lady at home!" another one put in.

"What'll we tell Dex and Phil?" a third fellow demanded.

One of the twins made a hand gesture Leah didn't understand, and she walked faster behind them. When the door opened, the afternoon sunlight revealed black bras beneath the twins' close-fitting tops—and they had matching tattoos of Tinker Bell on the backs of their left shoulders.

Leah was too startled by these discoveries to say another

word as Alice and Adeline unhitched Minnie and clambered into their rig.

Pierced ears and tattoos. So much for what Margaret knows about her granddaughters, Leah thought as she mounted Mose to follow them home. *Where are the girls getting money for these English clothes and jewelry and—and those colorful tattoos? How can I tell Jude what his daughters have been up to?*

How can I not tell him?

Chapter 8

Jude drank deeply from his glass of cold water, preparing to sell one last lot of sheep to the crowd of area farmers gathered in the sale barn near Cedar Creek. Although the bidding had been unusually active and he'd sold more cattle, hogs, and sheep than usual for a blustery March day, his mind had occasionally wandered home . . . wondering how Leah's day with the twins had been going. When one of the Amish barn hands opened a side gate to drive the lambs into the fenced arena in front of the elevated booth where he sat, Jude shifted the microphone into place—and then gripped it hard.

On the other side of the fence, Jeremiah was taking a seat in the bleachers. And Stevie was with him.

A prickly feeling went up Jude's spine, but when his son waved at him, grinning widely, Jude waved back. He hadn't seen Stevie so happy in months, so the day had to be going better than most despite the serious set to Jeremiah's jaw.

"All right, folks, we've got a dozen nice Suffolk lambs," Jude announced, allowing his amplified voice to catch the attention of the attendees as he read from the small computer screen in front of him. "They're from Jake Sutter up in Trenton, so you know they're good. Starting the bids at a dollar fifty, do I hear two?"

Jude eased effortlessly into his chant, acknowledging the raised cards of the three farmers who bid first. Below him in the pen, young Bram Kanagy, who owned the sale barn, was walking between the lambs to keep them moving so folks could get a good look at them. Jude focused on raising the bids until one fellow and then a second one dropped out. "Sold! Six dollars a pound to number one twenty-four. On behalf of the Kanagy brothers I want to thank you folks for coming out today," he said cordially. "Mary, our cashier, is ready to help you settle up before Bram and Nate help you load your livestock. Have a great day and may God bless."

Jude switched off the microphone and said a few words to redheaded Mary, who sat beside him and had been keeping track of the sale transactions for her husband, Bram. He left the booth, wondering what sort of news Jeremiah had for him—and wondering why he had Stevie in tow. By the time Jude made his way through the jovial crowd of farmers who were lining up to pay for the livestock they'd bought, he saw that Vernon Gingerich had spotted his brother as well, and had gone over to chat with him.

"Great sale today!" the white-haired bishop called over to Jude. "I picked up a fine lot of Black Angus calves to fatten up."

"You had several to choose from," Jude agreed. He knew that livestock was the furthest thing from Jeremiah's mind, so he asked the obvious question. "What brings you boys to the barn today? It's a nice surprise to see you, Stevie!" he added as his son launched himself from the bleacher.

"Leah took me to Uncle Jeremiah's coz she went out huntin' the girls," Stevie blurted, landing against Jude's shoulder.

"Apparently, Alice and Adeline believe you're not their father—and they told Stevie the same thing this morning?" Jeremiah asked carefully. He, along with the rest of the Shetler family, had known the truth about Frieda's babies ever since she'd confessed it, and they had agreed to honor Jude's situation by keeping silent.

Even so, Jude's heart shriveled. Who could've foreseen the

consequences of entrusting the story of his past to Leah after she'd bared her soul to him? As he hugged his son—for Stevie *was* his boy in every way that mattered—he wondered what Bishop Vernon was thinking as he followed this conversation. When the bishop from Leah's Cedar Creek district had counseled them about the potential pitfalls of bringing a new wife into a home with teenage twins, he hadn't been privy to the details of Alice and Adeline's birth. Jude figured Bishop Vernon felt even less confident about the possibility of the Shetler family coming together than he had before Jude married Leah.

"Oh, my. It's been quite a day at your place, by the sound of it, Jude," Vernon said. He rubbed Stevie's back, smiling at the boy. "But I can see you've let God's love and light guide your feelings about your *dat,* Stevie—and that's a wonderful gift you've given us all."

Jude sighed, glancing around to be sure the other sale attendees couldn't hear their conversation. "It all started when Leah and I were pouring our hearts out in the wee hours, unaware that the twins were listening on the other side of the wall," he said, shaking his head. "The girls were upset, of course. They said that if I'm not their father and Leah's not their mother, they have no reason to listen to us—much less obey us. I would've given anything to stay home today to help Leah deal with them, but—"

"Leah seemed to be handling it pretty well, all things considered," Jeremiah put in. "She took out on her horse to—"

"*Jah,* and she's lettin' me raise the new baby goats that was borned in the night!" Stevie crowed as he grinned at Jude. "And I got to feed the calves this morning, too."

Jude's heart swelled with love for Leah—and gratitude to God—that, for whatever reason, Stevie had finally decided his stepmother was a woman he could trust. "That's exciting," he said, hugging the boy close as he gazed at Jeremiah. "Do we have any idea where she planned to look?"

"She was goin' wherever Tinker Bell was!" Stevie blurted out. His eyes twinkled with mischief. "I told Leah the girls let me watch a movie about Tink on their phone, and I wasn't supposed to say nothin' about that. But Alice and Adeline aren't s'posed to have that fancy kind of cell phone, huh, Dat?"

Jude's suspicions spun as he wondered how many more revelations his boy would make. "No, but that's another matter entirely," he said. He lowered Stevie until the boy was standing on the bleachers. "Our first priority is locating Adeline and Alice before trouble finds them, so—"

"I'd check at home first," Bishop Vernon said pensively. "Your girls are upset by what they overheard—and they'd be acting out even if their mother were still alive—but I doubt they had a destination in mind when they took off. They'll find out pretty fast that the English world doesn't offer many options to young people without ready cash or a car." He squeezed Jude's shoulder, nodding. "If anyone can ferret them out, Leah can. She's resourceful in ways most Plain women aren't."

"Let's hope so," Jude muttered. "We certainly didn't see *this* coming when we considered the problems our marriage might face."

Vernon's blue eyes shimmered with a hint of sadness. "My suspicions about Frieda's youthful inclinations years ago have just been confirmed," he said with a shake of his head. "You and Leah have taken the higher path, and I wish you all the best as this situation plays out. Shall we pray about it?"

Jude couldn't recall ever praying in a sale barn, but he bowed his head and motioned for Stevie to do the same. If Bishop Vernon and God could give him some assistance with Alice and Adeline, he'd be foolish not to accept it.

"Lord and Father God, You've loved Your wayward children since before Adam and Eve rebelled against You," Vernon intoned. "We ask Your continued assistance as Jude and Leah strive to reconcile their family's difficult situation. Bless

Adeline and Alice with the insight to follow Your ways and to believe in the blessings You've given them in the form of caring parents. Amen."

"*Denki*, Bishop," Jude said, pointing Stevie toward the door. "I'll head home as you've suggested, and hope the girls are there."

"If they're not, come and get me," Jeremiah said, clapping Jude on the back. "Between the two of us, we know of every possible place in Morning Star where they might be holing up. Your girls aren't the first Amish teenagers to run around doing questionable things during their *rumspringa*, after all."

Jude smiled. "*Jah*, but it feels like a hundred years ago when you and I were running under the adults' radar. And we were guys—without cell phones," he added. He held out his hand, pleased when Stevie grabbed hold of it. "Let's go home, son. You can tell me about the new baby goats and the calves along the way."

As they rode in the rig, Jude nodded and smiled at Stevie's enthusiastic rendering of his adventures with Leah this morning, but his mind was gnawing on a different subject altogether. *What if Alice and Adeline have taken off with those English boys folks suspect they've befriended? What if they've learned enough about getting around in the English world to fare better than Bishop Vernon has predicted?*

"—and then Leah told me about how come the calves and some of her cows are black with white faces even though the bull is red," Stevie was saying excitedly. "And she let me scoop their alfalfa pellets into the feeding trough!"

Jude focused on his boy, grateful to God for the purposeful shine in Stevie's eyes as he spoke with such enthusiasm. "What was so special about today—so different?" he asked softly. "You've been around Leah for a long time now, yet today's the first time I've seen you really excited about spending time with her."

Stevie's eyes widened as he considered Jude's question. "I

dunno," he said with a winsome shrug. "I guess I was really happy when she told me I could be a friend to the new goats. Alice and Adeline are always tellin' me I'm too little and too—too stupid to do stuff—"

Stevie's chin quivered as he took in Jude's shocked frown. "Uh-oh. Now they're gonna know I blabbed about somethin' else they told me to keep quiet about."

"No, they're not," Jude whispered, cupping his boy's face in his hand as he held Stevie's gaze. He wasn't surprised that the twins were showing Leah so little respect, but his heart curdled at the thought that they'd been convincing Stevie he was stupid or inadequate. "There's something else I need to know, and it's just between us guys, all right? Leah and the girls will never hear what you tell me."

Stevie's expression grew serious. "*Jah,* Dat. It's just you and me and Rusty—and horses can't carry tales," he added, crossing his heart with his finger.

Jude didn't spoil the moment's solemnity by chuckling at Stevie's way with words. For safety's sake, he guided his bay gelding to the shoulder of the road and eased the horse to a halt. "Stevie, do the girls ever tell you things about Leah that . . . that make you think your new step*mamm* is mean or scary?" he asked carefully. "Have you stayed away from Leah because you believed Alice and Adeline when they said Leah might hurt you?"

The boy's wide eyes spoke volumes, and Jude's heart twisted in his chest.

"Sometimes," Stevie replied in a faltering whisper.

Jude bit back a remark intended for his daughters, because his son shouldn't have to carry the burden of his disappointment. "You don't have to tell me what they've said," he muttered, "but I hope that after today, you realize that Leah would never hurt you or be mean to—"

"And Leah won't never tie me up in the closet with my mouth taped shut like the girls said, neither, will she, Dat?" Stevie blurted. "And she won't make me eat chicken poop for lunch coz she can't cook nothin' better. I *know* that, coz we have really *gut* grilled cheese sandwiches a lot of days!"

"Oh, Stevie, I'm sorry," Jude murmured as he pulled his son close. "I don't know why your sisters have put such awful ideas in your head about Leah, but I'm glad you've decided not to believe their hateful talk."

Stevie nipped his lip. "Even though Alice and Adeline was talkin' mean to Leah this morning at breakfast, Leah got real worried about 'em when they didn't come home," he said. "She wouldn't never tie *them* up in the closet, neither, Dat. Leah's not mean, even when the girls hurt her feelings. Anybody who loves animals so much can't be a bad person."

Jude closed his eyes, grateful again for his son's unwitting insight. "You're right about her, Stevie," he said as he lightly clapped the lines across Rusty's back. "Let's get on home, and we'll hope that Leah and the girls are already there."

"What if they're not, Dat?"

"We'll take Uncle Jeremiah up on his offer to help look for them," Jude replied.

A smile flitted across Stevie's face. "Boy oh boy, the girls'll be in *big* trouble if the bishop has to go after 'em!"

They're already in big trouble, Jude thought as the house came into view. He'd expected the girls to feel some resentment about his new wife, but where had such hatred and disrespect come from? Why had the twins given Stevie such awful ideas about being tied in the closet and fed chicken manure?

As Jude drove down the lane toward the stable, he dared to believe he saw movement through the kitchen windows. It would take every ounce of restraint he could muster not to lash out at Alice and Adeline when he saw them—so he reminded himself that the knowledge he'd gained from Stevie would be an effective tool only if he kept it to himself until a moment his girls couldn't deny it.

"There's the Tink buggy!" Stevie crowed as Rusty pulled them into the stable.

Jude slipped his arm around his son as the bay entered his customary stall and came to a halt. "We guys have to stick together," he reminded Stevie gently. "How about if you help me with the horse chores? And then, when we go inside, how about if you let me do the talking? I want to see what the girls say about their day—"

"So they tell on themselves," Stevie put in brightly. "You do that with me sometimes, too, coz you know *everything* about what I've been doin', huh, Dat? You know when I'm tellin' the truth and when I'm fibbin'.'"

Jude stifled a laugh, cherishing his son's innocent honesty. "Yup, I know a lot—and God knows even more," he pointed out. "That's why it's never a *gut* idea to lie. It makes us feel real nervous about keeping our story straight, and it makes God and other folks sad because they love us and they want us to be at peace with ourselves and with everyone around us."

Although such religious philosophy was deep for a boy who hadn't yet started school, Jude sensed that Stevie understood it at a gut level. As he and his boy unhitched Rusty and filled the horse troughs and feed bins, Jude recalled a time when Alice and Adeline had shone with the same exuberant, forthright beliefs . . . and he wished he could return them to such a time, before hormones and the loss of their mother had altered them so drastically.

When Jude opened the mudroom door, the aromas of beef and gravy enveloped him. The kitchen was a picture of rare domestic bliss: Alice and Adeline, dressed alike in Plain green dresses, were adding vegetables to a delicious-smelling pot of stew that bubbled on the stove while Leah was tucking a large pan of biscuits into the oven.

Relief nearly overwhelmed him. His girls were home, apparently no worse for the day's wear—and Leah wore a placid expression that hid a slew of secrets.

Adeline turned toward the door, smiling. "Stevie! We made your favorite green Jell-O salad with peaches and pineapple."

"And biscuits to go with the beef stew," Alice added with a purposeful gaze at Jude. "It's going to be a yummy supper."

"Sounds wonderful," Jude said as he crossed the kitchen to slip his arm around Leah. She was wearing his favorite brick-red dress and a secretive smile . . . and when he nuzzled her temple, her light brown hair smelled like cigarette smoke. "How was your day?" he asked, including his daughters in the question.

The kitchen rang with silence.

Determined not to cave in to his curiosity—or to reveal how appalled he was about the girls' attitude—Jude meandered over to gaze into the stew pot. He caught a whiff of English perfume, which didn't quite mask the same acrid aroma of smoke he'd smelled on Leah. Was it his imagination, or did he also smell stale beer as the twins bustled away from him to set the table?

"We girls were all very busy," Leah finally replied, her purposeful gaze suggesting that Jude would be hearing more details later. "*Denki* for fetching Stevie."

Jude nodded. Surely, Alice and Adeline would suspect that Leah had had a reason for dropping off their younger brother, but he kept playing along with his wife's ruse. "Jeremiah thought Stevie would enjoy watching the livestock—"

"And I got to hear Dat be an auctioneer!" Stevie crowed. "He talks really fast!"

As they set the food on the table, Alice and Adeline chatted with their brother about what he'd seen at the sale. In their crisp pleated *kapps* and modest dresses, the twins appeared to be models of Old Order propriety and cooperation, as though they'd gotten along with Leah since the first day she'd joined their family—as though they hadn't been eavesdropping this morning, and overreacting to a conversation not meant for their ears. After the silent prayer, Jude allowed himself to enjoy a truly delectable stew and light, perfect biscuits, as though he believed his daughters had remained at home and out of harm's way all day. The twins were quieter than usual.

"You ladies have outdone yourself this evening," he remarked as he took two more warm biscuits from the basket. He focused on Alice and Adeline, noting that they didn't meet his gaze. "What all did you do today, girls? I'm pleased to see such an improvement in your attitude, because I was awfully concerned about you when I left for the sale this morning."

The twins exchanged a quick glance, shrugging simultaneously. "Not a lot," Alice mumbled.

"Nothing special," Adeline put in without missing a beat. "Just another day."

Jude gripped the stew bowl to keep from slapping the table in frustration. Although he understood the value of hearing Leah's version of the truth before he interrogated the twins, he despised game playing—acting as though Alice and Adeline had remained at home cooking and cleaning or working on other constructive projects, as most Amish girls their age seemed content to do.

"But it was a special day, coz two little goats got born," Stevie said, conveying the wonder of birth in his observation. "And they're gonna be my little goats, coz Leah says I get to take care of 'em. And we had the best grilled cheese sandwiches for lunch, too. You shoulda been here, Dat!"

Yes, I shoulda, Jude thought, smiling at his son. Experience told him Stevie could only go so long before he blurted out everything he'd heard this afternoon, so he changed his usual evening pattern. "After being cooped up in the sale barn all day, I believe I'd like to take a walk in the fresh air and sunshine before I eat my dessert," he said, gazing purposefully at his daughters. "If you girls will redd up the kitchen, please, Leah and I will return in a little while. And Stevie, their work will go faster if you help them."

Disappointment flashed in his son's wide blue eyes, but he nodded. Alice's and Adeline's faces tightened with suspicion as they exchanged glances. They began scraping the dinner plates as though they might take off the dishes' simple designs along with the food.

"*Denki* for your help, kids," Leah said as she rose from her chair. "I'll grab my coat, Jude, and off we go."

Jude's pulse thrummed as he preceded her into the mudroom. He held Leah's barn jacket as she shrugged into it, thinking he owed her a million more signs of his love and respect, considering what she'd endured since the wee hours of their morning.

"I love you," he whispered as he let his hands linger on her slender shoulders. "I apologize for whatever you went through today—and I want to hear all the details."

Fatigue lined Leah's eyes, yet her smile radiated her love for him. "All in *gut* time," she whispered with a slight nod toward the kitchen. "The walls have ears, after all."

The mudroom door had no more than closed before Alice narrowed her eyes, pointing at her little brother. "What'd you tell her today, Stevie?" she demanded.

"*Jah*, how'd she know where to find us?" Adeline put in stiffly. "You're in deep trouble if you've let on about the stuff we say and do when—"

Stevie crossed his arms, looking away. "How could I tell anybody where you were?" he replied. "I couldn't carry no tales, because I didn't know nothin' about where you were or—"

"Don't play stupid!" Alice blurted out, grabbing his shoulder to shake some sense into him. "If Uncle Jeremiah took you to the sale barn, that means Leah dropped you off at his place—"

"And you just can't keep your mouth shut when you're around him!" Adeline finished. She stood beside her sister, both with their fists on their hips, glaring at Stevie. "How much do he and Dat know?"

Stevie seemed oddly calm for a kid who usually cried at the first sign of conflict. His lips twitched as though he was trying not to laugh. "I dunno," he said with a shrug.

"But you had to've heard every word they said!" Alice retorted.

Stevie shrugged again. "Maybe I did, and maybe they were talkin' in the other room so I couldn't hear," he said. "When Dat and I got home, he said he was gonna do the talkin' and I was supposed to keep quiet. That's my story and I'm stickin' to it. Me and Dat, we're a team."

"He's not even your father!" Adeline reminded him hotly. "Why should you do what he tells you instead of listening to us?"

Stevie looked ready to cry, yet he stood taller. "Maybe you're lyin' about that—like you've told me lies before," he said in a quavering voice. "He's my *dat,* and that's that. You're in big trouble, and it's not my fault. I'm goin' out to see the goats."

Stevie bolted before Alice could catch him. As the slam of the door reverberated in the kitchen, she exhaled loudly. "Well, are we going to hang around here and clean up the kitchen, or is it time to just *leave?*"

"Where will we go?" Adeline challenged. "If Dexter and Phil hadn't left us hanging at the pool hall—if they'd come back for us like they said they would—we wouldn't be in this mess!"

Alice laughed bitterly. "I have half a mind to call Phil and give him an earful, but then he and Dex would probably dump us for *gut.*"

"*Jah,* so much for them being our ticket out of here. At least today." Adeline glared at the bowls of congealing stew and green gelatin salad. "Let's clean up this mess and see what Jude and Leah lay on us when they get back. At least we'll know what they've found out about us."

"*Jah,* you know Dat—er, *Judah*—will spell it all out when he gets back from his walk, because Leah will tell him everything even though she promised she'd keep her mouth shut." Alice spat at the stack of plates on the table. "Two-faced liar. What does he see in her, anyway?"

Chapter 9

By the time Leah had revealed the knowledge she'd gained about the twins this afternoon, she felt much better. It was such a comfort to walk arm in arm with Jude, their pace slower now that she had shared the most appalling of the details about Adeline and Alice. When Jude stepped in front of her, stopping at the edge of the unplowed cornfield south of the house, his eyes glimmered like dark, hot chocolate.

"Leah, I had no idea my girls were so far gone," he said sadly. "You probably saved them from a fate worse than we want to imagine when you went after them today, and I owe you a debt I can never repay."

Leah's heart thudded steadily when he pulled her close and kissed her. The evening wind was picking up enough that she grabbed the strings of her *kapp* to keep it from blowing off, yet the cold didn't faze her. She always felt so safe and warm—so centered—when Jude held her this way. "What bothered me most was that the girls seemed so comfortable with their cigarettes and beer in that smoky old pool hall," she said, shaking her head. "Another girl around their age was so deep into flirting with two of the guys that they pulled her tank top down and—well, I—I was about ready to run at that point."

Jude sighed, resting his forehead against hers. "When I smelled smoke on you, the pool hall was the first place that came to mind," he admitted. "Back in my wilder days, Jeremiah and I spent some time there. I can only imagine how much tackier the place must be by now, and I can't imagine the clientele has improved over the years, either."

"Why would so many young men be spending their time there?" Leah asked in disbelief. "Why don't they have jobs, or families, or—"

"A lot of them work the night shift at the pet food processing plant down the road—not that such work makes them bad people," he added quickly. "It just means they have time to kill during the day, and at that age, young men tend to congregate at places where they can eat cheap meals and drink beer. I've known a few Amish boys who've worked at the plant—and a few who've spent some time shooting pool during their *rumspringa*."

Leah frowned, considering this. "I can't imagine Plain fellows wanting to endure such ridicule about their clothing, just to play pool and drink beer."

Jude smiled sadly at her. "They wear English jeans and shirts, just like Alice and Adeline, so they sort of blend in with the crowd," he explained. "Considering how Jeremiah and I did that now and again, I should've guessed my girls might be masquerading as English. I just never dreamed they'd have any reason to go to such a dive."

"Maybe those English guys they supposedly run with work at the pet food plant," she mused aloud. "I didn't see any sign of them, but I got the feeling the girls were waiting for them."

"With dangly earrings and Tinker Bell tattoos," Jude muttered, shaking his head as he gazed toward the house. "I have half a notion to cut down that big tree by their bedroom window, except it shades that whole side of the house in the summer."

Leah smiled sadly, tracing the lines that bracketed Jude's mouth until her fingertips teased his cropped, curly beard. "I suspect they'd find other ways—other times—to slip away, if they're so intent on being away from home to socialize with boys."

"*Jah,* well—their old man might just take them down a peg or two," Jude blurted out. "*Rumspringa* or not—no matter what they heard through the wall—I'm still their *dat,* and I'm responsible for their well-being until they marry. At the rate they're sliding downhill, no respectable Amish men will want to hitch up with them if they've become too worldly or too free with their favors."

Leah winced. Alice and Adeline might be sophisticated enough to pass for English at a pool hall, but that didn't mean they knew how to prevent a pregnancy. And because they did everything together, chances were good that if one of them was getting intimate with boys, the other was, too.

Jude would love and support his girls no matter what they did, but he would be crushed—and he'd become the topic of hot, disapproving gossip—if he had to send the twins away to have babies out of wedlock.

"What's our next move?" Leah asked softly. "Just so you'll know, I had to promise them I'd not tell you anything to get them to come home today."

"Puh! They lost the right to our silence the moment Jeremiah walked into the sale barn with Stevie today to tell me where you'd gone. Bishop Vernon was in on the conversation, too." Jude wrapped his arm around Leah's shoulders and started walking toward the house. "It's time for some tough talk on my part and some straight answers on theirs."

Although Leah knew they were doing the right thing by challenging the twins to own up to their questionable behavior and change their ways, she prayed that Jude would find words to straighten them out without further alienating them. She couldn't imagine how difficult it must be for them to question their lineage—to doubt their deceased mother's integrity.

Please, Lord, don't let them rush down the same primrose

path Frieda followed, getting too involved with those English boys just to spite their dat. *They have no idea how quickly their lives can spin out of control.*

As they got close to home, squares of soft yellow lamplight glowed in the windows, and the white house seemed to shimmer serenely in the blue light of the dusk. Leah's sense of peacefulness was shattered as soon as she and Jude entered the kitchen: Adeline and Alice awaited them at the kitchen table, their young faces showing they were spoiling for a confrontation.

"I suppose you told him every little thing," Alice accused, glaring at Leah and then at Jude.

"Why should we stay here, when no one respects our right to privacy?" Adeline put in without missing a beat.

"Matter of fact," Jude jumped in before the twins could continue, "you can stop blaming Leah right now, because your uncle Jeremiah—not to mention Bishop Vernon from Cedar Creek—had already caught wind of your mischief and informed me about their suspicions before Leah did. The Amish grapevine runs swift and spares nobody, girls, so rest assured that your reputations are already toast."

As one, the girls each raised an eyebrow in disbelief. "That is such a stupid threat that—"

"You can't tell me that anybody knows where we've been, so—"

"Leah found you, didn't she?" Jude challenged. He rested his hands on the tabletop, leaning low to gaze into Alice's eyes and then Adeline's. "You girls are grounded. You're not to leave home except to go to church unless you're accompanied by either Leah or me. No arguments." He held out his hand. "I'll be taking your cell phone, too, since you somehow latched onto a much fancier model than the bishop or I allowed you to have."

Their eyes widened as they indignantly sucked in air.

"But you can't—"

"While we're in *rumspringa,* you have no—"

"Like it or not, I'm your father and I'm responsible for you," Jude interrupted in a rising voice. "Girls who wear sheer blouses that show off their black underthings and Tinker Bell tattoos are already on the highway to hell, so starting now, your rights and privacy are the least of my concerns. You'll be staying home, so you won't be needing those tight jeans or dangly earrings—"

"You can't touch our stuff!"

"If you sneak into our room, so help me—"

When both girls rose indignantly from the table, Jude grasped their shoulders. "I'm serious. You can run off to your room, but not before you hand over your phone," he insisted. "I suspect it's in one of your apron pockets."

Glaring in disbelief, Adeline and Alice appeared ready to bolt from Jude even as he held their gazes and their shoulders. Finally, Adeline reached into her apron pocket and hastily tapped on the screen of the cell phone before pressing hard on a button on top of it. She tossed the phone onto the table.

With red faces and muttered curse words, the girls rushed from the kitchen. Moments later the angry thunder of their sneakers on the wooden steps and along the upstairs hallway filled the house with their resentment. Their voices were muffled, but after their bedroom door slammed, the strident tone of their conversation filtered into the kitchen.

Jude raked his hand through his dark hair. "That didn't go well," he muttered in frustration. "I suspect the only way I'll keep them home is to take the wheels off their buggy—or stable their mare over at Jeremiah's."

"I'm sorry," Leah murmured. "The moment we walked in, they were set on confrontation. No matter what you'd said, you weren't going to win them to your way of thinking."

"When did they get so cynical? And so *rude?*" Jude gazed into Leah's eyes, appearing totally baffled. "While Mamm was here, I saw nothing but compliant, well-behaved girls, but my mother was obviously as clueless as I've been. I can't believe all this foul talk and indecent clothing—and tattoos!—have come about in the three months we've been married."

Leah shrugged helplessly. "They were gone some, *jah,* but they were here most of the time—or so I thought. Maybe they've had us all fooled."

"They're thinkin' to hitch up with those English guys real soon. They don't wanna be Amish no more."

Leah's heart sank as she turned to see Stevie's shadowy form in the doorway of the front room. Jude groaned and pulled out a chair so he could sit down and lean his elbows on the table. "What else have they told you, son?" he asked gently. "Do you know these boys' names?"

Stevie entered the kitchen to take his usual seat beside his *dat,* so Leah sat down, too, at Jude's left. "Nope, they don't tell me nothin'. Sometimes I hear 'em talkin' in their room, when they're gettin' ready to leave and they're excited. They don't know I can hear 'em."

Leah pressed her lips together grimly. She couldn't imagine being anything but Plain, and she'd never entertained thoughts of leaving the Old Order. Even when she'd been a teenager and some of her friends had whispered about the exotic lives they might live if they found English husbands, she'd never believed those girls would really leave the Amish church. Indeed, those friends had been married to Amish men for years now and had large families. . . .

But this situation with Alice and Adeline sounded a lot more serious. "Do they want to leave because of me, Stevie?" Leah asked cautiously.

The boy shrugged, shaking his head. "I dunno, but I don't think so," he replied after he'd thought about it. "They're girls, and they get wild-hare ideas sometimes, like maybe once they get married their lives'll be perfect and they won't have no more problems."

Leah's eyebrows rose. Such an observation seemed beyond a five-year-old boy's comprehension, yet Stevie had obviously thought at length about his sisters' situation.

"What problems?" Jude asked, exasperated. "They have a comfortable home and—even if they don't like knowing that I might not be their birth father, they surely can't hate living here badly enough to go English. They have no idea—"

"*Jah*, they have no idea what they'd be getting themselves into," Leah echoed, grasping Jude's forearm in sympathy. "What they've seen of English life in the pool hall—or riding around with boys—is not reality."

"Thank God," Jude put in quickly. "It's one thing for teenage girls to keep secrets from their parents, but it's another thing altogether when they believe that getting away from home will guarantee them the happily-ever-after they apparently envision. You'd think they'd know that, after witnessing the stress and strain of some of the marriages they've been around all their lives."

Leah wondered if Jude was referring in part to the years he'd spent with Frieda, but it wasn't her place to ask. Her heart went out to Jude, who stared glumly at the table, scraping a little spot of food with his fingernail.

"I need to talk to them before they really go off the deep end," he said in a tight voice. He picked up the cell phone, shaking his head. "I should go upstairs right now and—"

Leah sensed Alice and Adeline were in no mood to listen to reason, and that Jude would only be deepening the chasm that seemed to loom between them and their *dat*. "Maybe in the morning, when we're all calmer, we'll have a better idea about what to say to them so they'll actually listen," she suggested, tightening her grip on Jude's arm. "You don't have a sale tomorrow, so we'll all be home together and we can hash this out."

Come very early in the morning, however, Leah was awakened by loud voices in the kitchen—and she realized that

Jude's side of the bed was cold, as though he hadn't been beside her for quite some time.

"You don't own me!" one of the twins yelled.

"You're not even our *dat,* so butt out of our lives!" her sister lashed out vehemently.

Fumbling for her robe, Leah hurried from the bedroom.

Jude had prepared himself for the worst, but he still couldn't believe his eyes. Around ten-thirty the previous evening, a rumbling truck had wakened him from a fitful sleep and on impulse he'd checked the twins' room. He'd known as soon as the door didn't budge that the girls had sneaked out despite his insistence that they stay home. When he'd pushed aside the dresser blocking the door, the open window told him all he needed to know—and the clothing strewn around the room and on the undisturbed beds scared him into remaining awake the rest of the night.

He'd been on the verge of going to fetch Jeremiah—but he'd reasoned that the girls wouldn't be at the pool hall this time. And when he'd gone to saddle Rusty, and he'd seen that the girls' rig and their mare were still in the stable, he'd thought better of rousing his brother for a wild-goose chase. If the girls had left with their English boyfriends in that backfiring truck, they had all the advantages on their side.

So he'd wrapped himself in a blanket and waited in the girls' room, watching for them in the moonlit night. He spent a lot of the time pushing and prodding on the cell phone he'd confiscated, but the screen remained blank—he had no idea how to turn it on. Around four in the morning the girls had dashed in from the road, clambering up the tree like lithe monkeys. He'd stepped into the corner of the room until they were safely inside, slipping the phone into his pocket.

"We're going downstairs to talk about this right now," he'd said, hoping not to waken Stevie and Leah.

Alice and Adeline's shrieks could've roused the dead, but somehow he herded them downstairs and into the kitchen.

Waves of resentment rolled off them as he lit the lamps—and even in the low glow of the lantern he set on the table, he saw the irrefutable evidence of the trouble they were in. The makeup they were wearing was smudged and their long hair hung rumpled around their shoulders—and when they removed English-style jackets he'd not seen before, telltale bruises on their necks completed a picture he didn't want to witness.

Despite the fear that curdled Jude's stomach, his anger got the best of him. "Care to tell me why you defied me by sneaking out in the night?" he demanded.

"You don't own me!" Adeline blurted out.

"You're not even our *dat,* so butt out of our lives!" Alice cried out defiantly.

Memories of the night these girls had been born flashed through Jude's mind. How could he make them believe that despite their mother's duplicity, he had loved them—had considered them blameless and innocent and utterly wonderful since the moment he'd first laid eyes on them?

"I'm sorry you see it that way," Jude whispered. He prayed for a calmer mind-set in which the right words would bring the three of them to resolution—or at least help them speak in more civil tones. "If we can stop placing blame for a moment—if we can acknowledge that no one in this room was responsible for the fact that I'm not your birth father—maybe we can talk about the more serious situation we're in right now."

"And if you think you're old enough to run off with English boys—to marry them and escape your Amish life," Leah asserted from the doorway, "then you're old enough to answer our questions truthfully."

Jude sighed, regretting that the girls' clamor had awakened Leah—yet he was relieved to see her tying the belt of her robe and approaching her seat at the table with a resolve that bolstered his courage. Even with her pale, tired eyes and her long, loose hair pulled hastily back in a kerchief, she'd never looked stronger or more beautiful to him.

"What do you want to know?" Adeline challenged.

"You won't like the answers," Alice warned them archly. "You probably won't even *understand* the answers, seeing's how you know a lot more about ducks and goats than you do about being a wife or a—a mother."

Leah blanched and Jude grasped her hand. "Let's also remember that Leah wasn't around when you were conceived, so you don't need to include her in your resentful accusations," Jude insisted. "For starters, why'd you get those tattoos? And why Tinker Bell?"

The twins exchanged secretive glances. "Our English guys think tatts are sexy," Alice purred. "So they took us to the tattoo parlor and paid for them."

Jude swallowed hard, reminding himself that he was bound to see and hear more than he'd ever wanted to know during this conversation.

"Tinker Bell's our mascot—our role model," Adeline continued with a furtive chuckle. "She can *fly*—so she can leave whenever she wants to."

"With just a wave of her wand, her pixie dust makes everything right again," Alice added breezily. "Tink loves to have fun—and so do we. And to our way of thinking, you can call them *frolics,* but a bunch of women getting together to clean house or cook for hundreds of people coming to a wedding—"

"Or canning vegetables in a hot kitchen, or even spending a day hunched over a blasted *quilt,* gossiping," Adeline interjected with a sneer.

"—is *not* our idea of fun or frolic," Alice finished quickly. "There's more to life than working all the time! All Amish women ever do is *work*."

Leah sighed. She was no stranger to such observations, because she'd escaped what she'd perceived as women's work by spending her time with Dat and the animals. True enough, raising livestock had been her livelihood, but even on cold, snowy days she'd considered barn chores a lot more fun than the canning, cleaning, and quilting the twins had just mentioned in such disgusted tones.

"When I was your age," Leah began carefully, "I thought marriage would be the perfect answer to the problems I perceived in my life—"

"Hah! Who did you think would marry you?" Alice sassed.

"*Jah,*" Adeline put in with a laugh, "most guys probably thought of you as being one of them! More a man than a—"

"That's enough of such talk!" Jude blurted out. "When did you become so crass? So insensitive to everyone else's—" He sighed loudly when Leah rose from the table wearing a perplexed expression. How he wished he'd been able to quash the twins' talk before they'd hurt her feelings again. "Honey, please sit down," he pleaded. "I thank God every day that I recognized you for the fine woman you—"

"Don't you hear it?" Leah demanded as she hurried toward the front room. "I think there's a baby crying outside."

Chapter 10

As Leah stepped outside, the backfiring of a car made her look down the lane in time to see a pair of red taillights turning onto the road. In the darkness, she saw a container near the edge of the porch, from which came the frantic wail of a baby—a sound that had always made her feel helpless and utterly inadequate. Other women had known since they were girls exactly what to do when a wee one cried, but Leah had grown up as a tomboy, without siblings. She was so unfamiliar with babies that she'd joked with her *dat,* saying she'd probably put the diaper on the wrong end—and then stab the poor thing with the safety pins as well.

Shivering in the predawn chill, Leah quickly grabbed the container—a big basket, it was—and carried the crying child inside. She hurried through the dark front room to set the basket on the kitchen table, where the lamps lit the twins' amazed faces. Jude rose to shift the lanterns out of the way as the baby's ear-splitting cries filled the room.

Leah could only stare at the poor little wiggling figure, wrapped in a worn blanket and wearing a tiny white cap. Jude must've read the barely disguised terror in her eyes, because he immediately scooped the infant from the basket and held it against his shoulder.

Adeline watched as he began to walk around the room and murmur comforting words, while Alice snatched a piece of paper from the laundry basket. " 'My name is Betsy and my *mamm* can't keep me,' " she read aloud. " 'Will you please give me a loving home?' "

Leah's heart lurched. "Who would abandon a poor, helpless baby on somebody's porch—and then sneak away like a thief in the night?"

"A *hungry* baby, I suspect," Jude put in as he swayed with the wee child. "What else is in the basket? Any bottles or formula?"

"Nope, just a few folded clothes," Adeline replied as she lifted the items from the basket and placed them on the table. "We gave all the bottles and diapers and other baby stuff to *mamm*'s youngest sister a couple years ago, remember? Mamm said she was finished having babies."

When a pained expression flickered over Jude's face, Leah had a feeling Frieda had made her announcement—unusual for a Plain woman, unless she was ill—without giving Jude any say in the matter, or maybe without telling him beforehand. Her head was beginning to throb with the noise of the baby's cries, so she went to the mudroom to put on a barn coat over her nightclothes. "I'll get some fresh goat's milk," she said as she tied on her black bonnet. "It's the best we can do until we figure out what else to feed her."

The silence of the chilly night relieved Leah's headache as she hurried out the back door toward the stable. *If the girls and Jude think I'm running from that crying baby, well, so be it,* she thought with an embarrassed grimace. *The mother who abandoned Betsy must've been terribly desperate—and obviously had no idea how unprepared I am to deal with a wee one—when she dumped her off in a laundry basket and drove away. Her use of the word* mamm *seems Amish, yet I can't think a Plain family wouldn't care for such a sweet, wee baby. . . .*

Once inside the stable door, Leah lit the lantern hanging on the wall. As she walked past dozing horses toward the pens of goats in the back, her thoughts cleared. Gertie and her new twins were settled in their straw, appearing peaceful and content, their eyes reflecting the lamplight as they glanced up at her. In the adjoining pen, the goats Leah raised for their meat roused from their sleep, watching her continue to the pen where she kept the three milk goats.

Daisy, Tulip, and Buttercup rose slowly to their feet, assuming it was time for their morning milking. Leah quickly fastened Tulip into the milking stand, poured some feed into the attached trough, and grabbed a bucket. As the milk hit the metal in rhythmic spurts, she was keenly aware of how she could tend her animals without even thinking about it, yet she had no idea how to proceed with little Betsy—except that the poor abandoned baby needed food, diapers, and other supplies as soon as they could gather them. She felt confident about feeding Betsy goat's milk diluted with some water, because she'd supplied milk for a couple of neighbor ladies who'd been unable to nurse their wee ones, but beyond that . . .

Why on earth did that woman leave Betsy here? She could've chosen any number of other homes in Morning Star where folks already had young kids and babies.

When she'd milked the three goats, Leah took a big plastic bottle and its nippled lid from the cabinet. She sighed, replacing it. Even though the bottle and lid had been sterilized between uses with orphaned lambs, she didn't dare risk infecting Betsy by using her livestock equipment.

Lord, I hope You're giving Jude and the twins some ideas about how to proceed from here, she prayed as she strode toward the house with her covered bucket of goat's milk. When she stepped into the mudroom, Betsy's cries sounded quieter. She saw the twins at the stove with a pan of boiling water.

"We found an eye dropper, and the girls are sterilizing it," Jude explained. He was rubbing Betsy's back as she rested against his shoulder. "After we've had breakfast and tended the animals, we'll visit some neighbors to borrow diapers and such—and we'll let Jeremiah know we have an abandoned baby."

They make it sound so simple, Leah mused as she took off her barn coat and bonnet. "I have to pasteurize this milk—boil it and then cool it quickly with an ice bath," she remarked. "Meanwhile, would some water make Betsy feel better?"

Jude smiled gently. He looked completely at ease handling the tiny baby, even as he picked up on Leah's nervousness. "The girls have changed her diaper, so as soon as that eye dropper is cool enough, I'll give Betsy some water, *jah,*" he said softly. "I can't imagine why her mother would've dropped her off—let alone left her without even the basic necessities. She's a sweet little thing. Probably no more than three months old, best I can tell."

Leah swallowed hard. The tension that had hardened Jude's face while he was squabbling with his daughters had disappeared, and he now appeared totally smitten by the tiny girl he was rocking from side to side. As his gaze met hers, Leah saw desire in his dark eyes—not sexual desire so much as the yearning to hold his own baby . . . a baby he'd fathered with her.

Leah had anticipated Jude's wanting to start a second family, and despite her lack of experience with babies, she was eager to have his child—because she'd figured on having about nine months to prepare herself for motherhood. In the harried hours since the twins had confronted Jude about not being their birth father, Leah had fleetingly wondered if he was unable to father children, considering the long gap between the twins' births and Stevie's. That wasn't a subject she wanted to ask him about, however—and now that baby Betsy had arrived so unexpectedly, they had more immediate issues to deal with.

The longer Jude gazes at me this way, the less anything else matters, Leah realized as her insides fluttered. Because the love she shared with him was so much more wonderful than what she'd imagined before the wedding, she knew she was truly a blessed woman—even if Alice and Adeline despised her. *Jude will know what to do about Betsy. And maybe having a baby in the house will inspire the twins to behave more lovingly. More responsibly.*

"What's goin' on? Who's cryin' so loud?" Stevie asked hoarsely.

Leah smiled at him. As he stood in the kitchen doorway, his thick brown hair stuck straight up on one side, and his short flannel pajama pants suggested that he'd grown a lot since someone—probably Margaret—had sewn them for him. "We got a surprise package this morning," she explained. "The baby's name is Betsy, and her *mamm* left her on our porch."

Stevie's eyes widened. "Her *mamm* just up and left her? In the middle of the night?"

Leah nodded as she got out the large pot she used to pasteurize her goat's milk. "It makes me wonder, though, if Betsy's *mamm* is Amish, because she drove off in a noisy car. I saw its taillights on the road just as I stepped outside."

Alice's and Adeline's eyebrows rose as they stepped away from the stove and removed the eyedropper from the boiling water. "Odd," one of them said, and the other echoed the sentiment.

Jude watched his daughters' faces as he continued his walk with Betsy. "Any idea who might've been driving the car? One of your friends, maybe?" he asked. "If Jeremiah and I can reach Betsy's mother—"

"Not a clue," Alice insisted.

"Nobody we know," Adeline put in quickly. "We'll get our clothes changed and make breakfast, so we can round up some baby clothes from the neighbors."

Stevie appeared fully awake, his face lighting up. "So we get to keep her?" he asked eagerly. "I wanna help take care of her! Can I, Leah? Please, can I?"

Leah's heart swelled at the boy's generous offer before she

poured the goat's milk into the big pot on the stove. "I think that's a fine idea, Stevie," she replied softly. "But if we find Betsy's mother, we might not be keeping her—"

"*Jah,* don't get your heart set on having a little sister," Adeline warned as she and Alice left the kitchen. "Babies really do belong with their mothers."

As Leah exchanged a glance with Jude, she sensed he thought the twins might know more than they were saying. The tone of Adeline's remark also suggested that she wasn't keen on having Betsy around—but then, Jude's girls had displayed a negative attitude about a lot of things.

"Get your clothes on, Stevie, and we'll do the barn chores," Jude suggested. "The work always goes faster when you help me, son."

With a grin, Stevie took off through the front room. As his footsteps thundered in the stairwell, Jude approached Leah with Betsy. The baby had stopped crying and was resting comfortably on his broad shoulder. "Want to hold her, Leah?" he asked softly. "The only thing you need to be careful about is supporting her head with your hand—like this."

Leah focused on clipping the candy thermometer to the side of her pot, momentarily flummoxed. When she saw how Jude was gently stretching Betsy along his forearm so her tiny head rested in his hand, she knew a new definition of *strength*. Her husband wasn't much taller than she was, but he was muscled from working with livestock all his life—she'd watched him hang on to frenzied horses and cows that outweighed him two or three times over, with just a tether and his own powerful grip. Yet he'd never seemed stronger than at this moment, when he held Betsy's life in his hands.

"Go ahead and hold her, honey. You won't drop her."

Leah exhaled nervously. Slowly she accepted Betsy, holding her the same way Jude had. "Oh my, she hardly weighs anything, compared to a fawn or a foal," she murmured.

Jude stroked Betsy's forehead, his fingertip following the rim of her knitted cap. "She's so tiny and innocent," he whis-

pered, shaking his head sadly. "She knows she's among
strangers, and she might even sense that her mother has abandoned her. It's up to us to give her our best until we can get to
the bottom of her situation. I know she'll be in *gut* hands while
the girls and I borrow what we'll need from the neighbors and
visit with Jeremiah."

Leah's heart fluttered at the depth of his trust in her. "I—
I'll do my best."

"That's all any of us can do," Jude said, kissing her cheek.
"And for all we know, Betsy's *mamm* feels she's done *her* best
by bringing her child here. Life can take some unexpected de-
tours, so we shouldn't judge a mother who's desperate
enough to entrust her precious child to strangers."

Leah thought back to the brief note in the clothesbasket.
"What if we're not strangers? What if Betsy's mother chose
us because she knows us?"

Jude shrugged. "I can't think of any women—or young
girls—in our church district who'd be in such a predicament.
That's why I want to chat with Jeremiah. Sometimes he learns
of these situations through the grapevine of bishops and
preachers in other districts hereabouts, and he can put out
the word about Betsy with those men, too. The fact that she
used the word *mamm* in her note suggests she's from a Plain
community, even if she drove off in a car. We'll figure it out."

Jude wrapped an arm around Leah and placed his other
hand beneath hers, enfolding her and little Betsy with his
warmth. "At least that young woman understood the value
of bringing her baby to be cared for by a *family*. No matter
what my daughters seem to believe these days, only our love
for God matters more than love for our family. I'm a blessed
man because you're my wife, Leah."

When Stevie burst into the kitchen, dressed and ready to
do chores, Jude placed Betsy in the laundry basket on top of
her folded clothes. He slipped into his barn coat, kissed
Leah's cheek, and went outside with his son just as the milk
began to bubble and steam.

Leah watched the thermometer. When the milk had reached one hundred sixty-one degrees and boiled for more than twenty seconds, she removed the pot from the stove. As she was pouring the milk into clean metal canisters, Alice and Adeline returned. Dressed in their matching purple cape dresses and white *kapps,* they cast wary glances at the baby in the laundry basket before taking a skillet and a large bowl from cabinets near the stove.

"I still think it's odd that somebody would drop a baby *here,*" Adeline remarked with a shake of her head.

"*Jah,* who would do that?" Alice asked. She wrinkled her nose. "And who would want to drink goat's milk? It smells awful."

Although Leah once again suspected the twins knew more about this situation than they were telling her, she decided not to press for ideas about who Betsy's mother might be. "It does smell a little gamy, compared to cow's milk," she agreed. "But I know a lot of babies who've thrived on it when their mothers couldn't feed them breast milk. It'll smell better after it cools."

Leah carried the canisters to the sink in the mudroom. She fetched a large bag of ice cubes from the deep freeze and arranged the ice around the canisters so the milk would cool quickly. Betsy was beginning to fuss, and the girls were focused on frying bacon and mixing biscuits, so Leah went to stand beside the laundry basket. The baby's face was pink and puckered as she let out a squawk. Her flailing limbs were so tiny and thin compared to other infants' that Leah wondered if the poor thing had been neglected and underfed.

"Just pick her up!" Adeline challenged from the stove. "Don't let her start bawling again."

"*Jah,* she's a little kid—not a rabid dog that'll bite you," Alice chided as she rolled out biscuit dough. "Don't tell me you've never handled a baby."

Leah lifted Betsy tentatively and rested the baby against her shoulder. It occurred to her that the girls would've been about eleven when Stevie had come along—old enough to help Frieda with his care, even though they showed no interest in this abandoned child. She walked into the mudroom to test the temperature of the goat's milk, but also to hide her red-faced embarrassment. How did Jude's girls home in so effortlessly on her weaknesses? Why did they delight in making her feel lacking as a woman—and so unwelcome in their home?

The milk was at a drinkable temperature, but how much did a baby drink at one time? Lacking a bottle, Leah returned to the kitchen and poured some milk into a cereal bowl. No doubt the twins knew a better way to feed a baby, but they were making a point of ignoring her while they cooked, so she didn't ask their advice. She picked up the eyedropper, but had second thoughts about using it. What if Betsy sucked hard enough to break the glass?

Carefully cradling the baby in her arm, Leah took a spoon and a towel from the kitchen drawers and then retreated to the unlit front room and the comfort of Jude's cozy corduroy recliner. She set the bowl of milk on the nearby table. Why did the simple act of feeding a baby require so much thought and effort?

You poor thing, having to put up with my clumsiness, Leah thought as she positioned Betsy in the crook of her arm. *We both wish your* mamm *was taking care of you, don't we?*

When Betsy gazed at her, so tiny and trusting, Leah's heart melted. Somehow she spooned a small amount of milk into the baby's mouth without spilling it, and when Betsy gulped it eagerly, Leah kept feeding her slowly and methodically. The aromas of bacon, biscuits, and percolating coffee drifted from the kitchen, but it was Jude's masculine scent in the chair's corduroy that kept Leah centered and calm. After a while she heard the mudroom door close behind Jude and Stevie. The daily routine was going on around her, yet Leah sat mesmerized, watching Betsy's bow-shaped lips and eager swallowing.

Stevie approached the recliner slowly, his eyes wide. "She was really hungry, huh?" he whispered.

"*Jah,* she's finally slowing down and getting sleepy," Leah replied. She smiled at the boy as he gazed at the baby's closing eyes. "Did you wash your hands? We have to be very clean around Betsy."

"*Jah!*" Stevie held up his hands, smiling. His mood grew more serious as he gazed at the baby, who was drifting off in Leah's arms. "Her *mamm* left her, just like mine did," he said sadly, stroking the knit hat. "We gotta take *gut* care of Betsy and be her family now, ain't so? She really needs us."

Leah blinked back tears. Stevie's heartfelt words—and the way Betsy was now breathing deeply, so peacefully—convinced her that God had brought this helpless, innocent child to them to soothe their frazzled souls. Just when Leah had been at wit's end, wondering how to endure Adeline's and Alice's disrespect, a baby had arrived to remind them that the members of the Shetler family depended upon one another, just as all of God's children looked to Him for support and guidance.

When I'm feeling anxious, God, remind me that You're in charge and taking care of us, Leah prayed quickly. *Bless us all as we try to do what's best for this precious baby.*

Chapter 11

Around noon, Jude returned home. His enclosed double buggy, built to hold an entire family, was so full of borrowed baby necessities that Alice and Adeline had to sit facing each other on the back benches, surrounded by boxes and bins. When he parked near the mudroom door, the girls quickly carried armloads of items inside and he followed them with a bassinet.

"We'll fix dinner now," Adeline called out.

"*Jah*, you and Leah can figure out where to put all this stuff," Alice chimed in. "We don't have a clue where you want it."

As Jude passed through the kitchen and into the front room behind his daughters, he was pleased to see Leah seated on the sofa, holding little Betsy in a blanket, with Stevie leaning against her. The boy quickly put a finger to his lips, signaling for their silence.

The twins stacked their boxes on the floor around the recliner and returned to the kitchen, which gave Jude a moment to drink in the precious sight of his wife and son, both engrossed in the baby who dozed in the cradle of Leah's bent arm. With her hat off and her thin face framed by a froth of wispy curls, Betsy closely resembled Alice and Adeline when they'd been babies.

Someday that'll be my child Leah's holding, he dared to dream as his heart swelled. *If You'll grant me that one favor, Lord, my life will feel wondrously complete.*

He had no room to complain to God about the fullness of his present life, yet Jude yearned to expand his family—and the serenity that filled the front room lightened his mood, lifted his hopes. He stopped a few feet in front of the sofa. "Looks like I got here just in time with this bassinet," he whispered. "Shall I put it in the room next to ours?"

Leah's expressive eyebrows rose as she watched the twins carry in more plastic bins. "Let's go upstairs and figure that out," she said as she scooted to the edge of the couch. "Looks like you came home with quite a haul."

"*Jah,* the neighbors are all buzzing like bees now, wondering who abandoned this wee girl," he said as he offered her a hand up. "Jeremiah was alarmed to hear that such a desperate mother lives hereabouts—and he has no idea who she might be. Stevie," he added with a smile for his son, "I'd appreciate it if you'd drive the rig into the stable after it's emptied out, please."

The boy's eyes lit up, for he loved to drive the short distances Jude let him navigate around the home place. "*Jah,* I can do that!" he said in a loud whisper.

Jude gestured for Leah to precede him up the steps with Betsy. When they'd reached the upstairs hallway, he said, "Looks like you three were having a cozy time of it while the girls and I were gone."

Leah beamed at him. "Stevie's already wrapped up in this baby girl," she said. "He says they have a lot in common, because their *mamms* have both left them."

Jude's heart lurched, and he had to blink to clear his vision.

"So your visit with Jeremiah went well? And how's your mother?"

Leah's question brought him out of his momentary sorrow. "I saw firsthand just how accomplished my daughters are at playing charades," he muttered. "As we sat in the kitchen telling Jeremiah about finding Betsy on the porch, Adeline and Alice were sitting as primly as a pair of schoolgirls in church—as though they knew nothing about sneaking out last night, or defying my orders to stay home. Mamm fell for it," he added with a sigh. "She remarked how pleased she was to see that the rumors about them hanging out in the pool hall couldn't possibly be true. The twins just smiled sweetly and went along with Mamm's bent for looking the other way."

Leah's eyebrows rose. "She didn't see those bruises on their necks?"

Jude shook his head as they stepped into the guest room next to the room he shared with Leah. In years past this room had served as a nursery for the twins and then for Stevie until they'd graduated to their own rooms and regular beds. He'd always hoped that someday, another baby would need this room. "Alice and Adeline sat on either side of her, positioning themselves so those marks were on the sides Mamm wasn't looking at as she chatted with them," he explained. "They sounded sincerely interested in Betsy's welfare, and eager to gather the supplies we need for her."

"Hmm." A wide range of emotions played upon Leah's face. "When you and Stevie were doing the chores, they were a lot more interested in telling me how inept I am with a baby. You could've taken Betsy to sleep in the barn and they would've been fine with it, as long as she stopped crying."

Jude's eyes closed in regret as he slipped an arm around Leah. "I'm sorry the girls are treating you so deplorably. I'll have to have another talk—"

"Let it go, Jude," Leah whispered. "They're not entirely wrong, because I *am* at a loss when I'm around human babies. But if I let the twins' rude remarks upset me, they'll continue talking that way because they've found my weakness. If I counter them—or ignore their insults—they'll tire of trying to get my goat. So to speak."

Jude smiled sadly at her humor. Leah was proving to be one of the wisest—and strongest—women he knew. And at this moment, she looked totally comfortable with Betsy dozing on her shoulder. "*Jah*, but that doesn't excuse me from setting them straight," he said softly. "If they've allowed those English boys to kiss them so roughly on the neck, I'm concerned about where else they might have bruises . . . and what else they've been doing."

"*Jah*, there's that." Leah nodded glumly, gazing around the small room. "What if we put the bassinet in the corner of our bedroom? I'd hate for Betsy to wake up all by herself in here and wonder if she's been abandoned again. Baby animals begin to shut down from stress when they realize they've been orphaned, so why should we assume that human babies don't do the same?"

Jude hugged her close, kissing Betsy's soft hair. "God knew what He was doing when He sent Betsy's *mamm* here," he said with a gentle smile. "I'll bring the bassinet upstairs. While Betsy sleeps, you can decide where to put all those diapers and clothes the neighbor ladies loaned us."

He quietly slipped toward the door, and then turned. "By the way, I took the liberty of calling your mother," he said. "She sounded delighted about coming here for an extended stay to help with Betsy, so I—I hope you don't mind."

"Mind?" Leah's face lit up the dim room. "Oh, *denki* for thinking of that, Jude! Betsy's only been here a few hours, but I already understand why mothers with wee babies and children can't possibly have enough hands—or hours in the day."

After Lenore parked her buggy in the lane on Sunday afternoon, she walked toward the Shetler home with a twinge of apprehension, but her eager anticipation of spending time with Leah propelled her to the door. Neither the church in Cedar Creek nor the one in Morning Star had a worship service today, so this visiting Sunday was the perfect time to begin her stay with Leah's new family. She hoped she could bring harmony and healing to a household she sensed was in chaos after the startling details Jude had shared with her over the phone on Friday.

Lenore was pleased to see that the porch was swept and that the house had been painted recently. The lawn was well maintained, too, and the outbuildings were in good repair—signs that Jude was prosperous and was taking good care of his family. Often during the past few months she'd wished for an invitation to come to her daughter's home, yet she suspected Leah had been too busy—or too overwhelmed—keeping up with Jude's teenage twins and little Stevie to ask her over.

I could've come here any time and I would've been welcome, Lenore reminded herself. *But I didn't want to interfere while Leah settled in as a new wife and stepmother . . . even though she sounded as if she were keeping her troubles to herself whenever we talked on the phone.*

The front door opened and Stevie stepped out onto the porch. He gazed at her shyly at first as Leah joined him.

"Mama, it's so *gut* to see you!" Leah blurted out as she hurried across the porch. "And it's so nice of you to come help us with baby Betsy, too."

Leah's embrace dispelled Lenore's doubts about coming and restored her lonely soul. "How could I stay away when Jude told me you suddenly had an abandoned baby to care for?" she teased as she returned her daughter's hug. "That sort of thing doesn't happen every day, thank the Lord."

"*Jah,* we don't know who Betsy's *mamm* is, so we're her family now," Stevie piped up from the porch. "We got baby goats and ducklings, too! Wanna see 'em?"

Lenore released Leah to focus on the young boy. He still regarded her cautiously, but he'd become much more confident since the wedding, when he'd spent the day clinging to Margaret. "Baby goats and ducklings?" she repeated eagerly. "I'd love to see them sometime, Stevie, because I sort of miss having those animals at my house. Right now, though, I could use some help carrying boxes and bags—and then you can park my rig for me and tend my mare, Flo."

With a little whoop, Stevie sprang from the porch and shot toward her buggy. Lenore chuckled. "Stevie's come a long way," she remarked as she and Leah followed him. "I hope Alice and Adeline are as eager to please as he is?"

Leah let out a humorless laugh. "You warned me, Mama," she said sadly. "Jude and I are pulling out our hair over the twins' escapades. They're home today—but only because he took the back wheels off their buggy."

Lenore's eyebrows shot up. "Oh my. So the rumors about them running with English boys are true?"

"*Jah,* not that we have any idea who those boys are." Leah stopped a few yards from where Stevie was taking a plastic bin from the rig. Her eyes took on a sad desperation as she shook her head. "They despise me, Mama. But you're here now, so let's not waste a minute churning sour butter. Plenty of time for details about the girls on a day when they're not home—although Jude has grounded them indefinitely."

Lenore sighed with regret. *See there? You should've been coming for visits all along, knowing Leah would be too proud—or stubborn—to admit all the trouble she's been dealing with.*

"*Gut* heavens, Mama! Your rig's chock-full of boxes and bins," Leah exclaimed when she peered inside it. "What all did you bring?"

"I think she's stayin' a long time!" Stevie said as he headed toward the house with a bin of fabric. "I saw two suitcases and a whole lotta other stuff!"

Lenore laughed, gratified by the boy's excitement. "Well, I had more jars of peaches and vegetables than I can possibly eat this season—and I figured I'd make myself useful by sewing some clothes for the baby, as well as for you and Jude and the kids," she replied. "So I brought fabric and—"

"Oh, Mama." Leah's embrace was tighter this time, and she was breathing shallowly . . . as though she was trying not to cry. "*Denki* so much for thinking of us all. I'm so sorry I didn't invite you here sooner, but—but I didn't want you to know just how awful things have been with the girls. There. I've said it."

Lenore wrapped her arms tightly around her daughter and rocked her gently, as she'd done when Leah was growing up. Her daughter might have grown into an adult body, but inside she was still vulnerable and sensitive and just enough like her *dat* that she would never ask for help. "I'm sorry you've had such a tough time of it, Leah," she murmured. "I'm here to help in whatever ways you need me to, sweetheart."

Leah eased out of Lenore's arms to flick away tears with her thumb. "Unfortunately, Margaret doesn't share your helpful attitude—nor does she believe Adeline and Alice would sneak out of the house or get matching tattoos, amongst other things. But those are stories for another day," she added as she reached into the rig for a sturdy cardboard box filled with jars of food.

Tattoos? On Amish girls? Once again Lenore couldn't imagine what Leah and Jude had been going through, and she felt even more determined to make her time here count for something positive and productive. This visit would be a gift only she could give to the daughter she'd missed so badly the past three months.

When Lenore followed Leah to the back door and into the kitchen, she immediately noticed the empty baby bottles drying in the sink drainer, along with the deep pot used to sterilize them on the stove. A plate of cookies on the counter caught her eye, too. "Those snickerdoodles look heavenly," she said as she set her suitcases on the floor. "I confess that I haven't baked cookies since you left home, Leah, because it would take me forever to eat a whole batch."

"I could help ya eat 'em!" Stevie blurted as he grabbed two of the cookies from the plate. He smiled mischievously at her. "I like Alice's snickerdoodles, but peanut butter cookies with chocolate chips are my favorite—in case you're won-derin'."

Lenore laughed out loud, delighted by Stevie's way with words. "I'll keep that in mind," she said. "After all, baking cookies is one of the things a *mammi* does best, ain't so?"

Stevie's hand stopped halfway to his mouth, his cookie suspended as he considered what she'd said. "*Jah,* if you're Leah's *mamm*—and she's my *mamm* now—that makes you my *mammi,*" he reasoned softly. "That's *gut* to know."

Lenore's heart stood still. For years she'd dreamed of spoiling grandchildren, while wondering if Leah would ever marry. The way Stevie gazed at her with his eager blue eyes, wrapping her in his wondrous, innocent love, suddenly made her feel like the most special woman in the world. "You have your *mammi* Margaret, too," she pointed out.

"*Jah,* but she doesn't wanna live with us no more—and Mammi Lovina moved away to Ohio, wherever *that* is," Ste-vie said wistfully.

"She and your Dawdi Cletus went east to live with their son after your *mamm* passed," Leah clarified gently.

"Oh. *Jah,* that's how it was." Stevie's face lit up with boy-ish joy as he looked at Lenore again. "So, see there? We had an opening for another *mammi,* and here you are. I'm gonna see what other stuff's in your rig!"

Lenore's hand fluttered to her heart as she watched him run outside. "My word, who would ever have thought that little boy would be so—"

"Amazing? Lovable?" Leah asked with a little laugh. "He's been a real bright spot, and he's so devoted to Betsy. Come in and see her before she wakes up crying for her bottle."

As Lenore entered the comfortably furnished front room, she smiled at a white wicker crib near the picture window. The sight of Jude napping in his recliner with a tiny baby sleeping on his shoulder tugged at her heartstrings. "The poor man looks exhausted," she said quietly. "I hope Betsy hasn't been keeping you both awake since she arrived."

"He's lost a lot of sleep over Adeline and Alice lately," Leah whispered with a shake of her head. "After another lecture at the dinner table today, he sent them upstairs. He . . . he took to Betsy the first moment he saw her. She's such a blessing to us."

Lenore nodded. She'd always liked Jude, and his unconditional acceptance of other men's children made him even more admirable, in her opinion. She walked carefully toward the pair, hoping not to waken them. "Ohh," she cooed as she leaned over to look at the baby. "What a precious little face—like a doll's, so pretty and pink."

Jude opened one eye. "That surely can't be *my* face you're talking about," he whispered. "Sorry I didn't hear you come in, Lenore. If you'll take Betsy, I'll go unload your rig."

Lenore gladly cradled the little baby in her arms, delighting in Betsy's tiny fingers and bow-shaped mouth—and her shining eyes when she opened them. "You know, babies this young all tend to look somewhat alike," she remarked softly as she began to sway from side to side, "but Betsy reminds me a lot of you when you were this age, Leah. Your hair was this shade of brown, and you had such a thin little face."

Her daughter looked startled. "I—I never thought about her resembling any of us, Mama. My face probably changed week by week when I was a baby."

"That's true of tiny faces," Jude put in as he rose from the recliner. "But I've noticed a few similarities between Betsy's face and yours, as well—and I've gazed at both of them enough to know, *jah?*" he added, gently touching Leah's cheek.

Lenore smiled, relishing the rise of color in her daughter's complexion. She was pleased that Jude and Leah still appeared to be crazy for each other despite the trouble Alice and Adeline were giving them. As Jude left to unload her buggy, she and Leah returned to the kitchen, where Leah took a metal canister from the refrigerator.

"It's a *gut* thing you've got goat's milk to feed this wee

one," she said. "So much easier on her tummy than store-bought formula. And you can't beat the price."

Leah smiled as she poured milk into one of the clean bottles from the drainer. "Stevie's new mission is learning how to milk the goats, so he can help with feeding her. I let him practice on Tulip, because she's the most patient."

As she imagined the boy seated beside Leah's goats, Lenore chuckled. "I suspect he's an *enthusiastic* milker—maybe more eager than your goats would prefer."

Leah laughed. "Stevie's enthusiastic about most things, bless him—and that's such an improvement over his earlier sadness," she added. A creak in the floor above them made her glance upward. "We keep asking God for an attitude adjustment to transform the twins, but I don't see it happening anytime soon. Incorrigible, they are."

"God answers our prayers in His own *gut* time, and often in ways we don't expect," Lenore said, gazing from the baby to her daughter. "Before the girls come downstairs, tell me what I can do that'll be the biggest help to you, Leah. If you've given Adeline and Alice certain duties, I don't want to interfere—or let them off the hook, if they're to be responsible for, say, the laundry or the cleaning."

"Will you cook for us?" Leah replied plaintively. "I really miss your breakfast casseroles and your meat loaf and chicken spaghetti, and your soft bread and cinnamon rolls and—well, it's high time I learned to cook the way you do, Mama. The twins can put food on the table, but their hearts aren't in it."

Lenore smiled wistfully. "I would love to cook for your family, Leah. I confess that all too often these days, I resort to a bowl of cereal or eating fruit straight from the jar, because making a regular meal for just myself seems like such a bother." She smiled at little Betsy, who was wide awake now and starting to fuss for her bottle. "You have a higher priority than cooking now, so I'll be happy to take over the meal prep."

"Wow, that's *gut* news!" one of the twins remarked as she entered the kitchen.

"*Jah,* making food has never really been our cup of tea," her sister said, reaching for a snickerdoodle. "Baking cookies is fun, but fixing a meal is such a chore."

Lenore turned to greet Alice and Adeline, who wore matching cape dresses of deep rose—with bodices so snug as to appear a size too small. "Hello, girls, it's *gut* to see you again," she began, carefully considering her response. She'd raised a daughter who hadn't liked to cook—but Leah had never seemed so eager to get out of working. Nor had she worn such immodest clothing.

Don't forget that these girls lost the woman who probably sewed for them . . . the woman who loved them as only a mother could.

When Jude came through the back door carrying two large, stacked plastic bins, Lenore was grateful for his timing. "Here's some of the fabric I brought along, thinking we could make everyone some new clothes," she said, gesturing for Jude to set the bins on the kitchen table. "Why not pick out the colors you like best, and we can start sewing tomorrow?"

"Fine idea," Jude said with a knowing nod at Lenore. "I suspect there's fabric in the closet of the middle bedroom where the sewing machine is, too, because Frieda made a trip to the Cedar Creek Mercantile a few days before she passed."

Lenore blinked. The twins' stricken expressions told her that this mention of their mother's death had caught them by surprise, as grief often did. "That means we'll have plenty to choose from," she said, smiling at Alice and Adeline. "With the three of us working at it, we should be able to whip up dresses and shirts for all of you—as well as diapers and clothes for Betsy."

The twins exchanged a doubtful glance. "The three of us?" one of them asked as she lifted the lid from a bin.

"I take it Leah won't be sewing?" the other sister remarked archly.

Lenore bit back a retort as she handed Betsy to her daughter. "As you can see, Leah's got her hands full, caring for—"

"Well, Alice, at least we've got some cool colors to choose from," Adeline said as she held up a large roll of magenta fabric. "Can't you see us wearing crop tops and capris made from this?"

Alice laughed and lifted other rolls of fabric from the bin. "And sleeveless minidresses made from this tangerine piece—with the kitten heels we saw in the shoe store last week!"

Crop tops and capris? Kitten heels? Lenore had no idea what the twins were talking about—except she was certain no Plain woman would be seen wearing the items the girls had mentioned. *I guess I'll be glad they at least like the colors I've chosen and go from there. Give me patience, Lord. I'm going to need a wagonload of it.*

Chapter 12

"I smell coffee," Jude said as he held Leah close beneath the covers.

"Maybe we've died and gone to heaven, because I smell cinnamon rolls," Leah teased. She squinted at the alarm clock on the nightstand. "It's barely four-thirty. Mama and I made the roll dough last night and put it in the fridge. I insisted we could scramble eggs—cook something easy her first morning here—but bless her, she's gotten up early enough to bake those rolls for our breakfast."

"Maybe she had trouble sleeping in a strange place."

Leah bussed Jude's cheek and swung her legs over the side of the bed. "The least I can do is go downstairs and help her—and make sure she's all right. After Dat passed, she took to sleeping in while I went out to tend the animals. I love having her here pampering us, but not at the expense of her getting enough rest."

"You go ahead. I'll see to Betsy," Jude whispered.

Leah smiled as she reached for the dress she'd draped over the back of the rocking chair the previous evening. With her mother in the kitchen filling the house with the aromas of her cooking, and Jude being so considerate about caring for Betsy, life felt really good again—even if having a baby around required a new kind of patience. From years of practice, Leah dressed quickly in the darkness and wound her hair into a fat bun at the nape of her neck. When she'd determined that Betsy was still sleeping soundly in the bassinet, she slipped into the hallway with her shoes in her hand.

Leah padded downstairs and into the kitchen, cherishing the sight of her mother in the lamplight. "Mama, *gut* morning! When I asked you to cook for us, I didn't mean you had to start in the wee hours," she said lightly. "I hope you slept well?"

Mama opened the oven door and removed two pans of high, puffy cinnamon rolls. She appeared troubled, and didn't reply until she'd set the pans on trivets to cool. "I slept fine until I heard activity in the twins' room—and the rumble of a big truck that pulled in from the road. It's a wonder they don't fall to their death climbing down that tree in the dark."

Leah sighed. The room she shared with Jude was on the opposite side of the house from the girls' room, and she was so tired by evening that she slept too soundly to notice them slipping out. "So much for them obeying their *dat*'s order to stay at home," she said as she slipped an arm around her mother. "I'm sorry they woke you. Oh my, but your cinnamon rolls smell *gut*."

"You can stir up the frosting for them," Mama instructed, pointing toward a slip of paper fixed to the refrigerator with a magnet. "I jotted the recipe for you. I wish it were as easy to write you a solution to Alice and Adeline's dangerous behavior. Amish girls have been slipping out with their beaux since before I was born, but . . . well, it doesn't feel as worrisome when girls meet boys who're driving buggies rather than big, fancy trucks."

Leah smiled at her mother's sentiment. *Plain boys have the same urges as English ones,* she mused as she took milk and butter from the refrigerator to make the frosting. But she would feel better if Adeline and Alice were dating Amish boys, because Plain fellows were more likely to share the same values and sense of responsibility Jude's girls had been raised with. *Not that the twins' values are shining through their current behavior.*

After she'd mixed the frosting with the rotary beater—noting how lumpy it looked, compared to the frosting Mama always made—Leah went out to tend her animals. In the shadowy barn, while milking her goats by lantern light and feeding her ducks and chickens, she felt a sense of peace and predictability. It was such a blessing to work with animals that trusted her and were truly happy to see her. She found herself wishing such barnyard harmony could be cultivated in the house. Leah had hoped that her mother's presence would inspire Alice and Adeline to be more tolerant and polite—at least for the first few days. Yet they continued to defy their *dat*'s decree about staying at home.

A loud rumble made Leah scurry to peer around the barn. A large pickup truck was pulling in off the road, forming a dark gray silhouette against the pale sky of dawn. Its taillights burned red and its headlights sliced the horizon. Before the truck came to a complete stop, the doors on the passenger side opened and were slammed shut. The twins cried out in harsh voices.

"*Jah*, we heard you—loud and clear!"

"Don't come back until you've gotten over yourselves!"

Leah sucked in her breath, wondering if Alice and Adeline would be safely out of the way before the truck shot backward. Its tires spun and sent dust flying up in a cloud before the driver reached the road and drove off with a loud squeal of rubber. The twins grasped each other's hands as they ran across the yard, their long hair streaming behind them. Their agitation was palpable even from a distance, so Leah felt compelled to set down her buckets of goat's milk. She sprinted across the lawn to meet them. "Girls—wait!" she cried out. "Are you all right?"

The three of them reached the big maple tree beside the house at about the same time. Alice and Adeline were crying, yet they glared at her.

"What do you care if we're all right?" one of them blurted.

"*Jah,* are you happy now, hearing that we've sent those guys packing?" her sister retorted.

Leah was relieved that they stayed on the ground rather than clambering up the tree, because their vision was surely blurred by their tears. "What happened that made everyone so angry?" she asked in a concerned voice.

"None of your business!"

"It's all Dat's fault, for taking our cell phone!"

"Well, see, it's *not* our phone—"

"And Dex—the guy who's paying the phone bill," the twin nearest Leah amended quickly, "is really mad that he can't call us or text us."

"So of course he wants the phone back."

"And we don't know where it is! Dat has it!"

Leah could anticipate her response being shot down, but she gave it anyway. "Seems the simplest thing would be to tell your *dat* whom he should return the phone to, and where this young man lives," she said.

"Right, like that's going to happen!"

"How stupid do you think we are? No way are we telling Dat where to take that phone!"

Leah smiled, shrugging as she went toward the back door of the house. "The next simplest thing would be for that young man to stop paying the bill—to shut off service to the phone. Ain't so?"

The twins jogged in front of her, their faces turning deep pink with exasperation.

"You think this is really funny, don't you, Leah?"

"*Jah,* and next you're going to say that it'd be better if we never saw those guys again, anyway—that we should go

back to being *gut* little Amish girls who don't raise their
voices or give their family any trouble!"

Leah stopped with her hand on the doorknob to look at
them. She still had trouble telling them apart, and she couldn't
deny that they were attractive—downright enticing in their
tight jeans and tops, with their long brown hair falling loose
around their pretty faces and shapely bodies. Although she
didn't wish they were ugly, she realized that her plainer appearance during her teen years—her lackadaisical attitude toward
the way she'd dressed, and her tomboyish activities—had probably kept her away from temptation and compromising situations.

"I'm very concerned about the places you go with those
boys, and the lack of respect they show you—and your lack
of respect for yourselves," Leah said quietly. "The last thing I
want is for you to get caught carrying babies those English
boys won't claim, and whom you're not ready to raise as un-
married teenagers. Have you learned nothing from the desperation of the young woman who abandoned Betsy at our
doorstep?"

Alice and Adeline sneered, their faces identical masks of
disdain.

"What gives you any right to preach at us?"

"You're not our *mamm,* so we don't have to listen to you."

With a sigh, Leah opened the door for them. As the twins
hurried past her in a huff, she chided herself for believing she
could make a difference in their attitudes, their lives. Even so,
she'd felt compelled to drive home the reality they might be
facing if they continued on their current collision course.
Wearily Leah returned to the barn for the buckets of goat's
milk she'd left there.

When Leah stepped into the kitchen, Betsy was wiggling in
her carrier basket, which sat on the kitchen table. Leah's
mother gazed at her sadly from her place at the stove. "My
word, but those girls can suck the life out of a room with

their negative attitudes," Mama said as she turned the sizzling strips of bacon in the skillet. "I had no idea their situation had escalated to such an extreme. It's a sad example of what happens when our young people pick up nasty habits from the English—not that English folks are all bad."

Leah set her buckets on the mudroom floor and removed her barn coat. "I could be wrong, but I suspect the boys in the truck are drawn to Alice and Adeline more because it's a novelty to date Amish girls than because they really care for them," she mused aloud. "And the twins enjoy playing with fire, partly to defy their *dat* . . . and maybe as a reaction to me as well. I have no idea how to fix this situation."

Mama concentrated on removing the bacon from the skillet to a platter covered with paper towels. "The twins remind me of this grease, so hot and unpredictable they might burn us—or themselves—without warning," she remarked. "Truth be told, I wonder if they have thoughts about jumping the fence. I've never known Plain girls to speak and behave so rudely."

Leah sighed as she poured the goat's milk into a large soup kettle and lit the burner beneath it. "Stevie has overheard them say they want to leave the Amish faith. Alice and Adeline think our way of life is all work and drudgery," she added as she clipped the candy thermometer to the side of the pan. "I really wonder if they'll settle down enough to help you sew our new clothes—so don't take it personally if they're nowhere to be found when you're ready to start."

Mama chuckled softly. "Well, after all these years I've gotten used to sewing by myself—don't take it personally, dear," she quipped quickly.

Leah laughed, grateful for her mother's sense of humor. She went to the table and lifted Betsy from her basket. Was it her imagination, or did the baby flap her arms and make excited little noises because she was happy to see Leah?

"Often when I'm working alone, I have the chance to sort

things through in my mind, and to pray over situations that trouble me," Mama continued in a pensive tone. "Something tells me it'll be easier to talk with God and listen for His suggestions if Adeline and Alice aren't in the sewing room because they *have* to be instead of because they want to be."

Chapter 13

When Jude bowed his head the following Sunday to begin the time of silent prayer during the church service at the Hartzler place, his fingertips reveled in the crisp, smooth texture of the new white shirt he was wearing. *Denki, Lord, for Lenore's sewing skills and for the way her presence has brought peacefulness into our home,* he prayed. *It's a pleasure—and a relief—to see my girls wearing dresses of a more appropriate size, and to watch Stevie blossom like a springtime flower in the sunshine of his grandmother's love.*

At the end of the prayer, Deacon Saul Hartzler stood up with the large German King James Bible to read the passage of Scripture that Bishop Jeremiah would expound upon during the morning's second sermon. Saul was a burly man, and his rolling voice filled the huge room, which had been expanded by the removal of some interior walls. "Today's reading comes from the twenty-fifth chapter of Matthew, beginning with verse thirty-one. Hear the word of the Lord," he said as he located the verse with his finger. " 'When the Son of man shall come in his glory, and all the holy angels with him, then shall he sit on the throne of his glory: And before him shall be gathered all the nations: and he shall separate them one from another, as a shepherd divideth his sheep from the goats,' " he read with gusto. " 'And he shall set the sheep on his right hand, but the goats on the left.' "

Stevie elbowed Jude, smiling brightly. "We keep Leah's sheep separate from the goats, huh, Dat?" he whispered.

Jude nodded, his finger across his lips as he hugged his perceptive young son. It was wonderful, how much Stevie had learned since Leah had become his mother, his teacher.

" 'Then shall the King say unto them on his right hand, Come ye blessed of my Father, inherit the kingdom prepared for you from the foundation of the world,' " Saul read in a grand voice. " 'For I was an hungred, and ye gave me meat: I was thirsty and ye gave me drink: I was a stranger and ye took me in: Naked and ye clothed me: I was sick and ye visited me: I was in prison, and ye came unto me.' "

Stevie's eyes widened. "Naked?" he mouthed in silent surprise.

Jude smiled, recalling how such a word captured a boy's attention—especially in church—at Stevie's age. It was such a blessing that his son was paying attention to this important story instead of doodling with paper and pencil, as he and the other young children often did during church.

Deacon Saul's eyes widened with the drama of the story, as though he were one of the puzzled disciples listening to Jesus' teaching. " 'Then shall the righteous answer him, saying Lord, when saw we ye hungered and fed thee? Or thirsty and gave thee drink? When saw we thee a stranger and took thee in? or naked and clothed thee? Or when saw we thee sick or in prison, and came unto thee?' " he asked as he gazed out over the crowd.

Everyone sat quietly, in focused expectation, awaiting the answer to one of the Bible's most important questions even though they'd heard the story many times.

Saul kept them waiting an extra moment before he continued. " 'And the King shall answer and say unto them, Verily I say unto you, Inasmuch as ye have done it unto one of the least of these my brethren, ye have done it unto me.' " Saul closed the big Bible with a satisfied thump. "Thus ends this reading of His holy word. Let all those who have ears hear it and believe."

When the deacon had taken his seat, Bishop Jeremiah stood and began the longer main sermon of the morning. Sunday clothing rustled as folks shifted on the pew benches. Jude peered between the heads of the older men who sat in front of him, and gazed at Leah, who sat about halfway back on the women's side, across the huge front room. She, too, wore new clothes today, and the pumpkin-colored cape dress Lenore had made showed off her lovely complexion. When she smiled and lifted little Betsy to her shoulder, Jude's heart sang at the sweetness of the picture they made. Someday soon, he hoped it would be their new wee one she looked after during church.

"Since we last met to worship Him, our Lord has provided yet another opportunity to care for someone to whom He refers as 'the least of these,'" Jeremiah began in a resonant voice. "You may have heard by now that Jude and Leah Shetler found a baby on their front porch a little while ago. I was pleased to hear that so many of you responded generously, loaning them baby clothes, bottles, and other supplies," he continued with a nod. "As we hold little Betsy in our daily prayers, let us also remember the young mother who felt so desperate and incapable of raising her child that she abandoned it."

All around him, Jude saw folks nodding—although a few, who were hearing about Betsy for the first time, raised their eyebrows in surprise.

"It also behooves us to talk about this situation with our young people, whether they be your children or your neighbors' children," the bishop insisted. For a moment, Jeremiah's gaze lingered upon his twin nieces before he scanned the rest of the congregation. "While it's not our purpose here to condemn the English, we must remember that their ways are not our ways—and that their worldliness often leads to temptations and a separation from God that might have caused Betsy's anonymous mother more problems than we can imagine."

Again Jude noted that folks were nodding in agreement, following the bishop's message with concern etched on their faces. Most families in the Morning Star church district had teenagers or kids in their early twenties. Over the years he'd known of a few girls who'd left town supposedly to care for elderly relatives—and had returned after several months with secrets they weren't telling. It was sad to think about the babies they'd given up . . . and unfortunate that other girls resorted to urgent courtships with unsuspecting young men who married them only to discover a different sort of secret shortly after the wedding.

Forgive me, Lord, for dredging up old resentments and for wondering what my life would be like had Frieda not deceived me, Jude thought with a sigh. *Remind me what a blessing Frieda's children have been through the years. Remind me that forgiveness demands more than lip service— that it's meant to wipe the slate clean and bring a peaceful resolution.*

Jude felt anything but peaceful, however, when he saw Adeline and Alice rolling their eyes at the bishop's words. Would they comply with Amish ways more willingly if their mother were still alive? It was a useless question, yet Jude had often wondered how much Frieda's passing had affected their daughters and how much of the twins' rebellion stemmed from their association with English boys.

"Young Amish men and women must realize the consequences of sexual relations outside of marriage—the ways a child conceived out of wedlock can disrupt their lives and their families," Jeremiah continued urgently. "I realize that generations of Amish modesty have often prevented parents from discussing the facts of life with their kids, but perhaps it's time to rethink our position of silence on this subject. We don't do our young people—especially our daughters—any favors by leaving them uninformed about sex and conception."

Several red-faced women in the room stared at Bishop Jeremiah as though he'd sprouted a second head. The men around Jude were shifting on the benches and glancing doubtfully at each other, too. Although their children often witnessed the mating of the animals on their farms and the births that followed, it was another issue altogether to discuss the specifics of human reproduction. Amish parents tended to let nature take its course, or to speak only in generalizations about proper behavior on dates and during courtship. Jude recalled that Dat had stammered only a few words about what the stallions and bulls were doing—and his *mamm* had never brought up the subject of sex to her two sons at all.

"What's he gonna talk about now? Birth control?" one of the men behind Jude muttered under his breath. "If the bishop gets *that* progressive, I'm walking out."

Jude bit back a smile when he noticed his mother's flushed, downcast face across the room. His brother seemed to realize he'd pushed the envelope with his sermon, because he clasped his hands in front of him and remained quiet for a few moments.

"Mostly I'd like us to remind our young people to keep God's commandments and to honor the Plain ways of peace and patience," Bishop Jeremiah continued. "If I've made any of you uncomfortable, I apologize—but I believe God chose me years ago to be your bishop because He felt I had important things to say about how to keep our Amish lifestyle relevant as the rest of the world spins faster and faster around us. If you have comments or complaints, I'd like to hear them while we're gathered for our common meal after the service."

"Easy for Bishop Jeremiah to say, seeing's how he's got no kids," Zeke Miller, who sat a couple rows ahead of Jude remarked to the man beside him.

"*Jah,* there were just no easy words—no convenient times—to discuss that subject when my youngsters were still at home," Carl Fisher, seated on Jude's other side, admitted softly. "The wife's better at that sort of talk, but as far as I know she only told the girls about female stuff when they came of an age to deal with it."

Jude nodded. "I suspect my brother has rubbed a few folks the wrong way, and that he's going to hear about it."

Bishop Jeremiah announced the number of the final hymn, so everyone picked up a hymnal and flipped through its yellowed pages. Carl's brother Dan sang the first phrase, leading the congregation in a song that Amish believers had sung from the *Ausbund* for centuries. The words were in German, printed in phrases resembling poems without any musical notation. The tune had been passed down through the generations since the early days of the faith, led by men with an ear for singing the age-old melodies on pitch.

As they sang slowly, purposefully, through more than twenty verses, Jude's mind wandered. He realized that this song—like many of their hymns—spoke not only about the necessity of loving God, but also warned against Satan and his wiles, describing the unwavering path a believer must follow to attain everlasting life. It occurred to Jude that the newest of the *Ausbund*'s hymns dated back to the 1800s, and most of the songs had been written in the 1500s.

Has God not inspired any new hymn writers for the past six centuries?

Jude blinked at this distracting thought. He hastily found the verse everyone else was singing and followed it with his finger, keeping his voice low as he sang. His question simmered on the back burner of his mind . . . because he'd also wondered now and again why no new books had been added to the Bible for the past several centuries. Did God have no modern prophets? Had no one since the apostle Paul and the four Gospel writers felt compelled to pen letters or accounts of God's presence and direction in their lives?

Jude sighed to himself. *Here's the real question: Would our Amish bishops even accept additions to the hymnal—or just let us sing these old songs faster? Would they sanction using a more modern translation of the Bible? How many of our young people do we lose because the Amish faith seems outdated and irrelevant to them?*

Even though Jude believed he was as faithful to God as every other person in the room, he knew of old, conservative bishops who might consider him a heretic if he dared to ask such questions aloud. And even though his brother was considered more progressive than most Amish bishops, Jude suspected he knew how Jeremiah would answer his questions, too—even though the future of their faith might be at stake.

What if God's been talking to us all along, and we haven't been listening? What must He think of us, His creation, if we no longer recognize His voice?

Jude sighed sadly. The Amish believed their faith was the one true way to gain salvation, yet no one dared to prophesy as the Old Testament prophets had, or to admit that he'd gotten advice directly from God—had clearly heard His voice. Once again Jude lost his place in the hymn they were singing, but it seemed inconsequential compared to the questions he was pondering.

When he glanced across the room, he noted that Alice and Adeline weren't singing or even looking at the *Ausbund* as the long, slow hymn finally came to an end. In recent months he'd wished his daughters would participate more fully in church activities—and their remarks this past week about the *burden* of the Amish lifestyle had startled him.

If the leaders of our faith are so resistant to change, I'll have to change my approach—the way I relate to my daughters and live as their example—if I'm to see them married to Amish men.

This revelation startled him.

After the service, everyone shared in the common meal and visited for most of the afternoon. As always, the young people went outside to socialize in the barn and play volleyball after they ate, the women clucked together in Anne Hartzler's large kitchen, and the men sat solving the world's problems around the tables that had been set up in the front room for the meal.

During the buggy ride home, Lenore sat in the seat behind Jude and Leah, with the kids filling the seat at the back of the family-size vehicle. Leah's *mamm* bubbled with enthusiasm. "I was so tickled that the ladies in your congregation were asking about my special quilts," she said, "and I was even happier when a few of them suggested we have a quilting frolic someday soon. What do you think of that idea, Leah? I know quilting isn't your cup of tea."

"Ah, but a frolic would be a *gut* way for me to get better acquainted with the women hereabouts," Leah said quickly, turning to look at her mother. "They're all very interested in Betsy now. And maybe having a baby to look after has made me seem less . . . odd to them."

Jude grimaced to himself as he drove, although he sensed the accuracy of his wife's remark.

"And truth be told," Leah went on, "I'd feel more comfortable about such a gathering if you were there to keep the conversation lively, Mama. And if you girls would see to baking and serving the refreshments, it would be a nice party—a nice break from our daily routine—don't you think?"

Alice sighed loudly. "*Jah,* whatever."

"I guess we could tolerate it if the Flaud sisters and the Miller girls come," Adeline put in. "It's a sure bet we'll be looking after Betsy and all the other little kids who'll come with their mothers."

"And speaking of kids and mothers," Alice said with an

edge to her voice, "you can forget about that talk you're supposed to have about baby making and sex before marriage and all that. We already know that stuff, so let's spare everybody the embarrassment, *jah?*"

Jude pivoted in the seat to gawk at his daughters, who had the nerve to smile at him as though sexual matters were an everyday, run-of-the-mill topic of conversation. "So who told you?" he blurted out.

Alice raised an eyebrow. "Our real mother. Years ago."

"Certainly not Mammi Margaret," Adeline said with a laugh. "She got so red in the face during Uncle Jeremiah's sermon, I thought she was going to pass out."

Jude turned around so he could keep his eyes on the road. His heart was hammering rapidly, even though he doubted the girls had received all that much pertinent information from Frieda. How was he supposed to respond to their nonchalance? Should he be worried that they'd gained their sexual information from close encounters with the English boys they'd been seeing?

"If that's the case," Lenore said boldly, "maybe we adults should have a question-and-answer session so you girls can fill us in on details we might not be aware of."

"Or at the very least, we should write out a quiz and you can put your answers on paper," Leah suggested without missing a beat. "It would be far less *embarrassing* to write about these matters than, say, to find out you're carrying a baby and you don't know how it happened—and you don't know how to tell your family about your predicament, either."

When Jude heard the girls suck in their breath, he reached for Leah's hand. "*Gut* answer," he whispered. "You nailed them, sweetheart."

As he steered the horse into the lane that led to their home, however, Jude realized that it would take a lot more than the present-day prophets and the quicker singing he'd pondered in church to keep his daughters involved in the Amish faith.

Any help You can suggest would be extremely welcome, Lord, Jude prayed. Then, with a smile, he added, *And I thank You for sending me Leah, who is truly the answer to the greatest questions of my everyday life.*

Chapter 14

Alice stood beside Adeline at their bedroom window, gazing out at the patch of lantern light that bobbed through the evening shadows toward the barn. "Let's get going, while Dat's doing the chores."

"Do you suppose Leah and Lenore will stay busy in the kitchen long enough?" Adeline whispered.

"It's a chance we have to take. We've *got* to find that cell phone before Dexter gets any madder at us for not answering it or texting him."

Silently, barefoot, the two of them slipped into the hallway. Outside of Dat's room, they paused to listen for noises downstairs before entering. Hearing nothing, they went directly to the dresser. They had agreed to leave the door open so the hinge wouldn't creak.

"It's got to be here," Adeline whispered as she silently opened the top drawer on her side. "Most likely Dat put it someplace obvious like his sock drawer, figuring we'd never dare come looking for it."

"Or maybe Leah hid it. It would be just like her," Alice pointed out as she began rummaging through Leah's *kapps* and black stockings. "Hmm . . . it's not here, so maybe it's in her underwear drawer—"

Adeline grabbed Alice's arm and sucked in her breath.

"Who was that?" she whispered frantically as she gazed into the dresser mirror. "I swear I heard something—saw a blur of somebody passing by in the hall. Please tell me it wasn't Leah spying on us."

"You're just jittery," Alice hastened to reassure her. "We can't lose our nerve—and besides, what can she say? That phone doesn't belong to us, and it was wrong of Dat to take it."

"But she'll tell him, and then he'll—"

"Quit worrying and keep looking!" Alice muttered as she opened another drawer. "We don't have much time."

"It would be easier if we could light the lamp."

"Like that's going to happen," Alice shot back. "Besides, what else would they have that feels slick and flat like a cell phone?"

Adeline shrugged, sighing loudly in frustration. She eased the third drawer shut and opened the bottom one.

"So whaddya doin'? Why're ya in Dat and Leah's room?"

Stevie's voice nearly made Alice jump out of her skin. She gazed at Adeline in the darkness and then stared into the dresser mirror. Their little brother stood silhouetted in the doorway, leaning against the jamb as though he might've been there for a while. "Just putting away laundry," she replied nonchalantly. She turned, flashing Stevie a smile.

"And when we saw how messy these drawers were, we decided to straighten them," Adeline added as she, too, turned to look at Stevie.

Alice's eyes had adjusted to the darkness, so she saw how Stevie's brow furrowed in disbelief. "Then why don't ya light the lamp, so's you can see what you're doin'?" he asked.

"We can put away laundry without wasting a match—we do it all the time, you know," Alice replied in a tone that brooked no argument. "Why aren't you out in the barn helping Dat with the chores?"

"But this is Wednesday, and ya washed the clothes on Monday," Stevie pointed out.

Alice's stomach tightened. Their brother didn't sound the least bit convinced by the tale they were telling him, and the minutes were ticking by. She looked to Adeline, hoping she'd say something that would convince Stevie to believe them and move on.

Adeline cleared her throat. "Leah sent us up here to fetch her some bobby pins so—"

"Because her hair is coming loose from scrubbing the floor," Alice added quickly. "She's getting the house cleaned for Lenore's quilting frolic, you know."

After a few moments of contemplation, Stevie shook his head. "Nuh-uh," he countered. "You're lookin' for that cell phone Dat hid. And I won't tell ya where he put it, neither. Not even for a hundred dollars."

Alice lurched forward, glaring at him. "You know where it is?" she demanded.

"You'd better—we *have* to have that phone," Adeline insisted, "or Dexter will come here and get really mad at us."

"*Jah,* and we'll tell him *you* know where it is," Alice said as she started toward the doorway. "Trust me, Stevie, you don't want to mess with the likes of Dexter and Phil."

"They'll throw you in the back of the pickup," Adeline chimed in as she kept pace with Alice. "And then they'll drive you way, *way* out of town and dump you somewhere totally strange. You'll never find your way home."

"So do the right thing, Stevie." Alice stopped directly in front of him, holding his gaze as she towered above him. "Just tell us where the phone is. We won't tell Dat you let it slip about where he hid—"

"*Jah,* why would we tell him?" Adeline asked. "It'll be our little secret."

Alice crossed her arms, driving her point home. "And if those English guys haul you away for holding out on them, not telling them—or us—where the phone is, we'll keep quiet about that, too. Dat and Leah won't have a clue what happened to you. It'll be like you just disappeared—*poof!*" she said with a dramatic snap of her fingers. "Days and weeks will go by—"

Stevie waved her off. "You girls are full of beans. Dat won't let those guys do nothin' to me."

When he turned and started down the hall, Alice grabbed his shoulder. "Stevie, *stop* it!" she whispered fiercely.

"How much do we have to pay you?" Adeline muttered as she took hold of his suspenders.

"I'm not sayin' nothin'. Not even for two hundred dollars." Stevie shrugged out of their grasp and backed away from them. "And if you're not nice to me from now on, I'm gonna tell Leah how I got bruises on my shoulders—I'll tell her what you said and what you did to me," he said, his voice ringing in the hallway. "And if you don't stop bein' so mean to Leah, I'm gonna tell her you were riflin' through her underwear, too."

Alice bit back a retort and watched him go into his room. If Stevie told Leah—or Dat, heaven forbid—what she and Adeline had been doing, there would be no end to the lectures and punishment . . . and they would probably have an adult monitoring their moves every minute of every day.

"We've got to make sure we closed those drawers," Adeline whispered.

Alice nodded, and they quickly stole back into the bedroom. Her stomach was clenched in a knot at the way Stevie had taunted them. "What if he just said that to irritate us?" she whispered as they quickly checked the dresser drawers. "What if he has no idea where that cell phone is?"

"Do you really think he's smart enough to threaten us that way, if he doesn't know?" Adeline mused aloud. "He's just a little kid. Not even in school yet."

"Maybe Leah put him up to it." The thought curled Alice's lip as the two of them slipped out of the bedroom and into the hallway. It seemed like something Leah would do, and the unfairness of it all really galled her. "Maybe she heard us walking around up here and—well, for sure and for certain she deserves a little payback for such meanness, and for using Stevie to trap us. I'm thinking she's going to be sorry she did that, come time for Lenore's quilting frolic."

Chapter 15

On the following Friday, Leah felt as nervous as a newborn colt. Neighbor ladies and their daughters were arriving to begin quilting her mother's newest quilt top—and it would soon become obvious that Leah didn't quilt, nor was she much good at the chitchat most women engaged in so effortlessly. Still, she felt happy. Mama was beaming, welcoming their guests, while Alice and Adeline took pans of cinnamon rolls from the oven to go with the cupcakes and brownies they'd already made.

"Oh, but it smells yummy in here!" Delores Flaud declared as she entered the kitchen with her two teenage daughters. "And look at this little angel you're holding, Leah. Why, I think she's grown since we saw her at church last Sunday."

Leah smiled, realizing that this frolic would be as much about Betsy as it was about Mama's quilt—and that made the day seem easier, because she wouldn't have to rack her brain for topics of conversation. "She's doing well," Leah agreed, bouncing Betsy against her shoulder. "And she's not a fussy baby, either."

"Such an angelic face!" Frannie Flaud exclaimed as she gently touched Betsy's cheek.

"And dressed all in pink, like a little doll," her sister Kate said with a big smile.

"Mama made this dress—and stacks of new diapers and other clothes," Leah said with a nod at her mother. "She's kept the sewing machine busy ever since she got here."

"I can't wait to work on your quilt, Lenore." Delores set a covered casserole on the counter, and she and her girls removed their coats. "It's a real pleasure to see the patterns and colors other gals use. My quilts for around home all seem to look the same, because I'm using up remnants of fabric from our clothes—and I'm not inclined to go looking for a new pattern every time I make one."

Mama smiled as she hung up their wraps. "Truth be told, this quilt top is made from scrap triangles left over from a lot of my previous quilts," she said. "If I didn't make a scrap quilt every now and again, I'd have to build an annex onto the house to hold my fabric pieces!"

The two ladies laughed as they poured steaming cups of coffee from the big urn Mama had brewed earlier. Leah enjoyed the easy way the Flaud sisters joined Alice and Adeline as they stirred a big bowl of frosting for the hot cinnamon rolls. Within the next few minutes, Cora Miller and her three daughters arrived—and when Emma, Lucy, and Linda joined the other girls, the chatter level rose immediately. It was so good to hear happy voices filling the kitchen after the intense, unpleasant confrontations with the twins these past weeks—and nice that the ladies always brought casseroles to these frolics for an easy lunch so the hostess didn't have to do all the cooking.

Soon Anne Hartzler and her mother-in-law, Martha Maude, arrived along with Rose Wagler and her little girl, Gracie. When the *maidel* Slabaugh sisters stepped into the kitchen, Leah forced herself to smile brightly as she welcomed them. Jude had suggested that she should invite them to the frolic to dispel their notion that she was a poor housekeeper—and bless them, Mama and the twins had spent a lot of time this past week helping her clean thoroughly. Leah couldn't miss the way Naomi peered around the kitchen while Esther set the pan of corn bread they'd brought on the counter.

"Mighty nice of you to invite us today, Leah. Supposed to get some snow later—even if we thought it was supposed to be spring—so we might as well be quilting," Naomi remarked stiffly. She sniffed the air and squinted through her rimless glasses at Betsy, as though she thought the baby's diaper needed changing.

"Been ever so long since we had a quilting frolic," Esther said, observing the girls across the kitchen as they spread frosting on the fresh rolls. "My word, Lenore, if all of us are working on this quilt, I hope you've got it on an especially long quilt frame."

Adeline and Alice turned toward them before Mama could respond, their frosting-coated knives suspended over the pan of rolls. "Not to worry, Esther, you'll have plenty of room," one of them said.

"*Jah*, we girls will be having our own little party," the other twin chimed in. "We wouldn't dream of crowding you ladies who truly enjoy quilting."

Leah bit back a smile at the way Alice and Adeline had responded just within the bounds of proper courtesy. Esther was heavyset, and her protruding backside was often the subject of quiet jokes folks made when she passed by.

"Matter of fact, we're all here except for Margaret," Lenore said graciously. "We might as well head into the front room so you can choose the side of the frame you'd prefer to sit on, in case anyone else is a leftie, like I am."

"That would be me," Martha Maude remarked with a chuckle. "I'm ready for some coffee and to get to work on your quilt!"

Jude's mother bustled inside at last, appearing flummoxed as she handed Lenore a covered bowl. "This was supposed to be a coconut cream pie in a shortbread crust, but the filling didn't set," she said woefully. "It was such a mess, I poured it into a bowl and chopped the crust into the pudding. We'll just have to call it a trifle."

"If there's coconut in it, it has to be tasty!" Lenore assured Margaret as she carried the bowl to the refrigerator.

"You can be sure I'll eat *my* share of it," Esther remarked jovially as she held her coffee cup under the urn's spigot.

Leah was relieved that everyone migrated into the front room without needing any prompting from her. Gatherings like these reminded her how socially inept she was compared to most women who'd attended and hosted frolics all their lives. She plucked a bottle of goat's milk from the pan of hot water on the stove and followed her guests with Betsy cradled against her shoulder, determined to make the best of this event for Mama's sake.

The ladies made a beeline for the quilting frame, and their compliments made Mama glow modestly.

"Lenore, what a beautiful color combination!" Cora exclaimed.

"And what a wonderful way to use scraps, instead of just piecing a nine-square pattern," Anne said as she ran her finger over the design. "Where each of the four joined squares form a pinwheel, the design seems to *move* when you look at it."

"I hope you'll let us copy your pattern," Martha Maude said, leaning closer to the frame so she could study the quilt top more closely. "I've never seen this one, and we have bins and boxes of scraps at home we could use."

Esther wasted no time settling herself into the largest chair while her sister studied the quilt with a critical eye. "Mighty showy, with all those bright colors and prints," Naomi remarked. "Surely can't be for a Plain home."

Mama appeared unfazed by this comment. "The English lady who ordered it provided the print pieces and asked me to make her quilt very colorful," she explained as she took the spot beside Martha Maude. "She says it's a gift for a niece who'll go off to college next fall."

As the other ladies took seats around the quilting frame,

Jude passed through the front room with Stevie beside him. He flashed a thumbs-up sign at Leah before stopping to look at the quilt the women would be working on. "Very cheerful," he commented before greeting each of the ladies. "I recognize fabric from some of the new clothes Lenore has made us."

"*Jah*, there's my new green shirt—and my new purple shirt!" Stevie chimed in as he pointed excitedly to pieces near the edge. "This would make a real nice blanket for the new goats, ain't so, Mammi Lenore?" he teased.

Mama laughed as she threaded her quilting needle. "It would," she agreed, "but don't go telling the goats about it, or they'll feel bad when I take it to the lady who ordered it."

"No auction today, Jude?" Margaret asked as she clipped thread. "Friday's usually a big day for sales."

"Nope, so we men are going to make a few repairs in the barns and outbuildings," Jude replied. "I can tell there'll be a whole lot of clucking going on here in the house."

"*Jah!* Bwahk-bwahk-bwahhhk!" Stevie crowed, flapping his bent arms like wings.

"That's what hen parties and frolics are all about," Lenore said as she rumpled the boy's hair. "You'll probably want to stop through the kitchen for a few goodies before you head outside. Might not be any left when you come in for lunch."

Leah sat down in the wooden rocking chair and gave Betsy her bottle, delighting in the way the baby ate with such gusto. Maybe it was her imagination, but lately Betsy seemed to recognize her—to reach excitedly with her dimpled arms. *Or maybe she's just hungry and ready for her bottle*, Leah reasoned as she smiled at the baby and rocked. *It's nice to have someone who's so happy to be with me . . . who needs me.*

Across the front room, the girls were seated around a rectangular folding table to play a game of Yahtzee. Leah was pleased to see that Emma and Lucy Miller were helping five-year-old Gracie, who sat between them.

The women at the quilting frame talked quietly, focused on making their tiny white stitches along the swirling lines

Mama had stenciled on the quilt top. As Leah burped the baby and sang softly to her, she had to agree with the girls: quilting seemed like such a tedious way to pass a day, even though the end result was always beautiful. As little Betsy drifted off, Leah smoothed her silky brown curls. Like most Plain babies, she was able to ignore the noise around her— even the repeated rattling of the Yahtzee dice in the cardboard cup, as well as the occasional cry of "Yahtzee!" when one of the girls rolled all five dice alike.

Leah glanced at the clock, sighing inwardly. The ladies had been quilting less than an hour, yet already she felt unsettled and somewhat bored. On a normal day, she would be putting Betsy in her basket and heading outside with it to clear the winter's dead leaves from the fencerows or to help Stevie tend the new lambs and kids. The girls were avidly engaged in their game, and the women were engrossed in their stitching . . . and even though Rose and Cora occasionally smiled at her and Betsy, Leah felt more than ever like a fish out of water.

She lasted an hour and a half before she had to get busy at something. Carefully she slipped Betsy into her padded basket on the kitchen table and set about filling a carafe with hot coffee from the urn. She cut the frosted cinnamon rolls and arranged some of them on two trays along with brownies and cupcakes, figuring she could at least be a considerate hostess.

Leah stepped out of the kitchen with the carafe just in time to catch Naomi running her finger along the bottom of a windowpane—and then raising her eyebrow as though she'd found a frightful amount of dust. Leah's throat got tight, and she hurriedly set the carafe on the sideboard near the quilting frame. As she returned to the kitchen, she tried to recall Jude's long-ago reassurances that he wasn't the least bit concerned about a little dust—or about the neighbors' opinions of it—but it still took her a few minutes to settle her nerves.

When Leah figured Naomi would've returned her attention to Mama's quilt, she carried one of the trays to the girls' table and was met with an enthusiastic response.

"I just got a Yahtzee!" little Gracie crowed as she smiled at Leah. "I rolled five whole sixes!"

"*Gut* for you," Leah said as she set the tray on the table. "I'm glad you girls are having fun together."

When Leah returned to the front room with the other tray of treats, however, the Slabaugh sisters looked up at her as though she'd committed the ultimate sin. "Food is never served near a quilting frame," Naomi informed her stiffly. "How do you think your mother's quilt would look if we had frosting on our fingers as we stitched?"

Esther's expression softened as she eyed the cinnamon rolls. "This would be a *gut* time for a goodie break in the kitchen, however," she said quickly. "You can only sit and stitch for so long before you need to get up and stretch."

Leah set the tray on the sideboard beside the coffee carafe, her eyes growing hot with unshed tears. Ordinarily she didn't let criticism bother her—she'd grown accustomed to folks thinking she was an odd duck—yet Naomi's brusque remark had only underscored her feelings of being different from other women.

"It was nice of you to think of us, Leah," Mama put in consolingly.

Cora rose from her chair to stretch. "My word, we've been stitching for more than an hour and a half," she said as she glanced at the wall clock. "The time just flies when I've got a needle in my hand—but my back will be telling me I sat in one position too long if I don't move around a bit."

As if they wanted to soften Naomi's remark, the other ladies stood up, too, but Leah had lost all interest in the tray of treats she'd brought them. Anne Hartzler smiled at her, her freckled face alight with kindness. "Little Betsy's asleep? She's such a quiet, sweet little baby, and you seem as comfortable with her as if she were your own, Leah."

"We—we're blessed to have her," Leah stammered, deeply

pleased about Anne's compliment. "I give thanks to God every day for guiding her desperate mother to bring Betsy to our home."

A short, humorless laugh on the other side of the room made everyone turn toward the table where the girls were playing. "The more I see you and Betsy together, the more I believe that you *are* her mother, Leah," Alice asserted loudly. "I mean, she looks just like you. I think you kept her hidden away while Dat courted you, and then had Lenore leave her on the porch with that fake note, to make it look like Betsy had been abandoned."

"Maybe that explains why you're always warning us to beware of guys who come on to girls and then get them pregnant," Adeline chimed in as she and her twin gazed accusingly at Leah. "Could be you're speaking from experience, ain't so? Keeping your secrets and sins from Dat until after he'd married you!"

The bottom dropped out of Leah's stomach. The front room rang with absolute silence as her guests stood wide-eyed, too flabbergasted to speak—while wondering if the twins had exposed the truth. As the blood rushed from her head, Leah fumbled for words to refute the twins' incriminating remarks, yet she sensed that her crestfallen expression—her tongue-tied inability to defend herself—confirmed her guilt to the women standing around Mama's quilting frame. The gleeful gleam in Naomi's eyes made Leah pivot and rush to the kitchen.

By the time she reached the door, she heard Mama reprimanding the twins, but it was too late—Leah was too mortified to remain in the same room with those hateful teenagers. As she ran across the lawn toward the barn, all she could think about was getting away from this place where she'd never felt welcome, never felt accepted by Jude's brazen daughters.

By sundown it'll be all over Morning Star that I deceived Jude, because Naomi's just waiting to spread the news! Alice and Adeline will never stop harassing me—and those ladies will believe their lies over anything an outsider like me can tell them, she fretted as she ran through the open barn door. Nearly blinded by tears, she headed straight for Mose's stall, where her gelding looked up from the hay he was munching. His big brown eyes took in Leah's agitation with an air of wise understanding that horses displayed so much more often than people

"Let's go, Mose," Leah blurted as she grabbed his bridle from its peg. "We're getting out of here."

Always eager to stretch his legs, the gelding whickered and stood still as Leah quickly fastened the bridle around his head. As she'd done in her younger days, she hiked up her dress and leapt onto the horse's back stomach-first before swinging her leg over him. Leah was vaguely aware that Jude was calling to her as she raced out of the barn, but the pounding of Mose's hoofbeats drove her on. Gripping the horse with her legs and leaning low over his neck, she gave the gelding his head and ran full-tilt toward the road.

Chapter 16

"Leah! Leah, what happened?" Jude shouted as he ran from the barn. When she didn't turn to look at him—urged Mose into a full gallop as though demons from hell were chasing her—apprehension overwhelmed him. His wife was no sissy. What could possibly have upset her so badly that she would race away from her guests?

"Dat, where's Leah goin' in such a hurry?" Stevie asked as he joined Jude outside to follow Mose's progress to the road. "She was cryin' so hard she didn't even see us."

Jude's gut clenched. His son had just confirmed a detail he'd missed because he'd been driving a nail when Leah had entered the barn. "I'm going after her—but you stay here, Stevie," he added quickly. "Don't worry, son, I'll bring her home and we'll get this situation figured out."

A few minutes later, Jude was urging Rusty down the lane, aware that his bay gelding was much more accustomed to pulling a rig than galloping with a rider on his back—and also aware that it had been years since he'd ridden a horse bareback. To keep from losing his hat, he tucked it under his thigh. When they reached the road, Jude steered the horse to the right, as Leah had done—but after that, all he had to go on was instinct. She was nowhere in sight, and the dust Mose had kicked up had already settled.

Where would Leah go? Surely she wouldn't head for her *mamm*'s place clear over in Cedar Creek . . .

If she's going there, she'll at least slow her horse to a walk; he can't run for the entire hour it takes to reach the Otto farm.

As the brisk wind caught at Jude's open barn jacket, it occurred to him that Leah hadn't been wearing a coat—her dress had been a deep red blur against the gray sky as she'd galloped away. Although he urged Rusty along the shoulder of the road, the poor horse was already huffing clouds of steam and slowing down as the wind whipped at his black mane—which made Jude think his chances of catching up to Leah were slim to none.

Be smart about this. No matter how upset she is, Leah will come to her senses before she'll risk injuring Mose—and she has to be getting terribly cold by now.

Jude allowed Rusty to find his own pace as they passed the Flaud place and the Hartzler farm. He gazed across the pasture where Saul Hartzler's Black Angus cattle huddled together for warmth, watching him curiously. The fences around these properties would prevent Leah from cutting across them—and as he studied the wooded area along the border of Jeremiah's land, he didn't think she would've ridden into the trees, either.

As Jude approached the main road of Morning Star's business district, his thoughts went into a tailspin. The sky was hung with heavy gray clouds and the first snowflakes stung his face. When snow came this late in the winter, it rarely stayed on the ground long—but today it was surely a nuisance. He halted his horse until a few cars went by, gazing to the right and to the left and ahead of him.

"Rusty, you have a better idea where Mose went than I do," he said as he stroked the gelding's warm cinnamon-colored neck. "From here Leah could've gone around to the south, or across town, or—well, I have no idea, fella," he added with a sigh.

When the way was clear, Jude followed his instinct and steered Rusty along the shoulder of the main road rather than crossing it into town. Considering Leah's emotional state, he didn't think she would've ridden in traffic or in front of Plain businesses where local folks might've recognized her—or called out to her about why she wasn't wearing a coat.

Maybe by now she's so cold she's turned back toward home.

Jude sighed and kept scanning the farmland he was passing. Leah hadn't been all that excited about the quilting frolic— had gone along with the idea because she knew her mother would enjoy the company of other women after living alone these past few months. It seemed unlikely that his wife would return to the house until she thought the neighbor ladies were gone.

She might've slipped into somebody's barn. Or maybe she went into a store in town to get warm. Now that Lenore's at our place, I can't think of a single woman Leah would run to while she's in such a state of turmoil. . . .

Leah's lack of female friends saddened Jude—but it occurred to him that sooner or later, his wife would return home because she was totally devoted to little Betsy. She was more able than most women to look after herself, even if she had taken off like a shot without a coat, so Jude relaxed a little . . . let his mind travel down its own paths rather than trying to force ideas to come.

Rusty had slowed to a walk. The snow contained tiny pellets of sleet and pinged against Jude's face as it sparkled like diamonds in the gelding's black mane, and it showed no sign of letting up. He hated to head for home without Leah, yet in his mind he could hear her scolding him for needlessly keeping his horse out in the cold while he was searching for her.

With a sigh, Jude guided his gelding east at the next intersection to go home by another way—*on another couple of roads Leah might've followed,* he told himself.

He brushed the snow from his hair and crammed his hat back on his head, his eyes never leaving the fields and lanes of the Plain farms he rode past. The evergreens in the Slabaugh sisters' windbreak were taking on the lace of a snow cover, and as Jude glanced at their white farmhouse, he thought it appeared as tightly fastened and austere as the *maidels* themselves. Beyond the house sat a prim white barn and another outbuilding—and then a flash of red out in the stubbled cornfield made Jude suck in his breath.

"Leah!" he hollered as he nudged Rusty into the Slabaughs' lane. "Leah, please wait!"

All Jude could figure was that Leah was trying to find a shortcut home, rather than following the roads—and at that moment he didn't care. The only thing that mattered was that he'd found her, and that she'd stopped Mose to look at him. He urged Rusty into a canter, thankful that his bay seemed to realize they'd fulfilled their mission and would soon be returning home to the warm barn.

Jude's heart was hammering as he sped across the closely cropped cornfield, his gaze fixed on Leah. Never mind that she sat hunched against the wind and snow and that her hair hung in wet, uneven clumps around her neck. To him, she'd never seemed more beautiful or a more welcome sight for his worried eyes. Only when he was a few yards away did he rein in the horse. When Rusty came up alongside Leah and Mose, Jude slung his arm around his wife's shoulders and pulled her close for a clinging, desperate kiss.

"I thought I'd lost you—couldn't understand why you'd—" Jude rasped before he kissed Leah again. "My stars, woman, don't ever scare me this way again! What would I do if you didn't come home?"

When he felt her shiver, Jude shrugged out of his barn coat

and wrapped it around her shoulders. Still holding her as close as the two horses' bodies would allow, he gazed around them. "Let's head for the barn. We've got to get you out of this snow, sweetheart."

Leah let out a sob and allowed Jude to take her reins and lead Mose to the barn. She'd been five kinds of foolish to rush off without a coat, and two kinds of stupid to allow Alice's and Adeline's cutting remarks to get the better of her. When Jude hopped off Rusty to slide the barn door open, she was grateful that Mose had enough sense to get in out of the nasty weather and that Rusty immediately came inside with them. Because she'd left home in a silly, mindless snit, she'd caused two fine horses—and her wonderful husband—needless pain and exposure to the cold. It would serve her right if she caught a horrible cold for running off like a goose.

Behind her, Leah heard a *pffft!* A glow lit the shadowy barn as Jude hung the Slabaughs' lantern from a long nail in the barn wall. He closed the big door and came up beside her, opening his arms. She fell into his embrace and began weeping against his shoulder like a woman who'd lost her last friend.

He came after you. He thought he'd lost you. Leah's thoughts spun in circles that slowly began to unwind, and she became aware that Jude was shaking, too, wrapping his arms around her beneath the coat as though he never intended to let her go. *Don't ever scare me this way again! What would I do if you didn't come home?*

When Leah raised her head, she was stunned to see that Jude's face was wet with tears. "I'm sorry," she whimpered. "I should've known better—"

"What happened, sweetheart?" he whispered urgently. "You're the bravest woman I know, so I can't imagine what upset you so badly."

Leah wiped her face against her arm. Her clothes were

soaked and clinging to her, chilling her to the bone. Her hair had come undone and was hanging in wet bunches around her shoulders—and somewhere along the way, her *kapp* had blown off. Jude's dark eyes searched hers relentlessly, yet desperately . . . lovingly. When he took the bandanna from his shirt pocket and began to blot her face and hair, Leah began to cry again—but this time it was love rather than fear driving her emotions.

And when have you ever allowed your emotions to get so far out of control? You could've told Jude about the twins' remarks in the barn at home and saved him a lot of bother.

Leah sighed and took a couple of deep breaths. Bless him, Jude spotted a barn coat hanging on a peg near the door and he brought it to her . . . eased his own soaked coat gently off her shoulders and helped her into the dry one. He wasn't pushing her for answers, or chiding her for riding off in such a huff. He simply waited for her to regain her mental balance, rubbing her chilled, raw hands between his large, warm ones. The horses wandered back into stalls, following their noses to hay and water and a Slabaugh horse that whickered a welcome.

At last Leah cleared her throat. "The frolic was going like it was supposed to—unless you count the way I was so clueless as to carry food out to the ladies who were quilting," she added with a sigh. "But when Anne remarked about how I was handling Betsy as though she were my own child—"

"*Jah*, the two of you together make a sweet picture," Jude agreed, encouraging her with his loving gaze.

"—Alice announced that she believes Betsy *is* my baby," Leah continued, closing her eyes against the pain of the twins' accusations. "And of course, Adeline chimed in, and between the two of them they—they speculated that I'd had Betsy out of wedlock and hidden her at Mama's while you were courting me, so you wouldn't know about my secret and my sins until after we were married."

Jude's mouth fell open. "That's the most ridiculous thing I've ever—"

"*Jah*, but the women just gaped and gawked, thinking that maybe the girls had it right," Leah protested. "I was so stunned—so tongue-tied—that I surely must've looked guilty to them. So I ran," she continued in a whisper. "I had to get out of there, Jude. I-I'm sorry—"

"No!" he insisted, gently grasping her arms. "You have nothing to apologize for, Leah. But when I get home to those girls—"

Jude turned from her, so angry that it took him several moments to regain his composure. He exhaled fiercely and then held his head in his hands. "I can't begin to imagine how humiliated you must've felt, Leah," he said in a voice she could barely hear. "My first impulse is to rush home and have the girls apologize to you and to your guests—"

"If they're still at the house," Leah said glumly. While she craved the opportunity for Jude to set things straight before Mama's quilting friends went home, a part of her cringed at the thought of facing them all again.

Jude shook his head, still upset about his daughters' accusations. He pulled Leah close for another hug, rubbing her briskly to get her warm. "But my first concern is *you*—getting you home and into dry clothes," he said. He exhaled as though trying to rid himself of anger so he could think clearly. "And you know what, Leah? Even if what the twins said were true—even if you *had* hidden Betsy from me while we were courting—it wouldn't change my love for you one bit."

Leah blinked. Jude surely couldn't be serious, after the way Frieda had deceived him by keeping the same sort of secret—twice. What man would want to know that his second wife had betrayed him as well?

"And besides," he continued, easing away to gaze at her,

"I've known you for too many years to believe you'd pull such a stunt—and your mother's not the sort of woman to go along with such a hoax, either. I'm grateful to God, however, that Betsy has come to us, and I intend to adopt her and make her a permanent part of our family."

Leah's throat tightened with such love that she couldn't speak for a moment. "Oh, Jude, I love you so much for—for believing in me," she whispered. "And for wanting to be Betsy's *dat*. I want us to adopt her, too."

When she sneezed suddenly, Jude gave her his damp bandanna so she could blow her nose. He glanced around the barn. "Are you up to riding Mose back home? Or shall I go back and fetch a rig so you'll be out of the weather—"

"What's a little more snow?" Leah asked as she held up the sides of her soaked skirt. "I can't really get any wetter than I already am."

Jude kissed her lovingly. "You and I are going home to rectify this situation with the girls," he stated, "and then we're going to make plans to get away for a few days. You know that B and B that's on the road to Cedar Creek? The one the Kanagy fellows' wives run?"

Leah nodded, a spark of expectation warming her. "The double house beside the auction barn?"

"Yup. We're getting a room there," Jude said, gripping her hand. "You deserve some time off for *gut* behavior, Mrs. Shetler—and I don't get to spend nearly enough time alone with you."

Leah threw her arms around him. How had she ever managed to marry such a loving, thoughtful man? "That doesn't sound like something an Amish husband would do for his wife," she admitted softly. "I don't know of anyone who's stayed there."

"Then it's time we show Amish husbands that romancing their wives with a little time away is *gut* for both parties involved," Jude insisted with a gleam in his eye. "The Bible tells husbands to love their wives as Christ loved the church, so how could anyone say I'm being too extravagant? Let's get you home, sweetheart," he added gently. "You've had a rough time of it today."

Chapter 17

When Lenore heard the back door open, she rose quickly from her seat at the quilting frame. "Leah, is that you, honey?" she called out as she headed for the kitchen.

The other ladies kept stitching, as they'd agreed to do, but Stevie jumped up from the table where he'd been playing a game of Uncle Wiggily with Gracie, the Miller sisters, and the Flaud girls. "Did ya find her, Dat?" he cried, racing past Lenore. "You've been gone a long time!"

Lenore smiled fondly and let the boy have a moment with his parents. The sound of Jude's low voice and Leah's greeting relieved the knot of worry that had settled in her chest—not that her daughter's return solved the larger problem they needed to address. When she peered into the kitchen, however, she set aside her chagrin concerning the twins' behavior.

"Leah, let's get you out of those soaked clothes—and you too, Jude," she said as she rushed over to the pair, who were removing barn jackets that dripped on the floor. "You're both courting pneumonia, being out in the cold and the snow for so long."

"I'm thinking a hot shower and some hot tea will go a long way toward curing what ails us," Jude remarked, glancing toward the front room. "Have the neighbor ladies left?"

"I—I'm sorry I spoiled your party, Mama," Leah said with a sigh.

"Nonsense! After I demanded that Alice and Adeline apologize and tell our guests the truth, Margaret sent them upstairs," Lenore said, shaking her head. "I have no idea where they came up with such a wild tale—or why—but I felt they should be humiliated in front of their friends, the same way they humiliated you, dear. I'm going to suggest to your brother the bishop that they confess on their knees the next Sunday we meet for church."

Stevie gripped his suspenders, his brow furrowed in thought. "I think they was mad coz I caught 'em lookin' for that cell phone in Dat and Leah's dresser the other night," he said softly. "After I left, I heard 'em sayin' they thought Leah sent me up there to spy on 'em, so they was talkin' about payback. Or somethin' like that."

Lenore swallowed hard. Jude's and Leah's expressions told her they had no idea about the twins being in their room—and Stevie's story only deepened her disappointment in Adeline's and Alice's troubling tendency to lie and to sneak around like feral cats. The pair appeared stricken as they draped the wet coats over the sink in the mudroom.

Jude recovered first. "We'll deal with the girls after we've changed our clothes," he said wearily. "Let's go upstairs, Leah."

Lenore's heart went out to her daughter as the couple entered the front room. Even with such a stalwart, supportive husband as Jude, who'd slung a protective arm around Leah's shoulders, facing the neighbors who'd witnessed her ordeal with the twins had to feel terribly awkward—painful, to someone as shy as Leah. Yet the neighbors were smiling, looking up from the quilt on which they'd made so much progress.

"Leah, we're so glad you're all right!" said Delores Flaud.

Esther sighed apologetically. "We really did appreciate the goodies you brought us," she admitted. "And we're sorry you missed them."

"Hope you don't mind that I'm taking a turn at cuddling

Betsy," Rose Wagler said from the rocking chair. Her freckled face lit up when the baby squawked and reached toward Leah and Jude. "And you know what, Leah? This beautiful baby *is* yours, in every way that counts, because you love her without questioning where she came from or why she showed up so unexpectedly."

Lenore's hand went to her throat. She'd hoped her quilting friends would offer Leah their reassurances when she returned, but she hadn't anticipated such an outpouring of support. And when Margaret stood up to gaze at Leah and her son, appearing very nervous, Lenore held her breath.

"Leah, I owe you an apology," Margaret said in a strained voice. "I've been blind—reluctant to believe what you've been saying about Adeline and Alice. What we all witnessed today has been a real slap in the face—a wake-up call about the outrageously rude way the girls have been treating you, and . . . and the way a lot of us have written you off as, well . . . unwifely. I hope you can find a way to forgive me."

"Anyone can see you're the perfect mate for Jude," Martha Maude put in emphatically. "You've stepped into a challenging situation and you're doing your best to be the glue that holds this family together. We've been too slow to acknowledge this, but we're all glad you've come to Morning Star, Leah."

Lenore felt enveloped in the love and acceptance that had filled the front room. Her heart still went out to Leah, for the days ahead held more challenges with the twins, but now the network of neighbor ladies would provide some support even after she returned to Cedar Creek.

"And now, young lady, you and your man need to get yourselves into dry clothing—and get your hair put back into place with a *kapp*," Naomi instructed as she playfully wagged a finger at Leah and Jude. "We'll wipe up those puddles you're making on the floor—"

"And I'll put water on the stove for your tea," Lenore added quickly. It was a relief to see Leah smiling at Naomi's lighthearted reprimand rather than assuming it was yet another of the *maidel*'s customary criticisms.

"*Denki* for loaning me your barn coat, Naomi," Leah said. "I'll wash it and return it as soon as I can."

Lenore's heart swelled as she watched her daughter and son-in-law climb the stairs together, hand in hand. It seemed the quilting frolic had accomplished much more than mere needles and thread could do, and for that she thanked God. "I'll put on a big pot of water, for whoever else wants hot tea," she announced.

"Or hot chocolate!" Stevie piped up excitedly. He hugged her legs, gazing up at her with his big blue eyes. "It's not a party without hot chocolate, right, Mammi Lenore?"

"You've got it right, Stevie," she replied as she stroked his mop of thick brown hair. "Come help me set out some more goodies so it'll be a real party. We have a lot to celebrate."

On the following Monday afternoon, Jude felt high on anticipation as he set a large suitcase inside the buggy. In a few moments he and Leah would be leaving for the Kanagys' Countryside B and B to enjoy four glorious days without anyone except themselves to keep track of—and he planned to stay lost in love for the entire time he was away. When he returned to the house, he felt compelled to say a few last words to everyone who'd remained in the kitchen to see him and Leah off.

Jude gazed at Adeline and Alice, who appeared so contrite—so very Amish—in the maroon cape dresses Lenore had recently sewn for them. They stood at the sink washing and drying the dinner dishes, their expressions still somber from his stern lectures and the extra household duties he'd assigned them over the weekend. After the ladies had gone home from the quilting frolic, the girls had apologized to Leah, and she had accepted their apology—but it would be a while before the clouds in their relationship with their step-

mamm had a chance of clearing. Adolescent resentment had roots as deep and widespread as trees, it seemed to him.

"Goes without saying, girls, that I expect a *gut* report when we get home," he remarked. "And Stevie, you're to be your uncle's right-hand man while I'm away, so there'll be no tomfoolery on your part, either, *jah?*"

"We're *gut* to go, Dat," the boy replied as he gazed adoringly at Jeremiah. "All the horses and Leah's animals are gonna be fed and watered just the way they're supposed to be."

"And nobody'll go hungry—especially this little punkin," Lenore put in as she shifted Betsy to her other shoulder. "We'll take extra-*gut* care of her while you're away."

"We *mammis* are looking forward to time with the kids," Jude's mother said with a nod—although she didn't include Adeline and Alice in her gaze when she surveyed the kitchen.

Jude was satisfied, however, that his mother and his brother would help Lenore maintain order while he and Leah were away. Jeremiah had gotten quite an earful from Mamm when she'd returned home from the quilting frolic, and the bishop had made it known that unless he saw a marked improvement in the twins' behavior—in the sincerity of their words and deeds where Leah was concerned—the girls would be confessing before the entire congregation come Sunday.

When Alice had protested that they couldn't be punished or shunned because they were in their *rumspringa*—not members of the church—Bishop Jeremiah had informed her that he'd already spoken with the preachers on this matter, and that the twins were on everyone's radar. No longer could they use their unbaptized state as an excuse to sneak around with English boys, tell tales, or torment Leah. Adeline and Alice had been stunned to hear that folks other than the ladies at the frolic had heard about their blatant lie concerning Betsy being Leah's child.

Maybe they've learned a lesson they wouldn't accept just

upon my teaching it, Jude thought as he watched the girls wash and rinse a few more plates. *Sometimes the messenger is as important as the message.*

When he caught sight of the eager smile teasing at Leah's lips, he set aside his concerns about the twins. "Guess we'll be going now," Jude announced as he reached for his wife's hand. "See you all Friday morning."

He felt like a kid skipping out of school. Even though snow still lay in the low spots and ditches alongside the road, Jude was in a springtime frame of mind once he and Leah were in the rig and heading toward Cedar Creek.

"This is so exciting," Leah said as she reached for his hand. "I kept thinking something would come up and keep us at home, but you saw to all the details—especially about corralling the kids."

Jude chuckled. "I figured if I didn't have Mamm and Jeremiah there as backup, Lenore wouldn't stand a chance at keeping track of the girls—and it pains me to say that about them," he added sadly. "If I knew how to find the fellow who owned that infernal cell phone that was partly to blame for this mess, I'd return it—along with a few choice warnings. But for now Jeremiah knows where I stashed it, out in the barn where your goats are."

Leah's eyes widened with comprehension. "You figured the twins would never look for it out there, because they don't want to be around my goats," she put in with a chuckle. "Does Stevie know where it is? He seems to overhear a lot about what the girls are keeping from us."

"He doesn't know the exact stall—and it's behind a board, in a spot he can't reach," Jude replied. "He has the best intentions, but I figured if the twins tried to worm the phone's location out of him, he might let it slip. He just knows it isn't in the house."

They were silent for a few moments, sitting close enough that their shoulders and thighs brushed as the buggy swayed.

"We're leaving all that drama behind us now, for four whole days," Jude whispered suggestively. "I can think of much more . . . tantalizing topics for us to explore. I chose a room at the back of the Kanagys' double house, facing toward the woods and a pasture. When I stopped by to make our reservation, Mary and Martha told me we'd have the guest areas to ourselves, because at this time of year most folks only come on the weekends." Jude smiled, saving the best temptation for last. "We also have the option of getting our breakfast delivered to the room if we don't feel like getting dressed to eat in the dining room."

Leah sat back against the buggy seat, her eyes wide. "That sounds downright sinful, lolling in bed—holed up in a nice room—when we'd usually be doing chores in the barn or cooking breakfast," she whispered, squeezing his hand. "I—I'm not sure I'll know how to do that."

"I can teach you, sweet Leah," Jude teased.

Leah giggled. "I bet you can."

Chapter 18

Leah cherished every moment of her time with Jude at the Kanagy place. She was astounded that before they'd even arrived, he'd arranged for those private breakfasts he'd teased her about during the drive—and he'd also paid extra to take their noon and evening meals with Bram and Nate Kanagy and their wives so she and Jude wouldn't need to venture into town for food.

"This getaway is one of your best ideas ever, Jude," Leah said as she gazed out their room's big window late Wednesday morning. "It was so thoughtful of you to see to our meals and get us this room overlooking the woods. I can't remember the last time I felt so relaxed, so carefree—and please don't think I don't love the kids—"

Jude kissed her temple as he stood behind her, holding her. "I would never think that about you, sweetheart," he countered. "Truth be told, I was ready for some time away from parenting, too—and I believe we'll both see the kids from clearer, better-rested eyes when we return on Friday morning."

Leah watched a small red fox wander just to the edge of the woods, staying in the shade and underbrush to take in its surroundings. She touched the window so Jude would notice the fox, too. "You know, he has the right idea," she said pensively. "There's nothing wrong with taking refuge—staying in your safe domain—while you assess what lies around you," she continued. "You are my safe domain, Jude. My home. Because you've loved me so well, I've grown beyond that dark, desperate place I was in three weeks ago when I told you I couldn't go on living with your family."

"The morning the twins were eavesdropping," Jude recalled with a sigh. "It's been such an emotional roller-coaster ride since they overheard the truth about Frieda. I'm sorry they've put you through so much, Leah."

"Ah, but I haven't been alone during this ordeal," she pointed out as she turned in his arms. "I've had you by my side. And I feel we've reached a resolution with Alice and Adeline, because now we have support from our mothers and your brother. We're not facing the girls' rudeness alone."

"Their misbehavior finally caught up to them, in front of tongues that wagged—and a bishop who won't accept excuses for bad behavior," Jude remarked softly. "I confess that I've wondered how things have been going for Jeremiah and our *mamms* these past couple of days—but not enough that I want to call home and find out!"

Leah laughed, reveling in the warmth of Jude's embrace—and in the strength he revealed by sharing his thoughts and misgivings with her. She suspected that many of her friends' husbands kept their feeling to themselves, and she felt blessed that Jude could show his vulnerability to her—could admit he didn't have all the answers, and that he wasn't always in control of his children or his fears.

"Mary and Martha must be cooking something really wonderful for dinner," she said, inhaling deeply. "Can you smell it? What do you suppose it is?"

"We should go downstairs and find out, so they don't have to wait for us," Jude replied. "Bram has been kind enough to take on a couple of sales I was supposed to call this week, so the least I can do is help him stay on schedule."

When they stepped out of their cozy room, Leah once again drank in the simple beauty of the Kanagys' huge double home, which had been designed so each couple had separate living quarters on either side of the guest rooms in the center. Mary and Martha's *dat,* Amos Koblentz, was a much sought-after carpenter, and he'd built many lovely features into the residence he'd given his twin daughters for their wedding gift.

The gleaming wooden staircase that spiraled down into the oversize dining room made Leah feel as though she were a queen descending to the main floor of a castle—even though Nate and Bram had pointed out that the staircase's design had saved considerable space, compared to what a traditional stairway with a large landing would've required. Hardwood floors added a luxurious sense of warmth to the room, which housed four extended walnut tables—with enough seating to accommodate the uppermost number of guests the Kanagys could host.

"I understand why our linoleum floors at home are practical," Leah said wistfully, "but this wood is so pretty. It adds such warmth to the room, even if it's more work to maintain."

Mary and Martha emerged from the kitchen with two large platters, their blue eyes twinkling with mischief. "You're Plain, so we'll share our decorating secret," one of the redheads teased.

"*Jah,* you're walking on vinyl flooring that's made to look like hardwood," the other twin put in. "After visiting a few other country inns, we knew our place had to have a look that English folks would feel was homey—"

"But we didn't want to spend a lot of time buffing and polishing wood floors. So Dat came to our rescue," her sister finished. As Mary and Martha gazed around their dining room with obvious delight, Leah recalled that Mary wore her *kapp* strings behind her head while Martha let them hang down the front of her dress—their subtle way of dressing differently so guests could tell them apart.

"This is amazing," Jude said as he knelt to run his fingertips over the flooring. "I'd install this sort of flooring at our place in a heartbeat, but my brother the bishop would be the first one to tell me I was being extravagant—showing off—if I replaced our gray linoleum with this stuff."

The sisters shared a chuckle, their noses crinkling identically. "Bishop Vernon helped our *dat* with the cabinets and finishing work, and he was amazed at how fine the flooring appeared, too," Martha said.

"*Jah*, he almost told us to send it back and get linoleum—until Dat showed him that it was an upgraded version of vinyl flooring," Mary recalled.

"Bishop Vernon is a special man," Leah said as she gazed again at the beautiful details of the room. "I doubt Morning Star's Bishop Jeremiah would allow Amish folks to operate a bed and breakfast."

"*Jah*, a couple of years ago one of our families had the opportunity to take over a local hotel, and Jeremiah nixed that transaction," Jude said. "He didn't like the idea that some of the guests rented rooms for a few hours in the daytime—couples who might've been married, but not to each other," he added with a raised eyebrow. "Not the sort of business Plain people should be involved with."

The redheads' eyes widened. "Bishop Vernon had a few qualms about that as well," Mary said with a nod, "but he gave us permission to run an inn because Nate and Bram have their auction barn on the property—and we're out here in the middle of nowhere—"

"And we require that folks make an advanced reservation with a deposit and stay at least one night," Martha put in. "Most of them stay longer."

"Bishop Vernon and his wife were the first guests to reserve a room, so they know firsthand about the accommodations," Mary said with a chuckle. "Some mornings he pops in for breakfast, too, because he likes to talk to the people who come here from so many places—"

"And because he thinks you girls bake the best breads and cinnamon rolls he's ever tasted," Bram teased as he came inside with his brother.

Nate, the taller and older of the two men, slung his arms around Mary's and Martha's shoulders. "Bishop Vernon also realizes that some of my clients find it convenient to stay with us when they're delivering or picking up horses I train for them—or when folks come quite a distance to attend an auction in Bram's barn," he said.

"*Jah,* it's not as though the small towns around here have many motels," Bram put in. He flashed a brown-eyed smile at Mary and Martha. "It seems our wives had the right idea all along, wanting to run a B and B. We only married them so they could support us on their profits!"

Martha and Mary laughed and returned to the kitchen. Within minutes they had carried more bowls to the table they'd set with simple blue woven placemats and dishes with a deep blue floral pattern. Leah sat down in the chair Jude pulled out for her, between their hostesses, and Jude took his place between Bram and Nate, across the table. After they'd bowed their heads in silent prayer, Leah surveyed their dinner hungrily.

"It's a real pleasure to sit down to meat loaf *and* pot roast with gravy," she said happily. "And the best part is that I didn't have to cook!"

Nate chuckled as he handed the platter of roast beef to Jude. "Bram and I have discovered that we get a lot fancier fixings when the girls are cooking for guests—"

"Not that we go hungry when it's just the four of us," Bram hastened to put in. He smiled endearingly at the young woman to Leah's left. "But I'll admit that our wives have a talent for making meals big enough that we eat twice from what they cook once."

"Planned-overs, instead of just leftovers," his wife explained.

"Mostly because we enjoy spoiling our guests with big breakfasts more than we like to fuss over dinner and supper," her sister explained. "By the time we clean guest rooms and help Bram with sales at the auction barn, there's not a lot of time and energy left to cook the big meals our *mamms* fixed when we lived at home."

"But our *mamms* weren't working at two other jobs on top of managing their households and kids," Nate pointed out, smiling indulgently at the redhead to Leah's right. "One of these days when the kids come along, Bram and I will hire extra help so our wives won't work at the auction barn."

"And that's when we might have to give up being innkeepers," Mary said with a shrug.

"But for now, we enjoy every moment of entertaining our guests," Martha added, grinning at her sister. "We're living our dream, the four of us. We'll have these days to look back on when we've become parents, knowing we allowed ourselves some time to do exactly as we chose . . . even if the bishop and our parents are starting to hint that it's time we took on adult responsibilities—"

"And gave them grandkids."

Leah smiled. Mary and Martha were effortlessly finishing each other's sentences, the way Adeline and Alice did. After she'd filled her plate with a slice of meat loaf, some pot roast, mashed potatoes, glazed carrots, and fried apples, she felt compelled to ask the redheaded, fun-loving twins a question. "So tell me," she began as she cut into her meat loaf, "did you girls give your parents fits when you were young? Mary, did you pretend to be Martha? Or were you sweet and well-behaved, always following the rules?"

Across the table, Nate and Bram burst out laughing. Their dark hair and eyes made a handsome contrast to their fairer wives' features, and their mirth filled the dining room.

"When we first met Mary and Martha, they played that very trick on us," Bram recalled fondly.

"*Jah,* and I walked away from their place in a big snit, believing we'd never be able to trust them if we courted them," Nate added. "Even so, I knew Martha was the woman for me—"

"Even if she sorta played us false—set us up by secretly calling Mary on her cell phone so she could be in on the game," Bram put in. "But their parents set them straight—and the girls set *me* straight about a few wild-hare ideas—"

"And not long after that, we were engaged," Nate said with a satisfied nod. "So now we're living the dream, like Martha said."

Leah shared a long gaze with Jude. Was it too much to hope that someday Alice and Adeline would grow into sensible, responsible adults, as Mary and Martha had? She didn't think the two redheads could be much over twenty, if that old, yet they were managing a successful bed and breakfast business while their husbands of about the same age also ran independent businesses. "My dream is to live in a home where our sixteen-year-old twins no longer crave English boys—or the cell phone that one of those boys provided," she admitted with a sigh.

"The girls' disrespect for Leah is the main reason she and I came here for a few days," Jude admitted sadly. "Adeline and Alice seem to have lost touch with everything our Amish faith holds dear, even the basic courtesies their mother—my first wife—instilled in them when they were children."

"*Rumspringa* can be rough on parents, I suspect," Martha said softly. "Although when you're fully immersed in having your run-around years before you commit to the church, you're not always aware of the havoc you wreak. We were seventeen going on eighteen when we switched places on Nate and Bram—and meanwhile caused our parents a wagonload of worry. Yet we didn't see our behavior as rude or unacceptable."

"Our *mamm* and *dat* came down hard on us, to hold us accountable for our deception," Mary put in as she rose to refill the empty potato bowl. "Teenagers have to be told what their parents expect of them—and also reminded that the world doesn't revolve around them. If our parents had let us run wild, I don't want to think about the sort of trouble Martha and I might've gotten into—"

"Not because they were bad girls, understand," Nate insisted quickly.

"But they liked to have their fun," Bram put in as he grinned at his wife. "And they were so irresistibly cute that Nate and I fell for them hook, line, and sinker—even though we knew they wouldn't become wives who agreed to do everything a typical Amish husband would expect of them."

Jude laughed softly. "*Jah,* from what I've observed, you two couples are anything but typical—and I'm seriously impressed with the life you've made for yourselves at such a young age," he added. "You give me hope that Alice and Adeline can turn themselves around and someday become responsible adults and *gut* wives."

"Don't give up on them," Martha said softly. "And don't forget to tell them when they do things right."

"*Jah,* they need you more than they know," Mary added solemnly.

When Jude steered the rig into the lane midmorning on Friday, his heart felt lighter—renewed by the love he'd shared with Leah in the company of the Kanagy family. "Look at this," he said to Leah as Stevie raced out of the house, running toward them full-tilt. "I think our boy missed us."

"Dat! Leah!" Stevie hollered. "I've been waitin' and watchin' for ya to come home!"

Jude stopped the rig and hopped out its door to catch Stevie, who rushed into his arms. He hoisted the laughing boy above his head, twirling him in the air just to hear the joyful sound of his laughter and to share his son's unabashed love and excitement. Jude lowered Stevie to his shoulder, hugging him hard. "So how'd it go with Uncle Jeremiah and your two *mammis?*" he asked. He figured his boy's account might be more accurate than the story the twins told him.

Leah had joined them, happily wrapping her arms around Jude and Stevie so the three of them formed an affectionate huddle. "It's *gut* to see you, Stevie," she said as she rumpled his thick brown hair. "We stayed in a nice inn, but it was very quiet there without you—and without any goats or ducks or cattle or chickens to tend."

Stevie beamed at them. "Me and Uncle Jeremiah took real *gut* care of the animals," he said, nodding vigorously. "I showed him how to feed 'em their rations, and he took me out every afternoon on his big ole horse—to get away from the girls and have some man time, ya know."

Jude laughed as the three of them climbed into the rig. Jeremiah's dappled gray Percheron was an impressive animal— he stood several hands higher than the bishop—so Stevie had no doubt been delighted to sit atop the huge horse with his uncle.

"Did Mammi Lenore and Mammi Margaret spoil you by cooking all your favorite meals and treats?" Leah asked, smiling as Stevie perched between her and Jude on the seat. "And how did little Betsy do?"

Jude noticed that Leah had asked about everyone except the twins, perhaps trying to extend their peaceful getaway for as long as possible—and he couldn't blame her. He had vowed to return to the Kanagy place with her every now and again because the placid inn in the countryside had restored their souls. And Mary's and Martha's remarks about dealing with teenagers had also convinced him to remain firm in his convictions about how to raise his rebellious daughters.

"They made us chocolate chip cookies and nanner cream pie—and 'sketti with cheese on top!" Stevie crowed. "It was awesome! Betsy's doin' real *gut*, too—and Alice and Adeline even *like* her now, maybe coz both *mammis* thought they should be payin' more attention to her."

Jude glanced at Leah over the top of Stevie's rumpled hair. He raised his eyebrows as if to ask, *Do we dare hope this improvement will continue?* Leah shrugged, her expression hopeful. It was indeed good news that the twins were finally spending time with the baby . . . because maybe if they paid more sisterly attention to Betsy, they wouldn't feel the need to sneak away from home with those English boys.

Jude steered Rusty into the stable, thinking of one more subject to discuss with his son before they entered the house. "Did your sisters stay home while we were gone?" he asked as he set the buggy's brake. "Did they rifle through any more rooms looking for the cell phone?"

Stevie smiled knowingly. "They still haven't found it. And they think Dexter and Phil are probably ready to throw them under the bus," he replied.

"Throw them under the bus?" Leah asked. "What bus runs out here in the country?"

"Dexter and Phil?" Jude queried. His heart pounded with the thought that more of Alice and Adeline's secrets might've just been revealed.

"That's the two English guys they've been chasin' after," Stevie confirmed. He shrugged as he looked at Leah. "I dunno about the bus thing. Do ya think they're gonna take a trip or somethin'? I haven't heard 'em say no more about that."

Jude climbed out of the buggy and let his son jump down onto the floor. If he'd chastised Alice and Adeline for listening through the walls, he should be consistent with Stevie— even if his son often provided pertinent information. "You know it's wrong to listen to the girls with your ear to their bedroom wall—or at the space under their door—*jah?*" he asked sternly.

Stevie raised his arms in an exaggerated shrug. "When they start squabblin' about how ticked off Dexter and Phil must be, coz of the cell phone thing, ya can't help but hear what they say, Dat," he protested. "Sometimes I'm just goin' down the hall to my room, mindin' my own business."

Jude bit back a smile. Stevie ran ahead of them to the house, and when they entered the kitchen the aromas of roasting chicken and vegetables made his stomach rumble. His mother and Leah's were rolling out piecrust at one end of the kitchen table while Jeremiah sat at the other end with a mug of coffee, reading the latest issue of *The Budget*. The three of them confirmed Stevie's assessment that all had gone well for the past few days.

"Your boy was the best assistant I could've asked for," Jeremiah remarked with a smile for Stevie. Then he lowered his voice. "And—as far as we know—the twins stayed put. Didn't see any sign of those English boys, either, so I see no need for Alice and Adeline to confess on Sunday. Maybe they've changed their ways."

"They didn't give us a moment of trouble," Lenore added with a nod. "I'm not sure what's come over them, but I hope it lasts."

Jude nodded, gratified that God had apparently answered some of his most earnest prayers. In the front room, he was pleasantly surprised to see that Adeline and Alice had found a wind-up swing for Betsy. During the moments before the twins realized that he and Leah had returned, their faces were alight with sincere affection for the tiny girl in the swing as she moved forward and back. When Betsy caught sight of Leah and let out a happy squawk, the twins looked up.

"You're back!" Alice said. "Have a *gut* time at the inn?"

"Look what we found at the thrift store for Betsy!" Adeline put in. "She could sit in this swing for hours—as long as we keep it wound up and moving."

Jude's pulse thrummed as he watched Leah gently lift Betsy from the swing to hold her. It seemed that a minor miracle had occurred since he'd left home on Monday, and he dared to believe that the relationships within their family might have a chance to heal.

"You girls are a sight for sore eyes—all of you," he added with a special smile for Betsy. Recalling what Mary and Martha had suggested, he added, "I'm really happy to hear that your time with Jeremiah and your *mammis* went so smoothly. I appreciate your cooperation with them while we were gone."

"You should see the cool patchwork jackets Mammi Lenore sewed for us," Adeline said happily.

"*Jah!* I'll go put one on so you can see how they look," Alice said as she scurried toward the stairway.

Whatever You did for the girls in our absence, Lord, I'm a grateful man, Jude prayed. *Help me preserve this peace and be the father these girls and Stevie deserve.*

Chapter 19

Two weeks later, Leah felt torn about telling her mother good-bye. On the one hand, Alice and Adeline seemed to have returned to being the cheerful, conscientious Amish girls she and Jude wanted them to be—but on the other hand, Leah had truly enjoyed her mother's company.

"I've had a wonderful-*gut* time here with your family, Leah," Mama said as she packed the last of her cape dresses into her old suitcase. "But it's almost the middle of April, and things need doing around home."

Leah heard a touch of homesickness in her mother's words. "I really wish you'd stay, Mama," she said softly. "Not just because you'll always be a better cook than I am, but because we all really love having you here—and because I worry about you getting lonely all by yourself on the farm."

Mama gently placed her hand alongside Leah's cheek, gazing into her eyes. "I'll be fine, sweetheart, and far too busy to be lonely. Now that you're an old hand at handling Betsy—and especially now that the twins have come around to being responsible young women—I want the five of you to become a family without me hanging around."

Leah blinked rapidly. She hadn't anticipated feeling so emotional at this moment because she'd always known Mama would return home, yet her eyes grew hot with unshed tears.

"You've given us all such a gift, Mama," she whispered. "Your time and assistance with Betsy and Stevie and the girls—your wisdom—has meant more to us than you'll ever know."

Mama must have been feeling sentimental, too, because she looked away—pretending to search the guest room for something she might've forgotten to pack. "It's what mothers do, Leah. My coming here was nothing compared to the way you've opened your heart to Betsy—and to Alice, Adeline, and Stevie, as well," she insisted softly. "Jude's a lucky man to have you running his household. I recall giving you a talking-to the night before your wedding, trying to convince you that marrying into this family would never work out. But it has."

Leah hugged her mother hard, knowing it had been difficult for her to admit she'd been wrong about the marriage. "I still don't understand what you and Margaret and Jeremiah did to turn the twins' behavior around," she said. "It was such a help to have you sewing their new dresses—and those patchwork jackets are amazing—"

"They were a great way to use up some solid-color quilting scraps," Mama pointed out with a chuckle. She eased away to study Leah's face. "I honestly don't know what changed the girls' ways. Maybe it was Jeremiah telling them they'd be on their knees, confessing in front of the congregation if they didn't straighten up and fly right."

Mama stepped away to look out the window. "Or maybe when Adeline and Alice told that outrageous tale about Betsy being your secret baby—and then realized how the Slabaugh sisters and our other guests would spread the word about their lies—they scared themselves . . . realized that everyone in town would think a lot more harshly of them than they would you."

"Or maybe," Leah put in hopefully, "those English boys have written them off." Even as she said this, Leah suspected Dexter and Phil were still eager to get the cell phone back—unless they'd reported it stolen, so they wouldn't have to pay the monthly charges for it. She hadn't wanted to ask Adeline and Alice about what had inspired their change of heart, fearing she might jinx their three-week run of model behavior.

"Maybe we won't find out until years down the road, when one of the twins mentions it in passing after she's been married to a nice Amish man for a while," Mama suggested. "And maybe we'll never know. Life is filled with maybes, and those possibilities either work out or they evaporate like the steam from a teakettle."

Leah nodded, sighing as her mother fastened the metal clasps of her suitcases. The sound had such finality to it—but when Stevie burst into the room, he drove out any possibility of Leah dwelling upon the way she already missed Mama's company.

"Mammi Lenore, do ya really hafta go?" he asked, opening his arms to her.

Mama leaned down to hug him, kissing his cheek loudly. "You're getting so big I can't pick you up anymore, Stevie," she said cheerfully, "but I sure am happy to see *you* so happy these days. And I'm leaving it up to you to look after your *mamm*, all right? Will you do that for me until I come back?"

"*Jah,* I'm on it!" the boy replied with a smile for Leah. "Me and Leah, we're a team!"

As the three of them headed down the stairs, Alice and Adeline came through the front room to meet them—and to take the two suitcases. They had bread in the oven, and they'd been in the process of layering meat sauce and lasagna noodles into a pan while in the corner of the kitchen, Betsy went back and forth in the wind-up swing set.

Adeline smiled. "We really love our new dresses, Mammi Lenore—"

"And those pretty jackets you made us!" Alice added as they carried the luggage out the door Stevie held open for them.

"We hope you'll come back and stay with us again!" one of them called over her shoulder.

"*Jah*, you're an awesome cook, Mammi Lenore!" the other twin chimed in.

Mama leaned down to smile one last time at little Betsy. "I'll see you again, wee girlie," she whispered. "It'll be a joy to watch you grow up."

After one last crushing hug, Leah released her mother. She watched from the porch, waving when Mama, her mare Flo, and the buggy were headed down the lane toward the road. Her mother's five-week visit had been such a blessing—a timely lifesaver—that Leah feared she would soon flounder again while trying to cook and clean and care for Betsy without Mama's help.

God's on it, she reminded herself as Stevie joined her on the porch. When he sighed contentedly and reached for her hand, Leah's heart filled to overflowing. Why was she so concerned about running the household, when she had such a devoted son and husband, and three girls who made her life shine like the sun now that they all seemed so happy and settled?

Friday morning was a picture postcard of a spring day. From the kitchen window Leah noticed the redbud trees in the yard bursting with pinkish-purple blooms, as well as the dogwoods that were so full of blossoms they resembled huge popcorn balls. Cheerful red and yellow tulips filled the narrow flowerbed alongside the barn, and when the sun hit the grass at just the right angle, Leah held her breath. Every green blade was topped with a sparkling drop of dew, so the yard seemed to be covered with thousands of tiny glass beads. She took a moment to admire a sight that only God could've created.

"What kind of cookies do you want, Stevie?" one of the twins asked.

"We've got the makings for peanut butter, or oatmeal raisin, or soft sugar cookies with frosting," her sister put in.

Leah turned in time to catch Stevie's mischievous grin. He was seated at the kitchen table with a deck of playing cards, very carefully arranging them on their edges to make a simple house, as Jude had showed him. "All of 'em!" he replied. "Ya know how many cookies me and Dat'll go through when he gets home from the sale barn this afternoon—and with the weekend comin' up, we gotta be ready for that, too."

Alice and Adeline rolled their eyes good-naturedly. "If we make peanut butter cookies, you'll have to roll the dough into balls and then in the sugar," Alice suggested.

"Because while you're doing that," Adeline said as she took the flour canister from the cupboard, "we can be making the dough for the sugar cookies."

"And if you do a really *gut* job on the peanut butter balls, *maybe* we could be talked into making oatmeal raisin cookies, as well—if you'll chop the walnuts for them," Alice teased.

When Stevie jumped down from his chair, his house of cards collapsed, but he was too excited to care. "I'm goin' to wash my hands! Fill up the nut chopper for me!"

Leah chuckled. It was such a pleasure to see the twins coaxing their little brother to help with the baking—and such a huge difference from the days when Alice and Adeline couldn't have cared less about what sort of cookies Stevie wanted. Leah didn't know why—and she didn't want to jinx the situation by asking too many questions—but the twins had been staying home and behaving as though they'd forgotten all about the cell phone Jude had hidden in the barn, and about the boys who'd tempted them with it.

Leah went to the swing in the corner and cranked it again, making Betsy squeal and wiggle with delight. "Mah-mah-mah," she babbled, waving her little arms. Even if it was probably too soon for the baby to form words, Leah wanted to think Betsy might be close to saying *Mama* . . . might be calling her that because she actually associated such a name with her, rather than just repeating the sound. Leah smiled at the happy baby, her heart filled with hope.

By the time Stevie returned to the kitchen and proudly held his clean hands up for Leah to inspect, she had poured walnuts into the jar with spring-loaded chopper blades built into its lid. "Here you go," she said. "I'm sure glad you wanted all three kinds of cookies, Stevie, because they're all my favorites, too."

When he beamed at her, Leah shimmered with love for him. He was such a helpful son, so eager to please. Stevie climbed back into his chair at the table and braced the jar against the tabletop so he could push and twist the jar's handle to operate the chopping blades. Adeline was pulling the metal cookie sheets from the cabinet, making quite a racket—but a louder noise outside made Leah look out the window. A faded red car with rust on its lower edges was coming up the lane. Before it stopped, the engine backfired again.

Leah watched a heavyset, dark-haired young woman in jeans and a sweatshirt climb out of the driver's side. She vaguely wondered where she might've seen the girl before. Perhaps she needed directions, or was looking for one of the Amish shops that were scattered along the back roads . . . except her face was set in a purposeful expression edged with youthful uncertainty. When the visitor walked toward the front porch, Leah went to answer the door.

As she stepped into the open doorway, the back of Leah's neck prickled. Did she feel apprehensive because English folks didn't usually come to the door? Or because Jude wasn't home? Or was it the stranger's direct gaze that made Leah feel like a target about to be shot at?

"I'm Betsy's mother. I came to take her home."

Leah clutched the doorframe, momentarily forgetting how to form words. "I—I beg your pardon?" she finally managed.

The young woman cleared her throat, pointing to the

porch floor. "I left my baby here last month," she said in a tight voice, "and now I want her back. It was a—a big mistake to leave her here."

Wishing desperately for Jude's assistance, Leah fought to focus her racing thoughts. "I don't have any idea who you are," she stalled. "Why should I just let you take Betsy—"

"Hey, there's a car out front!" one of the twins called from the kitchen.

The sound of footsteps coming from the kitchen—the grasp of Stevie's hand as he hurried up beside her—gave Leah a surge of courage.

"Who're you?" Stevie piped up. About that time the twins were peering out the door from behind him and Leah.

"Natalie? What're *you* doing here?" Adeline asked, exchanging a wary glance with her sister.

Alice took a step back. "Hey, if this involves something—or somebody—at the pool hall, we don't want to talk about it."

The pool hall. Leah suddenly wondered if this was the young woman who'd been flirting with the fellows the day she'd found the twins there—the girl who'd gotten her tank top yanked down over her shoulders.

"How many times do I have to say it?" Natalie demanded. "I came here to take Betsy home, so—"

"Come inside so we can talk about this," Leah interrupted nervously. "I need a lot more information before I even think about giving up a—a member of our family!"

"*Jah,* and I'm not letting the cookies burn while we listen to this ridiculous conversation," Adeline muttered as she and Alice strode back toward the kitchen.

Stevie followed his sisters, glancing warily over his shoulder at the young woman who came inside behind Leah. *Natalie can't be much older than the twins,* Leah fretted. *How can I even think of letting her take our Betsy away?*

While Adeline pulled two sheets of cookies from the oven, Alice stood beside the swing with her arms crossed tightly. Betsy babbled at her, but the girl was too intent on studying

Natalie to coo at the baby. "So let me guess," Alice said sharply. "You dumped Betsy on our porch last month because you wanted Nick or Alex to date you."

"And a baby got in your way," Adeline added in a scornful tone.

Stevie turned his attention from the hot pans of cookies to glare at their guest. "Is that any way to treat a poor little baby?" he demanded hotly. "I'm thinkin' we love Betsy a whole lot more than you do."

You took the words out of my mouth, Stevie. Leah was at a loss—feeling sick to her stomach—because she saw how Natalie's gaze was fixed on Betsy as the baby swayed back and forth in her swing. Betsy had filled out a lot, and in her sunny yellow dress and airy curls of light brown, she resembled a doll baby, pink and perfect—a far cry from the condition she'd been in when Leah had found her in a basket on the porch a month ago.

"I—I brought Betsy here because I knew you'd take care of her," Natalie said in a halting voice. Once again, she held Leah's gaze, beseeching her. "When you came to the pool hall that day to take Alice and Adeline home, I could see that you loved them enough to look after them, so I—I figured Betsy would be in good hands here."

"*Jah,* she is in *gut* hands here," Alice retorted. "She has a real family now."

Adeline frowned as she removed cookies from the pans with a metal spatula. "Why should we even think about letting you have her back, Natalie? Betsy's our sister now. We've made plans to adopt her—because her mother didn't want her," she added with a purposeful glare.

Natalie took a few tentative steps toward the swing, swallowing hard. "My family's been pretty tough on me for getting into this mess—they're Mennonites, and they're mad because I don't want to join the church. But—but I want to take care of Betsy now. She'll love me even if nobody else does, so I—I've *got* to have her back. Please! It's only right—

it's only *fair*," she insisted tearfully, "because now I realize what a mistake it was to abandon her."

"Mah-mah-mah!" Betsy chirped as the swing stopped moving.

"See there!" Natalie said ecstatically. "She remembers me! She knows I'm her mother and she's happy to see me!"

Leah knew better . . . but she also knew what she had to do, even if letting go of Betsy sliced her like a knife. God had surely guided Natalie to bring Betsy to their home last month, but He'd also brought the young mother to her senses—even if she seemed woefully incapable of giving Betsy a stable home life. *But who are you to judge? Not long ago Alice and Adeline were making our home life pretty miserable.*

"So, Natalie, where are you living now?" Leah asked in the firmest voice she could muster. "I can't possibly let Betsy go with you if you've not got a place for—"

"I'm at my parents' house, on the other side of Morning Star," Natalie replied quickly. "I'm ready to be responsible for my baby. Honest."

Leah felt as though she might faint. She closed her eyes to lean against the kitchen counter, struggling to do the right thing. "When you brought Betsy here, you didn't leave us any bottles or diapers or clothing. Do you have those things for her?" she asked. "Betsy's been doing well—growing like a weed—on milk from my goats. What will you be feeding her?"

"I've got a can of formula powder out in the car," Natalie quickly assured her. "But hey, if you could give me some clothes and diapers and stuff, I could sure use them."

Adeline stared incredulously. "Leah, you can't be serious!"

"You *know* Natalie can't take *gut* care of Betsy! She doesn't even have clothes for her," Alice chimed in, placing her fists on her hips. "Why should we let her take a poor, helpless baby—"

"Because she's Betsy's mother, and a baby belongs with her *mamm*," Leah put in, somehow managing not to burst into tears at the mere thought of what she had to do. "If—if you girls will help me pack the clothes and bottles, this will go easier. Faster."

Not waiting for their reply, Leah turned to go upstairs before she lost her nerve. Her heart was banging against her rib cage and the staircase blurred as her eyes filled with tears, but she knew Jude would make the same decision, even though he'd loved Betsy as his own child since her mysterious appearance.

He'll be devastated when he comes home and finds that Betsy's gone, she thought as she entered the bedroom. Leah heard the twins speaking loudly and none too politely to Natalie downstairs in the kitchen, so she quickly emptied the drawers of the cloth diapers, onesies, and little dresses her mother had so lovingly sewn. She didn't want Betsy to have time to get upset by the girls' confrontational talk—and she knew she'd cave in with despair if she stopped to think about what she was doing. She found a big plastic bin in the hall closet and stuffed the clothes into it.

Downstairs, Leah tucked as many baby bottles as would fit inside the bin and snapped its lid shut. She couldn't look at Betsy in Natalie's arms—didn't dare ask to hold her one last time, for fear she'd be unable to let go of the little girl who'd so effortlessly filled her heart and her days this past month. *And if Betsy sees me crying for her—or won't release me to go with Natalie—we'll all get more upset.*

"All right, Natalie, let's go. Let's get this over with," Leah whispered as she hurried toward the door with the bin. Summoning every ounce of strength she had, she headed outside toward the run-down car, sensing she would regret this decision—would mourn this day—for the rest of her life.

But she was doing the right thing. In the Bible story about the two women who'd each begged King Solomon for a disputed baby, hadn't the baby's real mother loved the child enough to give it up after the king had threatened to cut the child in half?

Leah reached the car and flung open a back door so she

could stuff the bin into the backseat. The car smelled musty and was littered with food wrappers, but that wasn't her immediate concern. "Don't leave yet," she rasped as Natalie came along behind her with the baby. "I still have your basket. She—she can ride in it instead of bouncing around loose on the seat."

Somehow Leah made it to the house and then to the car again. As Natalie laid Betsy in the towel-lined basket, Leah felt as though this girl had just ripped her world to shreds. When the baby began to cry and reach for her, Leah turned away and held herself. "I—I wish you joy and God's blessings as you raise your beautiful little girl," she blurted out. "We love her more than you'll ever know. *Denki* for sharing her with us."

Leah rushed back to the kitchen and fell into a chair—but the emotional toll of giving up baby Betsy propelled her to the bathroom, sick to her stomach. When she'd stopped vomiting, she stumbled weakly to her chair at the table again. The twins were so upset with her that they'd forgotten all about baking cookies.

"This is just *wrong*, Leah," Alice cried out. "Can't you see that?"

"Natalie has no clue about raising a baby!" Adeline added vehemently.

Leah understood their criticisms, but she tried to help them understand her reasoning. "Natalie gave us such a gift, entrusting her baby to us—think about what a hard choice she made, and how tough her life's been since she had a baby out of wedlock," she insisted softly. "We've become a stronger family because Betsy was here, because we all wanted her to grow and be healthy. We need to keep Natalie and Betsy in our prayers, and be grateful for the time we had with Betsy. She pulled us together, girls."

"And now Natalie's tearing us apart!" Adeline put in angrily.

Alice started for the door. "We're going after her. We've *got* to make her see reason."

The slam of the back door made Leah wince. She admired the twins' fierce need to retrieve Betsy—and it warmed her heart to see how far the girls had come since the baby's arrival, when they'd wanted nothing to do with her. Yet she felt Natalie deserved a chance to raise her child. Natalie would make mistakes and some questionable decisions, no doubt. But what parent didn't?

Stevie was in the front room crying, but Leah didn't yet have the strength to go comfort him. She sat holding her head in her hands, focused on the tabletop so she wouldn't have to look at the empty swing where, mere moments ago, Betsy had been laughing and babbling at them. Such a happy, healthy baby. The light of their lives.

I feel like these cards Stevie was playing with, Leah thought as tears ran down her cheeks. *Scattered and strewn, as though my house—my life—is suddenly empty and has collapsed around me. What am I supposed to do now, Lord? And how can I possibly explain this to Jude?*

Chapter 20

When Jude entered the kitchen late that afternoon, the atmosphere felt so dark and heavy that a thunderstorm might've ravaged the house and blown away all the usual signs of his family's presence. The house was so quiet, he could hear the soft *tick-tick-tick* of the battery clock on the wall. Although he saw—and smelled—no sign that supper preparations might be under way, the kitchen was a mess. Utensils were strewn across the countertops and bowls of what appeared to be cookie dough sat near the oven. A couple of cookie sheets were covered with a dozen evenly spaced baked sugar cookies.

Why did the girls leave in such a hurry? I've never known Stevie to leave cookies untouched—

Jude sucked air. What if someone had gotten so ill—or injured—that Leah had rushed them to the hospital? Or had somebody . . . died?

"Leah?" he called out as he passed through the kitchen. "Stevie? Anybody home?"

He entered the front room and stopped. Leah sat on the sofa, holding Stevie in her lap. Her face was pale, and both of them looked dejected. Wrung out. The twins were nowhere in sight.

Jude scowled. Where was Betsy?

Leah glumly looked up at him. "We, um, got quite a shock this morning when . . . well, Betsy's mother came and took her back."

The bottom dropped out of Jude's heart. "Took her back? Who was it?" he asked, his mind in an uproar as he approached his wife and son. He sat down on the sturdy coffee table directly across from Leah, gently grasping Stevie's leg.

"The girls knew her from spending time at the pool hall," Leah replied sadly. "It went against my better judgment, letting Natalie leave with Betsy—"

"She didn't even have no clothes for her!" Stevie chimed in forlornly.

"—but how could I refuse her?" his wife continued with a shake of her head. "She wanted her child, and it wasn't as though Betsy was actually ours—"

"But we loved her," Stevie protested with a hitch in his voice. "And now she's gone."

Jude let out a loud sigh. He recalled how mystified they'd all been when the baby had appeared from out of nowhere a month ago. Now the mother in question had an identity—not that he felt any better, sensing Leah's reluctance to let Betsy go with her. "I'm sorry," he murmured, because he could think of nothing else to say. "I wish I could've been here to help you—or to ask Natalie to reconsider."

"Would you have done anything different? We've always believed that babies belong with their mothers." Leah's stark sadness reflected her doubts, her longing for Betsy's bubbly, sunny presence. "When Natalie said she could use some clothes and supplies I—I sent them along with her. I didn't want to think about Betsy without her little dresses, or bottles to drink from, or—"

Leah's sudden sobs tore Jude to shreds. She cried so rarely, and the fact that nothing had gotten done since Betsy's departure told him exactly how bereft and empty she felt. "I don't see how you could've refused to let Betsy go with her mother," he assured her. He listened for a moment, noting the stillness in the rest of the house. "Where are the girls? Maybe we should try to go about our usual evening chores. We'll feel better if we're all together to discuss this over supper."

"Supper," Leah said with a sigh. She shrugged. "Alice and Adeline thought I was absolutely wrong to let Natalie take Betsy—not to mention the clothes and supplies. I tried to talk them out of it, but they were determined to follow Natalie and get her to change her mind."

"Maybe they'll bring Betsy home with 'em," Stevie said with a hopeful smile.

Jude patted the boy's leg and stood up. "Whether they do or they don't, we've got animals to feed, son," he said gently. "And whatever happens, we can be sure God's got a hand in it. Sometimes He—and the folks around us—do things we don't understand, but we just have to keep on keeping on until we have a better answer."

Stevie rose from Leah's lap and started for the barn, but he didn't look convinced by what Jude had said. Truth be told, Jude wasn't sure they would ever have a better answer, either. Manual labor would at least give him some motions to go through.

After the chores, Jude went to the phone shanty and called for pizza delivery, a treat reserved for special occasions—or when the women in his life had spent the day in a hot kitchen running the canners. When he returned to the house and saw the depressed, defeated expression that lingered on Leah's pale face, he went upstairs on a sad mission of mercy. He heard Alice and Adeline in their room and let go of his last shred of hope that Betsy might return.

Jude choked up at the sight of a few little clothes left in the white dresser that doubled as a changing table. *Leah was too blinded by tears to see them when she was whisking away the rest of Betsy's clothing,* he realized. He quickly tucked the tiny garments into the white wicker bassinet and carried it to the attic. After he'd placed the white dresser up there as well, he returned to the bedroom.

The corner of the room appeared as starkly empty as he felt.

After a moment, Jude thought he heard happy gurgling . . . could still imagine little hands reaching up to him from the bassinet. He suspected memories of Betsy would haunt them all for a long, long time.

Amazing, how such tiny hands took such a big hold on our hearts in such a short time, he thought as he went downstairs to sit with Leah. *Lord, You've got to help me comfort her. Maybe it would help if we knew another baby would soon be sleeping in that bassinet. . . .*

On the following Monday, Leah worked at a stainless steel table outside the barn, cutting a large batch of butchered and plucked chickens into serving pieces. She had already finished with the ducks, which she'd left whole—except for removing their innards—and they were iced down in a big cooler. On the days when she prepared her birds to sell to the meat locker in Cedar Creek, she rose earlier than usual so the butchering was done by midmorning. After that, she would shower and take her coolers of poultry into town for Bishop Vernon's nephew, Abner, to package and freeze—or to sell fresh in his butcher shop's meat case.

The mid-March dawn was chilly, and Leah's breath rose as vapor that glowed in the light of her lantern. Ordinarily, these early mornings when she worked outside soothed her soul. On this particular day, focusing on her task kept her busy enough that Betsy's absence remained a dull ache.

It's been three days since Natalie took her back. If I can just get through this morning, this day . . . my work will be my salvation.

When Leah was milking her goats—or when she was dealing with the mess of butchering birds—she believed she was doing the work God had intended for her to carry out, for wasn't she feeding people? She might not be a whiz in the kitchen, but she still provided food that would nourish the folks who bought her poultry and eggs.

Leah glanced up to savor the pink ribbons of the sunrise. The light in the kitchen window told her the twins were cooking breakfast. Jude would soon be doing the horse chores and other work around the yard with Stevie before he went to the sale barn to call an auction this afternoon. Their days weren't as full without Betsy's presence, but Leah took solace from the way the Shetler household had found a flow, an orderly attempt at comfort, now that Alice and Adeline weren't causing any trouble.

Rifle fire shattered the stillness, one shot followed by several more.

Momentarily stunned, Leah rinsed her hands in the basin and ran toward where the gunshots had come from. It probably wasn't the smartest thing to do, but she had to be sure her cows and calves were—

The roar of an engine and the squeal of tires made Leah run faster. She caught sight of a dark gray pickup truck fishtailing down the road as it sped away in a cloud of dust. *English—probably men,* she thought as she raced the last several yards to the enclosure where her calves were eating. *What would they be doing on our road—shooting a gun—at this hour of the morning?*

What Leah saw stopped her heart. The four black-and-white calves cowered against the back side of the fence with Maisie, but the rest of her herd—except for Ike the bull, pastured farther from the road—lay dead on the ground. Within seconds she'd lost Erma, Patsy, and the six steers she'd planned to market in the next couple of months. Because she butchered animals for the meat market, she was no stranger to the sight of blood, but seeing the sudden, senseless slaughter of her cattle made her sick to her stomach. Clammy and sweating, she turned toward the bushes to vomit.

"Leah, what happened?" Jude called out as he ran toward her. "I heard shots being fired and—"

The twins, who'd jogged from the house alongside their *dat*, took one look and turned away from the pen, wide-eyed and pale. "Why would anyone want to shoot innocent cows?" Alice asked in a strained voice. "They weren't bothering anybody—"

"They *couldn't* bother anybody," Adeline protested. "And they had nowhere to run from whoever had the gun."

"Hey, what's goin' on?" Stevie hollered as he caught up to them. Jude quickly grabbed the boy, hoping to keep him from seeing the carnage around the calves' enclosure, but when Stevie saw how upset Leah and the girls were, he squirmed out of his *dat*'s grasp.

The boy could only gape before he turned to hide his face in Leah's skirt. "Who woulda been mean enough to shoot our cows, Leah?" he demanded, his voice rising into a wail.

Leah inhaled the chill morning air to settle herself before she stooped to embrace Stevie's shaking body. "I'm sorry you had to see this, honey," she said as she held him. "By the time I got here, all I saw was the back end of a big gray pickup truck racing down the road. I—I couldn't read the license plate—"

"English," Jude muttered, glaring in the direction the truck had gone. "And cowardly bullies they were, too, figuring we Amish wouldn't retaliate or report their crime. I have half a mind to call the sheriff anyway."

When Leah raised her head to question Jude's judgment, she noticed that the twins were gazing at each other as though something rang a bell. "Girls, do you have any idea who might've been driving that truck?" she blurted. "It looked a lot like the one your English friends drive."

Alice immediately shook her head and started back to the house, while Adeline grabbed Stevie's hand. "Let's go in," she hastily ordered the boy. "You'll have nightmares if you keep looking at those poor cows."

"*Jah*, son, it's best if you go in with the girls," Jude agreed sadly. "Leah and I need to clean up this mess."

Leah sighed as she and Jude watched the kids return to the house. Suddenly chilly, she buttoned her barn coat. "Sure as you and I are standing here, Dexter and Phil shot my cattle," she stated. "But we've got no proof."

"The look on Alice's and Adeline's faces is all the proof *I* need," he muttered vehemently. "If this is those guys' way of catching our attention—trying to get that cell phone back— well, I won't let them get away with slaughtering your animals, Leah. That's just *wrong*."

Jude stopped his ranting to look closely at her. "Are you all right—I mean, except for this shooting spree?" he asked as he slung an arm around her shoulders. "Ordinarily you've got a strong stomach."

Leah shrugged, bewildered. "I don't know what came over me," she said weakly. "I'm fine now, really. The sooner we clean up this mess, the better I'll feel."

He nodded.

Jude hurried toward the barn, and after a moment Leah followed him. "Guess we'll be eating a lot of beef and veal for a while," she remarked glumly. "Maybe Abner will be willing to sell some extra steaks and roasts. I'll take some in when I deliver my ducks and chickens."

"I'm sorry this happened," Jude said as they walked back to the pen. "I know you were counting on a nice check when you sold the six steers—which is why I plan to speak with Sheriff Banks instead of just forgiving and forgetting. And what if Stevie or the girls—or you—had been hit by bullets passing through the fence?"

Leah's eyebrows rose. Jude was feeling protective of her and the kids, but it wasn't the Plain way to seek out English law enforcement to deal with vandalism or other troublesome incidents. "Why not discuss this with Jeremiah instead?" she asked. "What sort of information could you give to the sheriff that would help him locate those boys?"

Jude grunted. "This isn't just about today's gunshots. It's about the way I believe Dexter and Phil have been tempting the twins away from our faith."

"All the more reason to talk to Jeremiah, who understands that angle. The sheriff may well refuse to go on a wild-goose chase, trying to find a Phil or a Dexter who owns a gray pickup," Leah reasoned softly. She tried not to think about the size of the check she'd been anticipating . . . the hay, supplements, and veterinary expenses that money would've covered. "After all, we can either sell the meat or eat it ourselves. We're not facing a total loss."

Jude gazed at her, inhaling the chilly morning air to settle his agitation. "You're probably right," he admitted with an impatient sigh. "It just seems that we Amish pacifists are as defenseless as your cows, because we're targets for English pranksters who think we'll take whatever they dish out."

They paused at the gate to the enclosure. "I hope Abner doesn't turn away your beef, sweetheart," Jude said. "His regular English customers—and our Plain neighbors who butcher their own animals—might already have lots of meat in their deep freezes."

"*Jah,* I'd thought of that, but it can't hurt to ask. Maybe God will use this incident to bring about justice in His own way." As Leah looked at her forlorn remaining cow and the four calves alongside her, she sighed loudly. "Let's get the carcasses into a wagon so I can butcher them at the barn," she suggested. "That way, poor Maisie won't have to watch me."

"And then I'll call Abner for you," Jude offered. "No sense in taking him more beef than he can sell."

Nodding, Leah headed back to the barn to hitch Rusty to the wagon. She'd tried to make the best of this nasty prank, but one thing was certain: it would take a very long day of butchering to deal with the meat from eight slain cattle.

Chapter 21

"Not much farther," Alice panted as she jogged alongside Adeline. "Then we'll be able to see if the truck's in the parking lot."

"Cutting across the back pastures saved us a lot of time and distance, but I need to catch my breath before we meet up with Phil and Dexter." With a final burst of energy, Adeline topped the hill and focused on the backs of the last buildings before the main street of Morning Star turned into a county road. "This would've been easier if Dat had put the wheels back on our buggy, seeing's how we've stayed home like *gut* little girls these past few weeks."

"Puh! He'll be mad at us all over again now, for running off."

"Well, I can't let the guys get away with shooting Leah's cows, can you?" Adeline demanded. She inhaled deeply, shaking her head. "It's one thing for Phil to be mad about a missing cell phone. It's another thing entirely to gun down a bunch of defenseless calves and their *mamms*."

They crossed the last several yards of grassy pasture, toward the low rock wall that marked the back boundary of the car dealership. Once they'd clambered the wall and hopped down onto the asphalt behind a row of parked cars, they gazed toward the pool hall.

"There's the truck." Alice looked down, studying the condition of her clothes. "Let's be sure we've got all the loose grass off our jeans—"

"And we'll act like we're really glad to see Phil and Dexter when we spot them," Adeline strategized aloud. She smoothed her unbound hair and adjusted the blue tank top she wore under the quilted jacket Mammi Lenore had sewn for her. "Better to get them outside, away from the other guys, before we lay into them about what they did."

"Do you think they'll really admit they shot all those cows?" Alice asked as a worm of doubt squirmed in her stomach. "We know it was their truck, but if they deny they fired any shots, what'll we do?"

"We'll cross that bridge when we come to it. Let's go."

Adeline led the way to the edge of the car lot and a few moments later they were approaching the back of the pool hall. Even at this early hour, when most folks were eating breakfast, loud music throbbed inside the building. Several old cars were parked around it, which meant the usual crowd of night shift workers from the pet food factory had come for beer and platefuls of greasy bacon and eggs.

"Play it cool," Alice whispered as her sister grabbed the back door's knob. "Act like it's old times and we're back to being their girlfriends."

"*Jah,* if they get nasty about the phone, let's tell them Dat took it," Adeline said in a tight voice. "After all, it's the truth. We had nothing to do with that."

"If they get nasty about *anything,* we're heading for home," Alice insisted, holding her sister's gaze. "Now that I've thought about it, maybe it wasn't such a *gut* idea to hightail it over here by ourselves. But we're here. We'll go inside—"

"At least to hear whether they shot those cows," Adeline put in. She took a deep breath to keep her courage up, noting that Alice appeared nervous, too. "And then we should probably head for home anyway. We knew the guys could get rowdy, but I . . . well, I never dreamed they'd run around shooting defenseless animals."

After a late breakfast, Jude sighed as he stood at the girls' bedroom window, watching them cross the pasture in English clothes. "Like moths to a flame," he muttered as he lowered the binoculars. "I don't like it one bit that they're heading toward the pool hall to see boys that are not only English, but are armed. I'm going to fetch Jeremiah so we can put an end to this mess they've gotten into."

"Why would the girls want to keep associating with such violent boys?" Leah asked sadly. "I was hoping their improved behavior these past few weeks meant they'd put those fellows behind them for *gut*."

"I heard 'em talkin' after breakfast, while they was changin' their clothes," Stevie said from the doorway. "They were all riled up—really mad at those guys. They think Dexter and Phil should apologize to Leah and pay for the cows they shot."

That'll never happen, even though the twins are right. Jude turned, sorry his young son had seen Leah's slain cattle—and sorry that Stevie was getting drawn into the fray his sisters and their English friends were creating. He set down the binoculars and started for the door. "If the girls call home, I want you to phone Jeremiah's place right away," he said.

"I'll go sit in the phone shanty, so's I'll be ready when the phone rings," Stevie said, pleased to have a job.

"We'll let you know if Alice and Adeline come home, too," Leah put in. "Be careful, Jude. Now that guns are involved, this situation's a lot more dangerous."

"I'll see you both later," Jude promised. He kissed Leah and clapped his hand on Stevie's shoulder. "*Denki* for your help. Keep us in your prayers."

As he loped toward the barn to retrieve the cell phone, Jude's mind spun with a lot of ideas for bringing a potentially hazardous situation to a positive, safe conclusion. When he reached behind the loose board and grasped the phone, he scowled at it. *I should've located Dexter and Phil and returned this infernal thing a long time ago. Guide me and my brother, Lord, as we settle this situation once and for all.*

Alice put on her best flirtatious smile, the one that could always coax Phil to do what she wanted. As she and Adeline made their way between the noisy pool hall's back tables, she noted a similar strained smile on her sister's face. She ignored the remarks from the guys they passed, focusing on Phil and Dexter at a back table.

Would they be able to tell that she and her sister were scared out of their minds? It was best to play along with Phil's mood and act as though the sight of all those bloody cows and calves hadn't upset them. He and Dexter would tease them mercilessly—and play upon their fears—if they sensed she and Adeline were ready to run.

"Well, well, well." A cocky voice rose above the loud country music. "Here comes Alice and Addie, just like we figured on, Dex!"

"Yessirree, Phil!" Dexter crowed, saluting the girls with his fork. "Do we know how to get their attention, or what?"

"Maybe if they'd answered their cell phone, a lot of cows would still be grazing in that fence near the road," Phil added archly.

Hearing his belligerent tone, Alice wanted to grab her sister's hand and dash past the pool tables, out the front door, but she sensed the guys would chase them down. Phil, the taller and heavier of the two, chugged the remainder of his beer and slammed his mug on the table with a loud laugh while Dexter brushed aside his shaggy black hair to leer at them. Half-eaten plates of fried eggs and bacon sat in front of them, along with several empty shot glasses. It wasn't yet ten in the morning and they were drunker than Alice had ever seen them.

"Cat got your tongue, missy?" Phil taunted as the girls slowly approached their table.

"Or did our drive-by shooting get you so excited you just had to come see us?" Dexter teased. He grabbed the empty chair beside him and pulled it out. "Sit yourselves down, girls."

"Yeah, and if you're not gonna answer that cell phone I bought you, you can put it right there," Phil said, pointing angrily at the scummy tabletop. "Don't think for a minute that this relationship is over until I say it's over. We've given you girls some gifts, and a little repayment of our kindness is in order—wouldn't you say, Dex?"

"Yup, a little *interest* paid on our investment," Dex replied with a short laugh. "After all, those Tinker Bell tattoos weren't free—and we've hardly gotten to see them."

"It—it's not our fault we haven't answered your calls," Alice protested. Her throat was getting so tight she was surprised she could respond. She knew better than to pull away from Phil's grasp as he pushed her into the chair beside him. She'd seen these two get squirrelly when they were drinking, but they'd never before displayed such a hard, cold-blooded edge.

"*Jah,* our *dat* took the phone and hid it," Adeline reminded them earnestly. She perched on the edge of the chair beside Dexter, wincing slightly when he hooked his arm around her neck and gave her a sloppy kiss.

"Hey, you're nineteen. Your old man can't run your lives anymore," Phil shot back. "If you think I'm gonna keep paying the bill on that cell, you're wrong, girls. Dead wrong."

"Dead as those cows," Dexter remarked. He laughed raucously, as though he'd made a joke.

Alice felt the blood draining from her face as she stole a glance at her sister. Fibbing about their age had been a bad idea . . . just one of the questionable choices they'd made when these two English guys in their late twenties had first flirted with them.

"All right, fine. We'll go home and get your phone," Adeline asserted in a shaky voice. "Dat'll hand it right over when we tell him we don't want to see you guys anymore—not after the way you shot down our cattle!"

"*Jah,* he knows your names," Alice blurted out. "And Leah can identify your gray truck. She saw you drive off after you killed her helpless—"

"Shut up!" Phil slammed the table with his hand. His eyes were bloodshot as he glared first at Alice and then at Adeline. "You're ticking me off, girls. If you're planning to leave home like you said, why do you even *care* about those stupid cows?"

"And how many dozen gray trucks do you suppose there are around Morning Star?" Dexter jeered. He tugged at the front of Adeline's quilted jacket to see what she was wearing underneath it. "Me, I'm thinking it's time for a lot less of this talk and a whole lot more action. Get my drift, baby doll?"

"Yeah, it's time to hop in the truck and take a little ride," Phil chimed in with a nasty laugh. "There's a no-tell motel a couple miles down the road. I guarantee you that by the time we finish our business, you girls won't feel the least bit Amish anymore. Let's go."

Adeline's heart leapt into her throat as the big man across the table suddenly scooted his chair back. "I—I need to use the restroom!" she rasped.

"And I need a beer!" Alice said just as desperately. "You should let us catch up, because you're probably a couple of pitchers ahead of us."

Phil scowled and stood up. "That's the lamest excuse I've ever—you girls've been giving us nothing but excuses since—"

"So do you want me to pee on your truck seat?" Adeline challenged as she ducked out from under Dexter's arm.

"I'll go get us another pitcher and four frosted mugs while we wait for Addie," Alice said, smiling playfully at Phil. "You know we'll be a lot more fun if you pour a couple of beers down us."

"*Jah,* I'm peeing to make room for beer," Adeline assured them flirtatiously. She wiggled her fingers in a wave as she started for the back hallway beyond the bar.

"You know, this salty bacon's made me thirsty again," Dexter admitted, glancing into the empty pitcher at his elbow. "But don't think you can hide in the bathroom," he called after Adeline. "Three minutes, and I'm comin' in after you."

"And don't even think about leaving, because I'm watching the doors," Phil added ominously. "There's no way you can outrun my truck, anyway."

Alice didn't wait to hear any more. She started toward the bar, so scared she was barely able to breathe the thick, smoky air. *God, if You let Adeline make it to the pay phone to call home for help, I promise I'll never again stray from the path to Plain salvation. And please, please help me distract the guys with this beer.*

"Hey there, sugar, long time no see." Rick, the paunchy, middle-aged man who owned the pool hall, gave her a gap-toothed grin as he ran beer from a spigot into a plastic pitcher. "Glad to see you girls show up to keep those boys from tearing the place apart," he said around the cigarette in his mouth. "They were pretty riled up when they got here."

As another loud country song from the jukebox filled the pool hall, Alice didn't know what to say. Rick was somewhat older than Dat, with stringy gray hair, and it creeped her out whenever he looked at her. He set the pitcher on a tray and then took four glass mugs out of the freezer behind the bar.

Alice took hold of the tray with both shaky hands, for fear she'd drop it. She planned to walk just to the end of the bar, to see if her sister was using the pay phone—except Phil suddenly planted himself in front of her, leaning heavily against the bar.

"Thought you might need some help carrying that," he said, narrowing his eyes. "Want you to save your energy for what comes next, once we get to that motel."

Alice swallowed hard. Phil had seemed so cute and appealing when he'd first pulled up alongside her and Adeline in the truck as they'd been walking down the road last summer, but the hard gleam in his eye today made her wish she'd never met him. She and her sister had enjoyed defying Dat's wishes with older, more worldly guys who made them feel so special with their gifts and promises for the future . . . and feel so beautiful with their deep, soul-stirring kisses. Too late, she realized that Leah had been right about these guys all along.

"Are we gonna go back and sit down while that beer's still cold?" Phil asked sarcastically. He grabbed the tray and made a point of walking beside Alice so she couldn't see what her sister was doing.

About the time Alice realized that Dexter was no longer at their table, she heard Adeline's shriek in the back hallway, followed by the loud slamming of the pay phone's receiver.

Why did you think you could fool these guys? Why did you believe you could come here and set them straight about shooting Leah's cows? Alice thought desperately. She sat down in the chair next to Phil's, feeling doomed. *They'll only get nastier after they drink more beer . . . God, can You please, please help us get home?*

When Adeline approached the table with Dexter's hard arm around her, she wore a frightened expression. She met Alice's gaze with the slightest shake of her head, as though to say she hadn't had a chance to talk to anyone at home, let alone leave a message.

Phil filled the four mugs with beer, his smug expression confirming the stupidity of Adeline's attempt to get help. "Bottoms up, girls," he said, leering at the innuendo in his words.

Alice flushed furiously. She nearly choked on her first gulp of beer, wondering why she'd ever pretended she liked it— and wishing she'd never pretended to be someone she wasn't. Adeline took a short sip, too, trying to make the glass of beer last long enough to plan a way out of this horrible predicament.

Rick came to the table with four jiggers of whiskey. He

was grinning as though he already knew that Phil and Dexter were about to win the prizes they'd been trying for ever since the day Alice and Adeline had first hopped into the truck. . . .

"Why don't you give us some more lessons on shooting pool?" Adeline gazed hopefully at Dexter as he tossed back his shot of whiskey.

Alice grasped for her twin's conversational straw. "*Jah*, as I recall, you fellows really enjoy leaning us over the table, showing us how to hold our cue sticks—"

"Why do you keep changing the subject?" Phil demanded after he, too, drained his shot of whiskey in a single gulp. "I want to talk about how you girls're going to—"

"I'm game." Dexter's smile was lopsided as he rose unsteadily to his feet. "If we do what the girls want now, they'll repay the favor when we take them down the road. Come on, Addie-baby. Let's show 'em how the game's played." He grabbed the shot glass in front of Adeline and gulped the whiskey in it.

Alice hurried to the nearest empty pool table. She stalled, fumbling while racking up the balls, acting clumsy as Adeline came up to help her.

"We're in a bad spot, Alice," her sister whispered before lifting the wooden triangle from the green tabletop.

"Keep them talking and drinking," Alice murmured. "If you can hold their attention, I'll try to slip away—"

"Too much table talk!" Phil interrupted as he grabbed Adeline's hand. "Get your little backside down there and I'll show you how to ram the cue stick so all the balls fly into pockets on your first shot."

Alice didn't mention that he'd chosen the wrong twin, because the bleary expression on Dexter's face told her that he, too, was confused about their identity. She and Adeline had traded places once without telling the guys—but Phil had immediately noticed a difference in the way Adeline kissed him.

Let's hope it doesn't get as far as kissing today, she thought, desperately wondering how to derail the guys' plans. It made her queasy to watch Phil press her sister over the end of the pool table, dwarfing her as he laid his arms over hers to guide the first shot.

When the front door opened, Alice wanted to cry out in relief—except Dat and Uncle Jeremiah were both gazing purposefully at her, shaking their heads slightly. They paused in the doorway to take in the scene.

"Amish farmer dudes?" Dexter called out with a drunken laugh. "Hey, won't you guys go to hell for being in a pool hall? We're drinking and smoking and carrying on here! We're baaad!"

From beneath Phil's bulk, Adeline caught Alice's eye while Dex heckled Dat and his brother. Alice quickly pressed a finger to her lips—and then pretended she had no idea who the two bearded men in black broad-brimmed hats and barn jackets could be.

Just one more favor, God, Alice prayed earnestly. *Please let Phil and Dexter be too drunk to realize why two Amish men have just shown up—and who they are.*

Chapter 22

It took all of Jude's strength to keep his fists at his sides. The sight of an unkempt—and obviously drunk—blond fellow pinning his daughter to the pool table in a very suggestive position was enough to make him punch first and think later. When Jeremiah tweaked his coat sleeve, Jude inhaled the smoky air to settle his nerves. He reminded himself to follow the game plan he and his brother had formulated as they'd ridden here in the back of the sheriff's cruiser, because it was the best way to insure that his girls stayed safe—and that he and Jeremiah did nothing they'd have to confess at church.

The smell of stale beer, cigarettes, and old walls that reeked of grease took him back to his *rumspringa*. *Nothing's changed,* Jude noted as he quickly glanced around. *You can pull this off if Rick doesn't recognize you—and if the girls don't give you away. Stick with the strategy Jeremiah suggested until Sheriff Banks comes inside.*

Jeremiah assessed the two men with Alice and Adeline and went to the wall to choose a cue stick. "I could use a little quick cash," he said above the wail of the jukebox. "What say you fellows team up and play me and my friend a little eight ball? Shall we go for fifty dollars a game?"

"Or shall we go for a hundred?" Jude picked out a cue stick and immediately dropped it, stalling so the sheriff would have time to search the gray pickup parked out front. He flashed a wide smile at the two young men. "Unless maybe you guys can't scratch up fifty bucks apiece."

"This should be good for a laugh," the blond jeered as he straightened to his full height and reached into his jeans pocket.

"Easiest fifty bucks I'll ever make," the other guy said with a drunken chuckle. He handed a fistful of uncounted bills to Adeline. "You girls can count the money and hold on to it, to keep everything fair and square."

"Hey, and bring our beer over to this table," the blond ordered Alice. "This won't take long, sugar pie, and then we'll be on our way to play a *real* game."

Once again Jude seethed, but the scenario was going just the way they'd hoped. His daughters were playing along, taking the money from the four of them and then sitting down at the table, out of harm's way.

Jeremiah took his time arranging the stripes and solids inside the wooden triangle, as though he wasn't sure how to rack the balls properly. "You guys might be better players than we are," he remarked apologetically, "so how about if we go first?"

"So we'll at least get a turn," Jude put in as he ambled to the opposite end of the pool table. As he chalked the end of his stick, he hoped his billiard skills would come back to him—just as he was counting on Sheriff Banks to come inside before the two English fellows realized they were being hustled.

Drew and Phil chortled as though Jeremiah's suggestion struck them as hilarious. "Sure, why not?" the shorter one replied.

"Fine by me," the burly blond said as he chose a different cue stick from the rack on the wall. "But you know, we play nearly every day, so if you guys're out to make a little money, maybe you should—"

"Shut up and let him take his shot," his friend snapped. "This game was their idea, after all. Easy come, easy go."

A MOTHER'S GIFT   213

Jude relaxed, leaning over the end of the table with his cue stick. As he'd hoped, these young men were full of themselves and skunk drunk. He focused on the tight triangle of colored balls and shot hard and clean, biting back a grin when the balls scattered all over the table.

"Guess we'll take the stripes," Jeremiah said as two striped balls fell into pockets. He easily sent a third ball into the center pocket as Jude studied the table and positioned himself to continue their turn.

Jeremiah turned to the tall blond fellow, who frowned at the direction the game was taking. "How many guys does it take to install the second lightbulb this swag lamp is supposed to have?" he teased, tapping the dust-encrusted beer advertisement with his cue stick.

Phil and Dexter appeared confused by this old joke. It was one of Jeremiah's diversionary tactics from when he and Jude were in their *rumspringa*—because even back in those days, none of the fixtures had been fully lit. The blond went over to sip his beer while the shorter guy peered up into the light fixture with a baffled expression.

"We'll probably never know," Jude responded in a conspiratorial tone. "Something tells me they don't keep any spare lightbulbs in this joint."

"Huh," the fellow grunted. He eagerly accepted the mug his blond buddy brought over and swilled about half of the beer in it.

Jude drove the white cue ball firmly against the table edge at an angle to knock another striped ball into a corner pocket. As his brother chose his next shot, Jude glanced at Alice and Adeline, who sat wide-eyed and silent. In their jeans, makeup, and dangly earrings, with their hair cascading over their shoulders and beer mugs in front of them, they appeared heartbreakingly English. At least the colorful jackets Lenore had made them covered their upper bodies, and they weren't smoking or drinking or glaring at him for coming to the pool hall. Jude couldn't be completely angry with his girls because they'd come here to right a wrong on Leah's behalf, so when they glanced at him, he winked.

"That's it for the stripes," Jeremiah announced when he'd taken his shot. "Go for the solids, little brother."

"Now just a freakin' minute," the blond protested over the blare of the jukebox. "I thought you two said—"

"In eight ball, our team gets to keep shooting until one of us misses a shot," Jeremiah pointed out firmly. "We're playing this fair and square, boys. You said we could go first."

Jude took great satisfaction in driving a blue ball the full length of the table into a corner pocket without the cue ball following it. As he stepped back to allow Jeremiah room for his turn, he glanced through the smudged front window. He was relieved to see a barrel-shaped man in a brown uniform approaching the door.

"Why did the chicken cross the road?" Jude asked his opponents, barely able to control his temper. What did his daughters find so alluring about these two belligerent, rude young men?

"To get to the other side," the shorter guy jeered.

"Nope," Jude said. "To get away from a couple of irresponsible guys with a gun."

Suspicion flared in the blond's eyes. When the sheriff stepped inside, both the young men sobered up fast. Neither of them spoke.

Clyde Banks assessed the situation and took his time approaching the table where the four of them were playing. He planted himself in front of the blond. "Phil Hainey, you're under arrest," he announced beneath the blare of the jukebox. "You have the right to remain silent—"

"And what's *this* about?" Phil demanded hotly. "I've been here all morning—and I've got all these witnesses—"

"Your truck was identified racing away from the Shetler place after you shot most of their cows and calves," the sheriff began. "When I received that call, I was just down the road from the Shetlers', checking out a call about a horse you shot—"

"You can't prove any of that!" Phil's buddy piped up.

Sheriff Banks shook his head in disgust. "The bullets that killed the cattle came from the rifle in the back of the pickup you fellows parked out front."

"You had no right to search my truck!" Phil shouted.

The sheriff calmly pulled a folded paper from his pocket. "Here's my search warrant, gentlemen," he said. "I found exactly what I was looking for—and it's not as though I haven't cited both of you for various offenses before," he added with a wry smile. "So again, you have the right to remain silent—"

The jukebox was suddenly shut off and Rick came out from behind the bar. "Hey, what's going on here?" he demanded as he crossed the room. "I don't take kindly to you harassing my customers, Sheriff. Everybody here's minding their own business, as usual, so—"

"Including these two young ladies?" Sheriff Banks interrupted, nodding toward Alice and Adeline. "I've warned you before about serving minors, Mr. Welch, and I've nailed you square-on today because these girls are only sixteen. Shall I shut your place down right now, or will you allow me to proceed with arresting Mr. Hainey and Mr. Stockman for shooting eight cows at point-blank range?"

The place got so quiet that Jude could hear the hum of the refrigerators behind the bar. All eyes were on the sheriff. Jude stepped back to stand with Jeremiah, behind the twins. Alice and Adeline had stiffened in their chairs, looking very scared.

Phil glared at the girls. "Sixteen? They told us they were nineteen, so—"

"You've got nothing on *me*," Dexter blurted out belligerently. "I was just along for the ride."

"Which tells me that one of you was probably driving the truck while the other fired the gun out the window," Sheriff Banks said in a voice edged with impatience. "That makes one of you the cold-blooded killer of those cows and the other one an accessory—and I'm betting you'd both flunk a Breathalyzer test, am I right? Before you answer that or say anything else, maybe you should come to my office and call your lawyer."

Phil and Dexter exchanged an angry glance, but before they could say anything more, the sheriff unhooked a set of handcuffs from his belt.

"You know the drill, gentlemen. One arm apiece, and you'll walk outside to my car together in an orderly fashion," Banks said in a no-nonsense voice. "Resisting arrest would just be one more offense to pile onto the others I'm going to write you up for, understand me?"

After a moment Phil stuck out his arm. He glowered at the twins and then focused on Jude and Jeremiah. "This was a setup," he muttered. "I want my money back from you—you *con artists* who came in here pretending to be Amish guys, playing us for suckers—"

Sheriff Banks shook his head as he fastened a metal cuff on each young man's arm. "Nope, this is none other than Bishop Jeremiah Shetler and his brother—whose cattle you shot," he added. "Ordinarily, Plain folks don't ask me to intervene in their affairs, but you non-Amish gentlemen should be held accountable for the crimes you've committed—the loss of income you've caused the Shetler family."

When Phil appeared ready to smart off again, stalwart Sheriff Banks stood within inches of the belligerent younger man. "I intend to see you punished to the full extent the law allows for this escapade, Hainey," he muttered. "Whatever you lost to the Shetler brothers in your pool game is a down payment for the damage you've done, the way I see it. Shall we go?" he demanded. "Or do we discuss the fact that your underage girlfriends have beer mugs in front of them?"

Jude's heart was hammering as he stepped toward the young men who were preceding Sheriff Banks toward the door. He pulled the cell phone from his pocket and thrust it toward them. "I believe this is yours," he said tersely. "Don't come around my daughters again, got it?"

Phil snatched the phone, glaring over at the twins. "Fat chance," he muttered.

"More trouble than they're worth, and liars, too," Dexter groused.

The sheriff lowered his voice. "Do you want to press charges, Mr. Shetler? No doubt in my mind they started this whole ball rolling—contributing to the delinquency of minors might be just the tip of the iceberg."

Sickening visions of Phil and Dexter with his daughters whirled in Jude's mind. "What else did you do to them—besides defiling them with those tattoos?" he demanded. "If you—"

Phil's face turned the color of raw steak. "Huh! You can't nail us for getting any action, because—"

"We haven't touched them!" Dexter cried out. "*Have* we, girls?"

Jeremiah grasped Jude's shoulder before the fracas intensified—not that Jude had the heart to hear his daughters admit to intimate involvement with these louts. "We'll be discussing this with Alice and Adeline at home," the bishop insisted in a low voice. "Right now, we just want to get them out of here."

Jude watched Sheriff Banks steer the two young men outside. He—along with Rick and several curious customers—watched through the windows until the young men were in the cruiser and the sheriff had closed its doors. At the far edge of the parking lot, a horse-drawn rig sat waiting.

Bless her, Leah came for us, Jude thought as he stepped away from the window.

"So you Shetlers have returned like a couple of bad Amish pennies, eh?" Rick asked tersely. "What am I supposed to do if Banks shuts me down because your daughters are underage—"

"That's between you and the sheriff and those two guys he arrested," Jeremiah replied quickly. "Had you asked for the girls' driver's licenses, you'd have realized they didn't belong here. You won't be seeing them again."

"You didn't ask to see *our* licenses back in the day, either," Jude pointed out.

Rick frowned as he thought for a moment. "Amish girls wouldn't have driver's licenses—"

"Aha," Jude put in with a purposeful smile. "Seems a spare lightbulb just came on, *jah?*" He looked over at the twins, gesturing toward the door. "Let's go home. I've had all I can stand of this place."

Chapter 23

After the short, strained buggy ride to the farm, punctuated by the twins' sniffles and Stevie's curious questions, Leah dreaded the conversation that was going to be held at the kitchen table. Jeremiah and Jude had stewed the whole way home, keeping the details from the pool hall under their broad-brimmed hats while Stevie was present.

"Sweetie, why don't you go play with the goats and check on Maisie and the calves," Leah suggested as the rig approached the stable. "I'll call you when it's time for dinner."

"But I wanna hear about—"

"Son, you're going outside," Jude said gruffly. "Do as your *mamm* has told you. And I want you girls to change into proper attire before coming to the kitchen to discuss what your uncle and I witnessed today."

With a heavy sigh, Stevie hopped out of the rig and started toward the barns. Alice and Adeline hurried toward the house, and by the time Leah had reached the kitchen, she could hear them upstairs in their room. She filled the percolator and set it on the stove to boil, preparing for what might be a long afternoon.

"So how did it go?" she asked when Jude and his brother had settled at the table.

Jeremiah smiled half-heartedly. "In some ways it was like old times, being at that smoky, greasy hole in the wall—with the same guy who ran the place when we were kids," he replied. "But thinking about Alice and Adeline being there—"

"With two fellows in their late twenties who were rude and drunk and trying to deny any involvement in shooting your cattle," Jude put in tersely.

"—well, it was a situation I hope I never have to repeat," Jeremiah finished. "Our plan to keep Phil and Dexter occupied at the pool table until the sheriff could find the gun worked as well as we'd hoped. I think Sheriff Banks will give those young men the what-for in ways we couldn't accomplish ourselves. It was the right thing to do, calling him in to deal with English troublemakers."

"Did you hear him talking as if Dexter and Phil were constantly on the wrong side of the law?" Jude asked in exasperation. "I only had to spend thirty seconds in the same room with those two to wonder what on God's *gut* earth Alice and Adeline ever liked about them. And why would the girls claim to be nineteen?"

"And why didn't Phil and Dexter figure out that they weren't really that old?" Jeremiah pondered aloud.

Focusing on Alice and Adeline as they came back downstairs into the front room, Leah sighed. They had changed into the royal blue cape dresses they'd worn early this morning, and their hair was once again coiled beneath their *kapps,* but the circles beneath their eyes were dark with wet mascara. "I suspect the girls wanted to seem older because Phil and Dexter flirted with them—made them feel special," she speculated. "And by the same token, those fellows willingly overlooked the truth about girls who were so eager to spend time with them, and who didn't make any demands or question their behavior."

Alice and Adeline entered the kitchen and slipped into their chairs at the table, appearing ready for a stern interrogation session. Leah's heart went out to them, now that they were safe at home, but she knew to remain quiet while the men did the talking. She got out flour and the other ingredients to make biscuits for the midday meal, which would be served a lot later than usual.

Jude cleared his throat. "What do you girls have to say for yourselves?" he asked sternly. "I couldn't believe my eyes when I saw you running across the pasture toward the pool hall, knowing Phil and Dexter had just killed Leah's cattle. And on top of that, you didn't admit to us that you knew they'd done it."

The twins hung their heads, sniffling. "We—we were mad at them," Alice began with a whimper.

"It was *wrong* to shoot her cows," Adeline put in sadly, "and we wanted them to know we weren't going to stand for it."

"Soon as we got there and saw how—how drunk they were, we knew we'd been stupid to go there and confront them," Alice admitted ruefully.

"We tried to fool them," Adeline continued. "I said I had to use the restroom—so I could call you from the pay phone—and Alice tried to distract them by ordering a pitcher of beer."

"But they figured us out."

"The phone hadn't rung but once before Dexter grabbed the receiver from me and slammed it down."

Leah cringed, recalling the smelly, noisy pool hall and the type of restless, shiftless young men who spent time there. "Luckily, Stevie was in the phone shanty and when he answered the call, he heard enough loud music to figure out it was you at the pool hall," she put in softly. "So we hitched up the rig and went there to be sure those boys didn't leave with you."

"Jeremiah and I had already called Sheriff Banks, and we were on our way, too," Jude continued. He sounded less irate now, but still stern. "We were counting on distracting Phil and Dexter with a game of pool they believed they couldn't possibly lose until the sheriff had time to search their truck for the gun."

"Thank the Lord it all worked out the way we'd planned," Jeremiah said, holding the twins' gazes. "But I was appalled to hear that you'd told those fellows you were nineteen. And having heard about the revealing blouses you've worn—and seeing you there with beer mugs, and your hair down, wearing so much makeup, I had a hard time believing you were the sweet, obedient nieces I know you to be. You looked like Jezebels. Harlots."

Leah cringed, but she understood why the bishop was telling the girls just how disappointed he was with their behavior. Alice and Adeline hung their heads, and it took them several moments to speak again.

"We're sorry, and we promise never to wear those clothes or go anywhere near Phil and Dexter again," Alice said with a sob.

"We had no idea they'd done so many bad things that the sheriff had arrested them before," Adeline put in.

Jude exhaled loudly. "I hope they told the truth when they said they haven't . . . violated you," he said. His voice was thick with worry. Silence hung like storm clouds as he awaited his daughters' response.

"We've always found ways to sidetrack them," Alice mumbled. "But today, if you hadn't shown up . . ."

"They were really drunk, and determined to take us to some motel down the road," Adeline finished in a tight voice. "I've never been so scared in my life."

"We were so glad to see you come in with Uncle Jeremiah, Dat," Alice admitted in a quavery voice. "You and Leah were right about them all along, and we were too stupid to see it. We—we didn't know it was illegal for us to be at the pool hall."

"*Jah,* we thought we were just being grown up, drinking beer like everybody else who was there," Adeline said.

"We don't even like beer," Alice whispered, grimacing.

Leah kept stirring biscuit batter to keep from crying. She

didn't want to think about how the morning might have gone had Jude and Jeremiah not arrived with the sheriff in time.

"Well, part of that was Rick's negligence for not asking to see proof of your age. Some things never change," Jude said with a disgusted shake of his head. "But some of the blame is mine. When we found out you'd been going to the pool hall, I should've told you straight out that underage drinking is against the law—and I should've read the riot act to Rick about it, too."

Adeline sighed, resting her head in her hands. "You and Leah did tell us we shouldn't go there—"

"But we didn't want to listen," Alice said glumly. "We thought being in *rumspringa* meant we could try anything. We never dreamed that Phil and Dexter would turn so mean."

"*Jah,* they said they killed the cows to get our attention because we weren't answering the cell phone," Adeline recounted shrilly.

"They figured we'd come to the pool hall, and we were stupid enough to play right into their plan," Alice said with a loud sigh. "I—I'm sorry we've caused you so much trouble, Dat. *Denki* for saving our hides today."

"*Jah,* can you believe us—trust us—when we say we've learned our lesson?" Adeline asked plaintively. "If you want us to confess at church, Uncle Jeremiah, we'll be on our knees."

"We need all the forgiveness we can get," Alice agreed. "From you two, and Leah as well."

After several moments of silence, Leah looked up from rolling and cutting biscuits. She believed the twins were sincere—and the torn expression on Jude's face told her he was near tears, relieved to hear what his daughters were saying after dealing with their misbehavior these past few months.

Jeremiah clasped his hands on the table and leaned toward the girls. "I believe God has already heard your confession," he said softly. "This might be a *gut* time for all of us to offer Him our thanks for His presence and guidance this morning."

Leah laid aside her biscuit cutter and stood at the counter with her floured hands clasped and her head bowed. *We owe You so much, dear Lord,* she prayed. *Help the girls go forward from this difficult morning to live their lives with Your purpose in their hearts and Your wisdom in their minds. Guide us as we parent them, too.*

When Jude released the breath he'd been holding, Leah felt the tension in the kitchen dissipate. The gurgling of the percolator reminded her that normal life could go on, now that Alice and Adeline realized what serious mistakes they'd made.

"I'm pleased—and relieved—to hear you talking this way, girls," Jude finally said to them. "I feel as though my real daughters have been restored to me."

Adeline and Alice nodded, thumbing away tears. It was a solemn moment, after confession and forgiveness had cleared the air and wiped the slate clean. But now that the serious talk had taken place, Leah had something to add.

She went up behind the girls and wrapped her arms around their slender shoulders, resting her head between theirs. "We've had our ups and downs, girls," she began in a voice thick with emotion, "but I want you to know how grateful I am that you took a stand for my cattle—for *me*—this morning. It's real progress that you got angry *for* me instead of *at* me, and I—I love you for it."

Alice and Adeline clasped her arms. Leah nearly fainted when they kissed her cheeks.

"Well, *there's* a picture," Jude said softly.

The girls chuckled nervously as they released Leah. "Guess we should help you fix dinner," Adeline said. "After all this excitement, I'm so hungry I could eat a horse."

Alice smiled wryly as she rose from her chair. "What *I* want to know," she said, "is how Dat and Uncle Jeremiah could play such an awesome game of pool! Dex and Phil didn't stand a chance."

Leah smiled and went to pour coffee before finishing her biscuits. Jude and Jeremiah were chuckling as they formulated an answer to the question.

"When we were growing up in this house, there was a pool table in the basement," Jeremiah began. "Our *dat* bought us a used table when we hit our *rumspringa,* on the condition that neither of us would learn to drive a car, or buy one and park it somewhere else so he and Mamm wouldn't know about it."

"It wasn't a common thing for an Amish family to own a pool table," Jude pointed out, "but our *dat* reasoned that learning how to make accurate shots would keep us boys at home, out of trouble, and it would improve our concentration."

"And because we weren't betting any money," Jeremiah continued, "we considered it a family game the same as Monopoly or Scrabble would be. Truth be told, your Mammi Margaret got to be a pretty *gut* shot—although she never talked about that with her lady friends."

Leah's eyes widened. The image of Margaret Shetler bending over a pool table with a cue stick in her hand was almost more than she could imagine.

"It's only fair that we confess to visiting the pool hall now and again, because it got sort of boring just playing members of the family," Jude admitted.

"And—as you girls saw today," Jeremiah said with a smile, "English fellows can't believe that we Amish would know the first thing about shooting pool, so we used that to our advantage now and again. Hustling wasn't an honorable way to win a little spending money—"

"But we were playing by the rules," Jude insisted, "and as long as we let some time go by between our pool hall visits, nobody called us out. English fellows didn't want to admit they'd been snookered by a couple of Amish boys. As long as we bought an occasional beer, Rick turned a blind eye."

Jeremiah nodded as he recalled those days. "We eventually grew up and sold the table, but I'm glad our pool shooting skills bought the sheriff sometime this morning."

"And I was glad Rick didn't realize who we were until Sheriff Banks made the arrest," Jude admitted. "It all worked out. And it'll be fine with me if I never enter that smelly old grease pit again."

Chapter 24

The next morning Leah was glad when Jude offered to drive her to Abner Gingerich's meat market and assist with butchering the rest of the cattle she'd lost. She felt tired and emotionally wrung out after their ordeal with the twins—mere days after Betsy had been taken away—and even though everything had turned out for the best, the idea of butchering all those carcasses alone overwhelmed her.

"Awfully nice of Abner to come fetch those cows yesterday," Jude remarked as the rig rolled toward Cedar Creek.

"I couldn't think of any other way to get all that meat refrigerated, once the twins took off for the pool hall, so I called him," Leah explained. "He's always been such a *gut* neighbor—so helpful to Mama and me after Dat passed."

Ordinarily the *clip-clop, clip-clop* of hooves upon the pavement soothed Leah, but she felt a headache coming on. She tried to dismiss it, because with all the cutting, processing, and packaging they had to do, there was no time for feeling puny. When they arrived at the butcher shop, Jude helped her down from the rig and she allowed herself the luxury of lingering for a few extra moments in his embrace.

"You all right, Leah?" he asked softly. "You don't seem to be your perky, spunky self this morning."

Leah sighed, resting her head on his sturdy shoulder. "I suspect my perk and spunk all went toward getting the twins back home safely and then rejoicing when they let me hug them," she replied. "It was a roller-coaster ride of a day."

"*Jah*, it sure was," Jude agreed. "I'm glad I don't have an auction to call today, because I suspect I'd be running out of energy by noon. I'd rather spend the day helping you, anyway."

When he kissed her lightly, Leah felt better. She took her butchering knives from the buggy, and as they entered Abner's butcher shop, a bell tinkled above the door. Leah heard two voices coming from the room behind the refrigerated glass cases that displayed whole chickens and cuts of beef, pork, and lamb.

Abner peered out at them, wiping his hands on a towel. "*Gut* morning, folks! Hope you don't mind that Uncle Vernon and I got a head start on your cows," he called out cheerfully. "I've got white coats for you to wear so you won't get your clothes dirty—and to keep you warmer."

Leah hadn't expected Bishop Vernon to be working with them, but another set of hands would make their butchering go faster. As she and Jude went down a short hallway and entered the refrigerated butchering room, she shivered. "Oh my, it's chilly in here!" she said as Abner helped her into her coat. "*Denki* for fetching the cows and keeping them cold for me. This way, we're certain the meat will be fresh, without any spoilage."

Bishop Vernon looked up from the large hindquarter he was working on. "I was mighty sorry to hear about the trouble you folks had yesterday," he said with a shake of his head. "I trust your chicks are back in the nest, hopefully sadder but wiser? Jeremiah called to share the highlights of your encounter at the pool hall, you see."

Leah smiled to herself. If the bishops of Morning Star and Cedar Creek had discussed yesterday's ordeal, it wouldn't be long before most of the folks in both districts got wind of their run-in with Dexter and Phil.

"I'm pleased to say that Alice and Adeline have turned over a new leaf," Jude replied as he donned his white coat.

"They were so repentant, they even offered to come with us today to help with the butchering, seeing's how they felt partly to blame for the way Leah's cattle got slaughtered."

"I was amazed at their offer," Leah put in, "because the twins despise anything to do with animal waste or blood. I suggested that they and Stevie could help us by planting more of the garden instead."

When the bishop nodded, his snow-white beard drifted like a cloud over his chest. "That's a step in the right direction. Any indication that they've seen the error of socializing with those English fellows? Jeremiah made it sound as though those two were on a first-name basis with the sheriff."

"*Jah*, they're a couple of bad apples," Jude said with a sigh. "I was appalled that my girls found them the least bit attractive—but that's behind them now."

"They've folded all of their English clothes, and we boxed them up to take to the Goodwill store—along with their jewelry," Leah added as she sharpened her knives. "I—I was amazed that Adeline and Alice allowed me to hug them, and that they no longer seem to consider me that impossibly stinky, stupid woman their *dat* hitched up with last December."

Vernon's laughter echoed in the cold concrete room. "I'm pleased to hear that," the white-haired bishop said. "The girls' attitudes were my biggest concern when you and Jude married, and it sounds as though you're finally on the road to becoming a happy family."

When Jude gazed at Leah, his smile made her quiver inside. "*Jah*, except for the house seeming way too quiet without Betsy, our home has already taken on a peacefulness I couldn't have foreseen a few weeks ago," he said as he began to strip the skin from the carcass on Abner's second worktable. "I believe the kids have accepted Leah as their *mamm* now. And I believe God will grant us even more exciting possibilities in the days ahead."

Rather than speculating on what her husband meant, Leah focused on removing the meat from a steer's neck and shoulder. The smaller pieces from the neck would be ground or cut into stew meat, while the larger sections around the shoulder would make nice roasts and steaks.

"I'll be pleased to sell as much of this meat as you'd like me to, Leah," Abner said as he deftly plied his knife around the flank he was butchering. "What I don't sell fresh in the next few days, I can package and freeze for selling later—or to keep for you folks, if you don't have space for it in your freezer at home. The meat from your grass-fed cattle is tender and well marbled, so the beef will be tastier than what folks can find in regular grocery stores."

"I'd appreciate that," Leah put in. "You've been such a help to us, Abner."

"Another possibility is donating some packages of the meat to a couple of families in the Cedar Creek district who've met with misfortune recently," Bishop Vernon suggested. "Over the weekend, Mose and Hannah Hartzler lost their home—including the jars of canned goods and their deep freezes—in a fire, and Rudy Ropp suffered a stroke I suspect he might not recover from."

Leah's eyes widened. "Oh my, I hadn't heard that sad news, what with all the goings-on at our place," she said. "*Jah*, I'd be grateful if you'd give those families a *gut* supply of this meat. They've got kids to feed."

The four of them settled into a companionable routine, with Jude skinning the last few carcasses while Vernon and Leah removed the meat from the bones and Abner cut steaks and roasts. The men shared talk from around the Morning Star and Cedar Creek church districts, but Leah had to force herself to concentrate on her work, despite the fact that she'd been butchering since she was a young girl. Her headache sapped her energy and she had the sensation of working inside a bubble, somewhat removed from the men, as she tried to convince herself she didn't feel queasy.

Something in the breakfast casserole the twins had fixed seemed to be upsetting her stomach. Trying not to draw attention to herself, Leah left the cold room and hurried to the bathroom in the hallway. She barely made it in time to vomit repeatedly in the toilet.

When she had nothing left in her stomach, Leah leaned against the wall for a few moments to settle herself. Why was she feeling so clammy and weak-kneed? She hoped she hadn't caught the flu or—

"Is there some *gut* news you're not telling us, Jude?" Bishop Vernon asked on the other side of the wall. "In all the years I've known Leah, I can't recall that she's ever gotten sick to her stomach."

"*Jah,* ordinarily Leah's got a strong constitution when it comes to butchering," Abner put in.

"I can't say for sure that we have happy news," Jude replied with a chuckle. "But I intend for us to find out soon, because this isn't the first time Leah's thrown up recently."

Leah's eyes widened. Could she possibly be in the family way? She hadn't been throwing up every morning, as she'd heard was common, yet she couldn't deny that she'd gotten sick to her stomach, dizzy—or just cranky—several times over the past weeks.

Leah rinsed her face with cool water and took a few deep breaths. It was embarrassing to think the fellows in the next room might've figured out her condition before she'd thought of it—but she hadn't dodged men's remarks and opinions before, and she didn't intend to start now. She returned to the refrigerated room as though nothing had been amiss and resumed butchering alongside Jude, Abner, and Vernon.

The men played along with her pretense. Leah felt better, more able to focus on the task at hand, and by the end of the morning all her cattle had been processed and packaged in white butcher paper. She and Jude loaded several boxes of meat into the rig and took off around twelve-thirty.

"What if I treated my girlfriend to lunch at Mrs. Nissley's Kitchen or Mother Yutzy's Oven while we're in Cedar Creek?" Jude asked as he steered the rig onto the county highway. "I always look forward to auctions where Beulah Mae or Lois provide the lunch. And then . . . do you suppose we should swing by the clinic and find out if a new little Shetler is upsetting your system?"

Leah's cheeks tingled with heat. "Do you think that's what's going on? It's kind of, well—*humiliating,* to think you and the Gingerich men guessed my condition before I even had a clue."

Jude gently cupped her face to bring it closer to his. "Nothing to be embarrassed about, sweetheart," he murmured before he kissed her tenderly. "You've had a lot on your mind lately, dealing with the twins and letting Betsy go back to her *mamm*—not to mention this ordeal with your cattle."

Leah's heart thrummed steadily as she rested her head against Jude's shoulder. "Maybe we should visit the clinic first and then celebrate the results over lunch."

"I like that idea."

"And—Jude?" Leah hesitated, yet she knew he would understand her request. "If there's a baby, let's keep it between you and me for a while, shall we? Just to be sure everything's going the way it's supposed to before we tell everyone."

Jude slung his arm around her, nodding as the rig rolled down the road. "Fine by me. I think I was more upset than Frieda those three times she miscarried my babies," he admitted. "It made me wonder if something was genetically wrong when she could carry another man's kids to term but not mine."

Leah sighed, hugging him around the waist. "I'm sorry about the sadness and doubt that situation with Frieda caused you. I—I would be ecstatic to find out I'm carrying your child, Jude, and I want everything to go right," she said earnestly.

An hour and a half later, Jude felt ten feet tall. Dr. Baumgardner had declared Leah about three and a half months along in a pregnancy that appeared normal and healthy, and they'd set an appointment to see him again in a month. Jude couldn't stop grinning, couldn't stop hugging Leah close and kissing her as they drove toward Beulah Mae Nissley's café on the outer edge of Cedar Creek.

"After the ordeals with the twins and your cattle this news turns our lives around and points them in a whole new direction," he declared happily. "We'll keep our secret a while longer, but I won't be surprised if people guess it when they see my smile and the glow on your face, Leah."

She blushed prettily. "If they guess, so be it. High time we had *gut* news to share with our friends and family."

Chapter 25

During the church service on Sunday, Leah found herself gazing raptly at all the toddlers and babies who sat with their *mamms*. Although she usually paid close attention to Bishop Jeremiah's sermon, her mind was full of fantasies as he spoke at length about the story of the ten lepers Jesus healed and how only one had returned to thank Him.

"We should never forget that our Lord hears our every prayer and knows the strength of our faith," Jeremiah said eloquently. "If we believe in His ability to heal even the most unfortunate and distasteful of conditions in our lives, we can anticipate great joy after heartache we thought might tear apart our very souls. God gives us things to be thankful for every single day."

Leah glanced across the room to the side where the men sat, catching Jude's nod. More than once this past week, he had given quiet thanks for the way Alice and Adeline had learned their lesson about running with those English fellows. When he caught Leah's eye, however, his boyish grin made her heart quiver. The sweet secret they kept had brightened both of their lives, and they had agreed not to tell Stevie or the twins—or even their mothers—that Leah was carrying a baby due in September. Such a special announcement deserved the right moment.

A muffled squawk made Leah glance at a wee one in the

row ahead of her. The littlest Plank girl rested against her *mamm's* neck and shoulder, watching the women on Leah's pew bench with alert brown eyes as she stuck her tiny fingers in her bow-shaped mouth. Leah wondered how she'd gone through so many years of her life not being particularly aware of babies' facial features, yet now she noticed every dimple and wispy curl.

Will my baby be a boy or a girl? Will he have Jude's dark curls, or will she take on my lighter skin tone and hair color? Shall I name her Lenore or Margaret, or give her a name all her own? Will our little boy be healthy and survive to a full-term birth?

Leah sighed when she wondered how Betsy was faring with her young, confused mother. The pain of that separation had grown easier to bear when she'd learned that Jude's child would soon bless their lives, yet Leah realized that she would never forget the sweet, warm weight of holding Betsy to feed her. Sometimes she dreamed vividly about the tiny girl, clearly hearing her voice and watching her dear little face light up when she caught sight of Jude or clutched her bottle of goat's milk and snuggled in Leah's arms to consume it.

"As we come to our time of prayer," Jeremiah said in a resonant voice, "let us each thank God for the special blessings He's granted us this week. Perhaps members of our families displayed great growth and understanding as they returned to the path of salvation, or maybe we got a medical report that was better than we anticipated. Could be that we realized a financial loss has actually turned out to be a blessing in disguise because God infused the situation with His grace."

Leah's eyes widened. Jeremiah knew about Alice's and Adeline's adjustment of attitude, and Jude had told him about donating some of the beef to a couple of needy Cedar Creek families . . . but had Bishop Vernon also shared his assumptions about her pregnancy? Or was Jeremiah speaking about another member's medical report? As the bishop finished preaching, Leah could only wonder how much Jude's brother knew and how much he'd surmised through his spot-on intuition.

"I would like to offer my personal thanks to our God because my nieces, Adeline and Alice, have asked to begin their instruction so they can join the church," Jeremiah continued, his face alight. "It's always a special blessing when our young people profess their faith and pledge their lifelong support of our Amish ways and beliefs."

Leah turned quickly—as many other women did—to flash an encouraging smile at the twins, who sat a few pews behind her. Alice and Adeline hadn't said a word to her or Jude about their decision, so Leah thrummed with excitement and relief. The girls' intention to join the church was the ultimate sign that they were indeed finished with the English men who'd caused the family such heartache. They were done with *rumspringa* and ready to become responsible, faithful adults.

As members of the congregation positioned themselves for a long silent prayer, Leah went to her knees smiling. *I love Your surprises, Lord, because they keep me guessing—and because they bless me and strengthen my family,* she prayed lightheartedly. *I'm grateful for Your power and presence in our girls' lives. I know You're watching over little Betsy and her mother, and that despite the way we miss her so badly, You have the power to turn her absence into a blessing we can't anticipate. Be with me as Your miracle grows inside my body.*

As everyone rose to sit on the pew benches after the prayer ended, Leah felt a great sense of gratitude and expectation. Peacefulness settled over her as she realized how far she and the rest of the Shetler family had progressed since the fateful morning when the twins had eavesdropped on her and Jude's intimate conversation about the circumstances of their birth. Leah thought back to her *maidel* fantasies of the perfect life she would experience as Jude's wife. She believed those dreams had a chance to come true now.

Leah's breath caught when she saw the way Jude was gazing at her from across the crowded room. When Stevie climbed into his *dat*'s lap and wiggled his fingers at her, her heart overflowed with love for the boy she now considered her son. She wondered if the women around her could feel the way she glowed.

How had she been so fortunate to hitch up with such a handsome, affectionate husband? Who could have foreseen the all-encompassing love she now felt for his children— and the way they had accepted her? The coming weeks and months would surely be filled with the goodness and mercy promised in the Twenty-Third Psalm, with blessings she couldn't anticipate, and Leah couldn't wait to see where God would lead her.

A couple weeks later, Leah watched Stevie as he scooped alfalfa pellets into the calves' feed trough. The May morning sparkled with sunshine and the breeze that whispered in the leafy trees tousled the boy's shiny brown hair. When he looked at her, Leah realized that he was beginning to resemble Jude more closely.

With practiced ease Stevie held out the two big nipple bottles to feed Erma and Patsy's orphaned calves. "Mama, do ya think Maisie and these calves miss the other cows that got shot?" he asked wistfully.

Leah sighed. Lately she'd been thinking that the pen and pasture seemed awfully empty, and unless she found another Black Angus cow or two, her little herd couldn't grow very fast. "I'm sure they do, Stevie," she replied softly.

"Pretty soon the calves will grow up and we'll be sendin' them to market, huh?" he asked plaintively. "I'll really miss gettin' to feed 'em and watch 'em every day."

"We'll keep the two little heifers as breeding stock, but we'll sell the two steers when they've reached a *gut* market weight," Leah clarified, even as she wondered what direction

Stevie's questions were heading. "By this time next year, I hope the heifers will be carrying their first calves."

"Oh." Stevie considered this information. "That's a long time to wait for more cows, huh?"

Leah nodded sadly. She'd tried to make the best of a bad situation—had tried to find the silver lining to the dark cloud that hovered over her livestock business—but having a lot of meat in the deep freeze and stored at Abner's locker wasn't the same as having the money she would've earned with the cattle that had been shot. Jude was a fine provider, but she didn't expect him to replace the cattle she'd lost by spending money that should go toward supporting their family.

"It's a lesson in patience, Stevie," she said. *And maybe God's giving me time to deliver my baby before I have to tend so many cattle again . . . or He's pointing my business in a different direction.*

As Leah combed the boy's warm hair back over his ears with her fingers, however, she brightened with a new idea. "But we'll still raise our goats and ducks and chickens—and when we get more cows and calves, I think we should let you be totally in charge of them. You would be responsible for tending and raising them—with your *dat*'s and my help. When you earn an income from selling the first batch, you can take over buying their feed and paying the other expenses. Someday I hope to turn the entire herd over to you, Stevie."

"Wow," Stevie said, awestruck. "You think I can do that, Mama? I'm just a little kid, not even in school yet."

Leah smiled proudly, her heart expanding with the thrill of being called *Mama* on a regular basis. "Your *dat* and I will help you keep your accounts, sweetie. We've both been managing animals since we were kids—maybe not handling the buying and selling yet, but our parents were pointing us in that direction."

The sight of the sheriff's car turning off the county road and into their lane made Leah nip her lip. Had there been trouble? Jude was calling an auction and the twins had gone into Morning Star to shop for groceries and sewing supplies, so Leah hurried toward the car as it approached the house. Sheriff Banks had spoken to her briefly in the pool hall parking lot the day he'd searched the gray pickup for the gun that had killed her cattle, so her thoughts spun around images of Dexter and Phil. Now that the twins were taking their instruction to join the church, she hoped those reckless young men weren't coming around again, causing Adeline and Alice more trouble. More temptation.

"Morning, Mrs. Shetler," the burly sheriff called out as he stepped from his vehicle. "It's a beautiful May day, and your place looks really pretty with the iris and peonies in bloom. I've got some good news for you."

Leah inhaled deeply to settle her nerves. Clyde Banks was a nice enough fellow, but she still felt a little nervous dealing with an officer of the law—especially while Jude was away from home. "Oh?" she asked, grasping Stevie's hand as he came to stand beside her. "I—I was hoping you hadn't come to report more trouble with those fellows who shot my cows."

A smile eased across the sheriff's weathered face as he handed her an envelope. "I know better than to say Dexter and Phil won't ever run afoul of the law again, but at least they've been held accountable for some of the damage they've done," he said cordially. "Seems their boss at the pet food factory told them they wouldn't have jobs there any longer unless they repaid you and your neighbor, whose horse they shot. When I told him you Amish folks don't believe in insurance to cover such losses, he decided to pay you forward, and he'll withhold money from their paychecks until he's been repaid. You're to tell me if this check doesn't cover your loss of income."

Leah's fingers shook as she pulled the check from the envelope. The total amount—the number of zeroes preceding the decimal point—made her suck in her breath. "But—but

I've already been paid for the meat I had Abner Gingerich process and sell at his butcher shop," she began hesitantly. "And he didn't charge me for processing the meat we kept—"

"Don't go selling yourself short," Sheriff Banks said with a kind smile. "The way you Amish folks make the most of misfortune has always impressed me—but it doesn't change the fact that you lost all but a few of the animals you raise for an income," he reminded her. "I believe we've seen some justice done, and I know you'll put Dexter and Phil's repayment to good use."

Leah stared mutely at the check. She'd always considered herself pretty capable of running her business, but the money she'd earned over the years by selling her eggs, goat's milk, chickens, and cows paled in comparison to the lump sum she'd just received. It boggled her mind.

The lawman's face creased with a friendly smile. "No doubt in my mind you folks will prosper and move ahead," he said. "I have to tell you that I bought some of your veal and roasts at Abner's shop, and the meat was fabulous—and nearly gone," he added quickly. "Abner said a couple of specialty restaurants in Columbia and St. Louis are offering local grass-fed beef and veal on their menus and they can hardly keep it in supply. I suspect there's a profit to be had for folks hereabouts who're raising cattle without corn or hormones these days."

After the sheriff left, Leah's mind was spinning in fast, tight circles. She carefully stashed the check in her coffee can in the pantry, where she kept her egg money, until she could deposit it in the bank. She and Jude would discuss how best to use all that money—thousands of dollars they hadn't anticipated. With a baby on the way, it would be good to acquire the furniture and supplies they'd need, but even after that, their bank account would have a substantial chunk of change in it.

Stevie gazed at her as she poured milk into glasses and took some cookies from the cookie jar. "Are we rich now, Mama?" he asked softly.

Leah sat down at the table beside him and pulled him close, savoring the feel of his solid, healthy body and the way he asked such astute questions. "Stevie, God has always provided our family with all we need," she replied as she chose a peanut butter cookie. "We have our home and our health. We have food on our table, and we have one another. The check we got today can't make us any richer in the ways that truly count, but *jah,* we now have a chance to expand our family's income—and to share more with folks who aren't as fortunate."

Stevie considered her words as he gulped some milk. When he smiled at Leah, his milk mustache made her chuckle. "So we're blessed," he said softly.

Leah hugged him close. "You've got it exactly right, son."

Chapter 26

"Mama, it's so *gut* to have you here again," Leah said as she preceded her mother up the stairs with her suitcase. "We have a lot to catch up on since you left a month ago."

"*Jah,* we do," Mama agreed. "I was glad you invited me here for Mother's Day this weekend—and to celebrate Adeline's and Alice's being baptized into the church in a couple of weeks. I hope it's all right that I brought some summer-weight navy blue fabric to make them new dresses for the occasion."

Leah laughed. "I suspect you'll notice an improvement in their attitude about Plain dresses, among other things."

Mama glanced into the bedroom Leah and Jude shared before heading down the hall. "Mighty sorry that Betsy's no longer with you," she said as she sadly shook her head. "I hope her young *mamm*'s taking *gut* care of her."

"I pray for her every single day." Leah entered the guest room and tossed the heavy suitcase onto the double bed. "And I pray for you, too, Mama, out there on the farm by yourself. How are you getting along, really? When I call, you sound cheerful enough—and you tell me you've got more quilt orders than you can handle—but I wonder how you handle so much time alone."

Mama hefted the suitcase she carried onto the bed beside

the other one. As she went to the window to look out over the yard and the blooming flowers, Leah watched her closely. She detected an air of loneliness camouflaged by Mama's stalwart smile . . . along with something else in her mother's sparkling eyes she couldn't define. Was it her imagination, or did Mama have a secret? Had a nice man been keeping her company perhaps, with the intention of marrying her?

"We're never alone when we live in our Lord, Leah," Mama replied softly. "*Jah*, the evenings and the long visiting Sundays without church drag on at times—but I didn't come here to whine. I intend to enjoy every moment I'm here with you and Jude and your kids!"

Leah knew better than to pry into Mama's life; sooner or later, all would be revealed. Instead, she opened a suitcase and began hanging clothes in the closet. She couldn't help noticing dresses sewn in fresh new pastels for summer, a sign that her mother was moving beyond her period of mourning Dat. "What a pretty shade of green, like tree leaves bathed in sunshine," she remarked as she held up one of the dresses. "And look at this deep pink one. Mama, are you trying to catch someone's eye? That would be a *gut* thing, you know— as I'm sure Bishop Vernon's told you."

Her mother waved her off and began arranging her under- things in the dresser drawers. "Don't be silly, Leah. *Jah*, Calvin Eicher and Ivan Beachy have been sniffing around, but why would I consider either of them?" she asked in a teasing voice. "They make a point of arriving at mealtime—unan- nounced—and when they're not spreading on the compli- ments too thick, they're asking if I'd do some mending. Or they invite me to their homes as though it'll be a really hot date to spend time cutting their hair or cleaning up their clut- tered kitchens. No, thank you!"

Leah laughed out loud. "With their families grown and scattered around, they want your company, Mama."

"They want my farm, Leah. And they both need a mother

more than a wife." Mama widened her eyes purposefully. "And compared to your *dat,* they have all the personality of dusty cardboard boxes. End of discussion."

The set of Mama's jaw confirmed that she had absolutely no interest in the two widowers she'd mentioned, so Leah let the subject rest. Her *mamm* planned to stay for a nice long while so there would be plenty of time for the mother-daughter conversation she craved . . . and time to share the secret that was beginning to swell beneath her apron as well.

"Our big news of late—besides Alice's and Adeline's joining the church, of course—is that the sheriff brought me a big settlement check from those two English fellows who shot most of my cattle," Leah said as she shook out the last dress in the suitcase. "And I mean a *big* check."

"Only right that those young men pay you for the animals they slaughtered," Mama insisted. "From what Abner and Bishop Vernon told me, they didn't leave you with many cows—not to mention the way they were corrupting the twins. Adeline and Alice will remain forever marked by tattoos their future husbands might not like much."

Leah wondered what else Abner and his uncle might have shared with her mother, but she didn't want to blurt out the news of her pregnancy. It was a happy topic best shared on the porch swing with refreshing glasses of iced tea rather than on the spur of the moment in a guest room that seemed stuffy from lack of use. She opened the two windows, allowing the breeze to circulate the fresh scent of honeysuckle and sunshine. "The girls will have a lot to admit to the fellows they marry someday," she agreed. "But I suspect they'll be attracted to the sort of Amish men who've had a few adventures of their—"

The loud backfiring of an engine made Leah stoop to stare out the window. Her heartbeat accelerated to a crazy rate when she saw an old red car rolling slowly up the lane toward the house. "Oh! Oh, could it be?" she whispered as she dashed for the door. "Mama, I think that's Natalie—little Betsy's mother!"

Leah raced downstairs so fast she didn't feel her feet hitting the steps. Stevie looked up from the kitchen table, where he was writing his alphabet and numbers to show his Mammi Lenore, but hope was making Leah's throat so tight she couldn't speak to him. As the screen door banged behind her, she was vaguely aware that the twins were in the garden hoeing weeds, but she only had eyes for the car door that was swinging open with a loud creak.

The sound of a high-pitched cry inside the car made Leah's heart shrivel. "Natalie?" she called out to the girl emerging from the vehicle. "What brings you here? It—it's *gut* to see you," she added.

When the dark-haired young woman gazed at her, desperation tightening her young face, Leah stopped several feet away from her. Natalie's complexion was splotchy and she'd put on enough weight that her T-shirt and jean shorts appeared a couple sizes snugger than Leah remembered. For a moment she just stood beside the car, plucking nervously at the hem of her shorts. Then she burst into tears.

Leah approached her slowly, sensing that the young girl's life had gone sadly awry. "Natalie?" she asked softly. "How can I help you, dear? Shall we get Betsy out of the car and go inside for something cool to drink?"

With a loud sniffle, the young woman reached into the car and pulled out a basket—the same basket she'd left on the porch on a chilly March morning, except Betsy had grown so much that she barely fit in it. The baby was crying, sounding hungry and frustrated, yet Leah hesitated to rush over and pick her up. Natalie appeared determined to handle her noisy child her way—which meant she started toward the house as though she didn't even notice that Betsy was upset.

Leah felt torn. It wasn't her place to ask Natalie if Betsy could return to them, yet her arms yearned to hold the wee girl and comfort her. Thinking quickly, she held the door for

Natalie and then grabbed a container of goat's milk from the spare refrigerator in the mudroom. "I—I'm not sure we have any baby bottles, because I sent them along with you when—"

"I can't keep her." Natalie set the basket on the kitchen table, oblivious to wide-eyed Stevie.

At that, Leah set aside the milk and scooped Betsy out of the basket. The baby wrapped her little arms around Leah's neck, clinging for dear life even as she began to relax. The twins and Mama had come into the kitchen, but Leah focused on the girl in the unbecoming English clothes. "What do you mean, you can't keep her?" Leah said breathlessly. Her heart throbbed in her chest as she awaited Natalie's answer.

"My family kicked me out because I refused to join the Mennonite church," Natalie replied in a dull voice. Regret and envy shadowed her face as she saw the way Betsy was quieting down as Leah swayed from side to side with her. "I've run out of money, so I sold those bottles and baby things to—you've got to take Betsy back. *Please*," she begged.

Leah's pulse ran a wild race with her thoughts. "Of course we will, Natalie," she whispered quickly.

Natalie swiped at her tear-streaked face. "I tried really hard to be a good mom but—I just couldn't seem to—"

"You *sold* your baby's clothes?" Adeline demanded in disbelief.

"How'd you think you'd feed Betsy if you sold her bottles, too?" Alice chimed in angrily.

With a sob, Natalie turned and bolted out the door. Leah wanted to laugh and sing and shout for joy now that she was once again cradling Betsy in her arms, but other matters needed tending to. "Stevie, go after her," she urged him. "Tell her I want to help her—hurry before she drives off!"

Grinning at Betsy, the boy shot out the door in pursuit of Natalie, with Mama following behind him. Leah allowed herself the luxury of cuddling Betsy, kissing her curls, and for a few minutes the rest of the world ceased to exist. She was aware that the little girl needed a bath and clean clothes, but first she needed nourishment.

With Betsy balanced against her hip, Leah turned to the girls. "Go find the pot we used for warming her bottles—and anything else that didn't fit into the boxes I sent with Natalie," she said. "I suspect Betsy's so hungry, we don't even want to think about when her last meal might've been."

Alice and Adeline shared a disgusted look before heading toward the basement stairs, muttering about Natalie.

Leah looked out the screen door, relieved that her mother and Stevie had convinced the skittish young woman to return to the house. "Oh, Betsy," she whispered against the little girl's cheek. "Betsy, we have to say everything just right, honey, before we get our hopes up. Have you really come back to us for *gut* and forever?"

She opened the door to admit Natalie, who came inside with a red face and a sorrowful expression. "I—I don't mean to be any trouble," she mumbled.

"We just need to be sure we're on the same page," Leah said, gesturing toward the table. "Let's get you and Betsy something to eat, and we'll talk this through. Have a seat, dear. Mama, if you'll slice some bread and get the cold cuts and cheese from the fridge, I'll start warming this goat's milk."

"Goat's milk," Natalie echoed with a sad shake of her head. "Where on earth was I supposed to get that? I've been feeding Betsy formula, but it's so expensive and—and it really upsets her system, too."

Leah sighed. She'd seen goat's milk in cartons at the grocery store, but she suspected Natalie had reached the point where she was so desperate and dejected she couldn't see things that were right in front of her. *Thank God she realized she and Betsy needed help and came here to get it.*

The twins came up from the basement bearing the tall stockpot they'd used for warming bottles, and Leah gave thanks that two glass baby bottles were still in it. While Mama made Natalie's sandwich, Leah quickly ran water into the pot and set it on the stove burner. The twins washed the bottles and then filled them with goat's milk.

While Leah waited for the milk to warm on the stove, she sat down at the table beside Natalie. Betsy was resting against her shoulder, hiccuping now instead of crying, so it was easier to have a normal conversation. "When you say you want us to take Betsy back," she began hesitantly, "do you mean you want us to have her as our own child again? Or will you be popping in for her whenever the whim strikes you? You tore our family apart—left a gaping hole in our hearts—when you took Betsy away from us last month."

Her questions sounded harsh, but Leah wanted to clarify the details—and she wanted Natalie to realize that her actions had serious consequences.

"It's not *gut* for any of us—especially for this wee girl—when you disrupt our lives and her routine," Mama pointed out firmly. "*Jah,* she's your child, but—"

"But I know now that I can't raise her," Natalie interrupted miserably. "As you're all my witnesses, I want you to have her—to raise her without any more interference from me—because I can't begin to guess where I'll go or how I'll be getting by."

Even as Leah's heart thrummed with joy, she felt sorry for the young woman who slumped awkwardly at the kitchen table. Nodding her approval, Mama set a sandwich in front of Natalie.

"All right then, you have our word that we'll raise this child as our own," Leah said, relishing the words she'd longed to say for weeks. "Jude and I will adopt her—"

"*Jah,* it should be legal and clear-cut," Mama put in firmly.

"—and we'll expect you to abide by your side of the agreement," Leah finished. She shook her head. "I can't imagine how horrible it must feel to be cast out by your family. I'm sorry you're going through such a rough time, Natalie."

Natalie was devouring her sandwich hungrily, obviously trying to hold herself together emotionally. As Mama prepared another ham and cheese sandwich for their distraught guest, Leah accepted the bottle of goat's milk Alice handed her. When she'd tested its temperature on her inner wrist, she placed the bottle in front of Betsy. The little girl grabbed it and began sucking down milk as though she couldn't drink it fast enough.

When Betsy had drained the bottle, Leah stood up to walk around the kitchen with the child resting against a dish towel on her shoulder. It felt heavenly to hold the baby again, even though Leah could feel some of her tiny ribs and her hip bones. Adeline and Alice came up to coo at Betsy and stroke her cheeks, and Stevie stood on tiptoe beside Leah to gaze up at the baby, too. The moment felt especially blessed because Leah sensed their family was complete again. The aching hole in their hearts had been filled, and the balance of their family restored.

Natalie hastily finished her second sandwich and stood up, looking at Betsy with mixed emotions as the little girl giggled in recognition of the twins and Stevie. "Well, there's no point in me hanging around here when you folks are obviously better at—"

"Wait." Leah stepped into the pantry and grabbed the wad of bills stashed in her coffee can. "I want you to have this, Natalie. It's not all that much, but maybe it'll help you get groceries and a place to stay."

The young woman appeared too flustered to count the money—or to meet Leah's gaze again. "Thank you," she whispered before hurrying toward the door. "I'm such a mess, I don't deserve your kindness."

Moments later the car's engine churned, and Natalie backed the noisy vehicle down the lane and onto the county road. Leah closed her eyes and embraced little Betsy, feeling her cup of joy and blessings was ready to overflow. Jude would be ecstatic when he came home from the sale and learned what had happened.

"So how much did you give her?" Alice demanded.

Adeline let out a grunt of disapproval. "Knowing Natalie, she's headed toward the pool hall to impress the guys with her money—"

"Or to blow it all on beer," Alice said in a disgusted tone.

Leah thought carefully about her response as she gazed at her daughters, neatly dressed in their crisp *kapps* and matching lavender cape dresses. "I suppose there might've been three or four hundred dollars in my can from selling eggs and that last batch of chickens," she replied softly. "I felt it was the least I could do to help that poor girl. Your *dat* and I would've given every dollar we had to save you two from a fate similar to Natalie's, you know."

Adeline's and Alice's mouths clapped shut as Leah's words sank in.

"*Jah*, I was mighty concerned that things had gotten way out of hand," Mama said as she cleared Natalie's plate from the table. "I was so relieved to hear that you finally realized those English boys were more trouble than you might've been able to get yourselves out of."

After a moment, Adeline sighed. "You know, Natalie said something when she came for Betsy last month," she mused softly. She gazed steadfastly at Leah. "She told us that after she'd watched Leah come to the pool hall to take Alice and me home, she could see that you loved us enough to look after us—even if we didn't want to believe that at the time."

"Even though we treated you terribly and called you names, you stuck by us," Alice chimed in with a quavery smile. "You gave us the tough love we needed, Leah. We're really sorry for the way we acted—"

"And really glad you didn't give up on us," Adeline added with a nod.

Leah was speechless. Tears of gratitude stung her eyes as she looked from one twin's face to the other. Betsy seemed to sense it was a special moment, too. She patted Leah's damp cheeks with her hands and said, "Mah-mah! Mah-mah!"

Everyone chuckled and cooed at the baby, bursting the balloon of airless tension that had held them all suspended.

"Betsy knows who loves her," Mama said as she reached for the baby. "I think she's every bit as glad to be amongst us again as we are to have her."

Leah nodded, blinking back tears as she released Betsy. "Natalie has given us the greatest gift of all," she murmured. "It took a lot of gumption to come back here and admit she couldn't raise her child—and to give up the baby whose love she needed so badly when she took her away last month. Natalie's made the ultimate sacrifice, and we'll forever owe her our prayers and gratitude."

Stevie tugged at Leah's apron. "Can I sit on the couch with Betsy and give her that other bottle?"

Smoothing his thick hair, Leah smiled at the boy who was beaming up at her. "That's a fine idea, and a *gut* place for her to be when she nods off—maybe before she's finished the bottle," she added.

It made a sweet picture when Stevie settled on the couch with Betsy in his lap, her head resting on a pillow as she drank more slowly from her second bottle. Leah pulled the curtains against the bright sunshine, and within minutes the baby was breathing deeply, slipping into sleep.

We can't thank you enough, God, for the surprise You've given us—the precious lamb You've returned to our home, for keeps this time, Leah prayed as she gazed at Betsy. *Like Natalie, we don't deserve Your grace and gifts, but we're forever grateful that You stand by us despite our shortcomings.*

Chapter 27

On Saturday morning, Jude savored some extra time in bed with Betsy cradled in one arm as he held Leah against him. A warm breeze stirred the curtains, allowing quick glimpses of the pale, predawn light—and casting a glow on the white bassinet that had resumed its place in the corner.

He sighed languidly. "It feels like the perfect morning," he whispered as he kissed Leah's soft forehead. "Betsy is back. You're not throwing up anymore—and you're starting to show. I wish we could just stop time so this moment would last forever."

Leah chuckled, snuggling closer. "You forgot the part about the scent of Mama's cinnamon rolls drifting upstairs," she said, "but otherwise, you got it just right. Our life is perfect, Jude. Just like we dreamed it would be when we married."

Jude smiled. "Feels *gut* to prove our naysayers wrong, ain't so?" he teased. "If you've got a few minutes, I have an idea about how to use that chunk of money you received for your cattle. Seems a shame to get up and waken Betsy."

Leah rose onto one elbow, a sleepy smile warming her face as she gazed at the baby he held. "With Mama cooking breakfast, I have nothing but time for you, Mr. Shetler. What's your idea?"

Jude considered his words carefully, because the large

amount of money he was discussing belonged to Leah. The last thing he wanted was to take control of her earnings, as a lot of Amish husbands tended to do—or to usurp her right to run her business the way she wanted to. Time and again she'd proven that her instincts for investing in livestock were as strong as her intuitive handling of the animals themselves.

"When you told me what Banks said about those high-dollar restaurants featuring local grass-fed beef on their menus—and that they'd bought most of the meat Abner had processed," he began, "it made me think that raising your cattle on a larger scale might be a great alternative."

Leah's eyebrow rose as she considered what he'd said. "What do you mean by *larger scale?*"

Jude smiled. "Well, we've got that six and a half acres of pasture land down by the creek, where I was thinking of running some sheep, and Jeremiah has a nice tract of pasture he'd consider renting to you as well," he replied. "So why not restock your herd and enlarge it? And why not have Abner do all the processing to sell the meat to restaurants, so you both earn some nice money?"

"Oh my," she whispered. "I like the sound of that—but we'd have to reinforce the fences, not to mention reseeding those areas and buying enough Black Angus cows to—"

"And you have the money to cover all that now," Jude pointed out, loving the way Leah's mind worked. "I know of a couple breeders up north who've been raising their cattle on grass, too."

"—and with Betsy back, and our baby coming, I'd have to consider a more efficient feeding system for them—and maybe you won't want me spending so much time tending animals anymore," she continued. Her voice was low and urgent, betraying her keen interest in this venture even as she anticipated the extra effort another baby would require of her.

Jude cleared his throat. "You're right, of course, and I'm all in favor of streamlining your operation—which Stevie will jump into with both feet," he added quickly. "He's so excited about the way you want to put him in charge of your new animals, and I think that's a fabulous idea that'll work well with a little help on our part. And because you're reinvesting that chunk of money in livestock, it'll be a tax deduction. A really nice tax deduction."

"Ah. I hadn't thought about that." Leah's smile widened as she rested her head on his shoulder again. "But I don't want you to think I'm shortchanging the new baby, or the housework, or the cooking, or—"

"That's the least of my concerns."

Leah raised herself up again to gaze into his eyes. "But you know we won't have the twins helping us out with the house-work one of these days, after they marry," she insisted. "And what'll the neighbors say? They already think I spend too much time doing men's work—"

"I've never given a hoot about what the neighbors say, so why should I start now?" he countered with a chuckle. "If you want to give your cattle business a bigger, better shot, go for it. I'm saying this with utmost, unconditional confidence, sweet Leah . . . because I know things you don't. Details that'll be revealed in their own *gut* time."

She swatted at him playfully. "Who do you think you are, keeping secrets from me?" she teased.

"I'm the man who loves you more than life itself," he murmured as he pulled her close for a kiss. "I'm proud of the way you do business—and I'm in awe because you've won over my kids and brought our family together despite the or-deals you've endured."

Leah's eyes widened even as she appeared ready to cry. "I love you, too, Jude," she whispered. "Where would I be if you hadn't believed in me?"

"Probably still at your family's farm with your *mamm*, doing just fine," he replied matter-of-factly. "You're one of the few women I know who could make a go of her life with-out depending upon a man—so *I'm* the lucky one. Do what you want about our herd expansion idea, but I suspect it'll be really profitable on a larger scale. You might do so well you'll give up your chickens and ducks one of these days."

"Oh my. I've been raising ducks and chickens along with my milk goats since I was a girl," she pointed out. "But . . . but maybe it's time to consider some changes. Dat always believed in latching onto new opportunities and letting go of the jobs that weren't worth his time anymore."

Jude smiled as he inhaled deeply. The baby Leah carried was already shifting her mind-set—and the yeasty-sweet scent of Lenore's cinnamon rolls was another sign that change was coming to the Shetler household. "No matter what you decide, it'll all work out, sweet Leah. Shall we go downstairs and start our day?"

Leah felt a tingly heat in her cheeks when Jude kissed her good-bye and left on a mysterious mission after breakfast. He was humming under his breath and he had a spring in his step that she hadn't seen since they'd married.

"There goes a happy man," Mama remarked as they began clearing the table.

"There goes a man with a *secret*," Leah countered. She wound up the swing for Betsy, delighted that they'd kept it—and that the little girl who filled their hearts with sunshine had resumed her place. "This morning he encouraged me to consider raising a much bigger herd of crossbred cattle and funneling them to market by way of Abner Gingerich's butcher shop. Then he left me hanging, hinting there are things he knows but refuses to tell me."

Once again, a furtive smile made Mama's lips flicker, as they had when she'd arrived on Thursday. "Maybe I know a little bit about that—and maybe I don't," she teased quickly. "But then, I suspect I'm not the only woman in this kitchen who's not telling everything she knows."

Leah's eyes widened. Had Mama guessed there was a baby on the way? Adeline and Alice were gathering ingredients to make the fried pies they were taking for the common meal after church the next day, while Stevie had come over to make funny faces so Betsy would laugh. Maybe it was time to tell the kids about the upcoming visit from the stork before she and Jude shared their news with everyone at church . . . so they could savor the family's secret before the neighbors heard it.

"I'll tell my secret if you'll tell yours, Mama," Leah said boldly. As she'd anticipated, her words had caught the attention of Stevie and the twins, who would probably pester her and their *mammi* until the revelations came out.

Mama set the stack of dirty plates on the counter beside the sink, chuckling. "All right, that's fair. You go first, Leah."

Leah paused. She'd imagined having Jude by her side when she first mentioned the baby to his kids, yet she felt confident that Adeline and Alice would receive this news much more graciously now than they would have when they were calling her names and taunting her with chicken bones. "Well," she began shyly, "it seems we'll have another little Shetler joining us, sometime in September."

The girls sucked in their breath and rushed over to her.

"A baby? Really, Leah?" Alice asked excitedly.

Adeline hugged Leah at the same time her twin did. "Oh, but this is *gut* news! And we've all had plenty of practice with Betsy!"

"We love babies!" Stevie exclaimed, clapping his hands. "But I want a brother, okay?"

Mama laughed knowingly as she, too, hugged Leah close. "I had my suspicions," she admitted softly, "and I'm ecstatic, Leah. Maybe this is why Jude's got a sparkle in his eyes, ain't so?"

"Puh! You're not getting out of telling your secret with *that* line, Mama!" Leah teased affectionately. "Seems to me you're the one whose eyes are shining. Out with it!"

Mama's face turned a little pink when she noticed the kids' expectant expressions. "I've decided to take Jude up on his offer to come here to live—if it's all right with you, Leah," she added quickly.

Leah's heart turned flip-flops as she grabbed Mama's shoulders. "All right?" she blurted out. "After you've made us such wonderful rolls for breakfast—not to mention all the clothes you've sewn and—well, do you really think we'd turn you away?"

"Yay!" Stevie cried out as he made a beeline for Mama's knees. "We love you, Mammi Lenore, and we'll do anything you say if you'll stay with us!"

Mama laughed as she stooped to hug him. "You've got a lot of witnesses who heard you say that, young man."

Alice and Adeline slipped their arms around Mama, too, eyeing her closely. "So what brought this on?" Alice asked.

"*Jah*," Adeline chimed in. "Did Dat tell you about the baby, so you decided to come help us out?"

"Or are you really coming to keep an eye on *us*?" Alice added with a laugh.

The twins gazed steadily at Mama—and so did Leah. Having her mother here to help with the cooking and household chores would be wonderful no matter why she'd decided to come, but now that Betsy had returned and a baby was on the way, Leah felt an enormous burden had been lifted from her shoulders.

Mama smiled as though all this close attention had caught her off guard. "Truth be told, Jude has asked me more than once to live here, but I wasn't ready—until Bishop Vernon suggested that Mose and Hannah Hartzler could live in the house—"

"They lost their home in a fire, I heard," Leah put in.

Mama nodded. "And it seems the bishop's been looking for more pastureland for his Black Angus," she continued. "Vernon has offered to buy the place, lock, stock, and barrel so I won't be bothered with collecting rent or maintaining the place. After I thought about it, it seemed as though God had dropped a huge opportunity in my lap. So now that you're all agreeable to having me here, I'll take the bishop up on his generous offer."

"Oh, Mama, this is wonderful-*gut* news," Leah said. "I like your secret almost as much as I like mine!"

Mama's smile took ten years from her face. "Truth be told, I *was* a little lonely on the farm by myself," she admitted. "And it seemed nobody *needed* me anymore. If I live here, I'll have folks to cook and sew for—"

"And kids to play with!" Stevie crowed.

"—and you folks won't have to clean out all my stuff or deal with my furniture, either," Mama added. "Except for my quilting supplies and a few other personal belongings, I can walk away from the place unencumbered because the Hartzlers lost everything in the fire. They don't care that my curtains are faded or that your *dat*'s tools and a couple of old buggies are in the barn, because they can use them."

The kitchen seemed to expand to twice its size to accommodate all the happiness Leah was feeling. Why hadn't *she* thought to invite her mother to live here? Had she been so determined to prove herself to Jude and his kids that she'd overlooked a very practical source of assistance?

This isn't about practicality, though, Leah realized. *And it's not about expecting Mama to do all the work I'm not so gut at, either.* Left alone much longer, Mama might've withered away like the last grape left on the vine after harvest— although she'd never let on that she didn't enjoy the life of an independent widow.

"Mama, it'll be so *gut* having you here," Leah said, gazing into her mother's eyes. "I've missed our talks, and the way your presence always calms me. What a blessing it'll be to have you here as we get ready for the baby, too."

Mama's eyes shone with tears. "I've waited a long time for grandkids," she said softly, "and now—why, I'll soon have *five* of them! I won't be living in a house that's too quiet any-more."

Leah chuckled, slipping an arm around Mama's shoulders. "I doubt Calvin or Ivan will be showing up here unannounced at mealtimes, either," she said in a low voice. "But if a nice man comes along wanting to court you—"

"We'll all be here to check him out!" Stevie interrupted brightly.

Mama burst out laughing. "If that happens, he'll either pass muster or he won't, and that'll be the end of it," she said. "It'll be such a relief not to listen to Ivan's long-winded stories—or to wish Calvin would shower more often."

When Alice and Adeline grimaced and went back to mak-ing their fried pies, Leah ran hot water to begin washing the dishes. What a morning this had been, and it wasn't yet eight o'clock! No matter what sort of mystery Jude might still have up his sleeve, it couldn't possibly compare to the news she and Mama had just shared.

And when Mama drove to Cedar Creek to bring back an-other load of her clothes and belongings, Leah didn't think anything of it. . . .

Chapter 28

Was it Leah's imagination, or did folks seem extra-happy to see her as the family arrived at Jeremiah's for church on Sunday morning? She'd anticipated that Betsy's presence would spark conversation among the women as they gathered in Margaret's kitchen before the service, yet she sensed another undercurrent, too . . . secretive glances, and snatches of whispered conversation that stopped when she came near. Leah could recall the same furtive behavior when she'd first married Jude, but this time the women seemed festive and cheerful rather than judgmental.

"Happy Mother's Day, all!" Margaret called out as she greeted Leah and the other ladies. "Won't it be nice to have the men setting out the food and cleaning up after the meal today?"

"I'm not a mother, but I enjoy this Sunday every spring!" Naomi Slabaugh said with a chuckle.

Esther's chins quivered with her chuckle. "*Jah,* it'll be a real treat to relax out in the shade with lemonade and extra dessert while the fellows do the work," she said. "And today we'll have Betsy to entertain us, too."

Leah was amazed when the two *maidel* sisters came up to her and tweaked Betsy's nose as though she were their favorite niece. The other women were also greeting Leah as they placed their pans of food on Margaret's counters and in the refrigerator. Soon everyone was filing into Bishop Jeremiah's expanded front room to begin the service. Gabe Flaud sang the first few words of the opening hymn.

As everyone's voices rose in the ancient song, Leah noticed how little Betsy brightened and began to gaze at the women seated around them. She wiggled happily in her basket on the pew bench, even though the hymn was rather slow and somber. Was the wee girl fond of music? Or did she simply enjoy being in the company of so many folks who smiled and paid attention to her? Either way, Leah couldn't recall feeling happier at church—especially considering how some of these ladies had once considered her an odd duck because she worked with animals.

Leah blinked. *I was indeed an odd duck, because I got along better with my goats than I did with most people,* she thought. *Now that I've chosen to be a part of Jude's family—and his church district—I'm more open to the company of women, and they accept me. I feel like I belong here now.*

It was a wondrous revelation. A few verses of the hymn went right past Leah before she found her place on the page of the *Ausbund* and joined the singing again. Her heart felt light, and as Betsy began to babble quietly, Leah couldn't help smiling. Surely, God had found favor with her, and He'd blessed her with a life she could've only dreamed about last year at this time.

After a time of kneeling for prayer, Bishop Jeremiah began the first sermon. Although Leah had always admired Bishop Vernon's wisdom and his way with words, she also appreciated the energy with which the Morning Star bishop addressed his congregation. His voice rang with enthusiasm as he told them the story of Jesus feeding the multitude that had gathered on the hillsides.

"With only a few little fishes and loaves of bread—certainly less food than we'll consume after church today—our Savior satisfied the hunger of more than four thousand people. And there were leftovers!" he exclaimed with outstretched arms.

"It was a miracle, for sure and for certain, and once again Jesus was showing those who followed Him that in God, all things are possible to those who believe—"

Leah sucked in her breath and sat very still, oblivious to the rest of Jeremiah's sentence. She'd felt a flutter deep inside. Could it be the baby moving? She closed her eyes and focused inward, praying for guidance.

This time the movement was more distinct, and Leah was filled with awe. The bishop might be expounding upon wondrous events of long ago and far away, but right here on the pew bench she was experiencing her own miracle. She'd witnessed birth dozens of times in barns and pens, yet now that she was the mother involved, the whole process took on a brilliance that rivaled the sun. Somehow Leah made it through the remaining hours of the service without exploding from sheer joy.

At long last, Bishop Jeremiah pronounced the benediction. "Do we have any announcements?" he asked with a knowing smile. "Any concerns or news about our family or friends?"

When Jude stood up with a boyish grin on his face, Leah met his brown-eyed gaze and fell in love with him all over again. "Guess you've noticed by now that Betsy has returned to us," he said happily. "And this time it's permanent—Leah and I will be adopting her."

Heads nodded and folks smiled at little Betsy, who now leaned against Leah's shoulder with an arm around her neck. When Betsy squawked, pleasant laughter filled the room.

"But that's not all!" Jude continued. "Our family will be welcoming a new Shetler come September, and we couldn't be more delighted."

This time folks applauded and took a second look at Leah, whose cheeks tingled with heat. The women seated near her grabbed her hand or grasped her shoulders, sincerely happy for her, and folks began standing up to congratulate her and Jude.

"Before we leave this room—before you men set up for

our dinner," Margaret said loudly, "we're not finished with announcements. Hush now, so everyone knows what's going to happen."

The murmurings ceased. All eyes focused on Jude and Jeremiah's *mamm,* who stood with a hand on her hip and an authoritative expression on her face.

Margaret smiled at Leah. "When Jude came over yesterday and told us Betsy had returned—with only the clothes on her wee back—Lenore and I decided to make this a Mother's Day we'd all remember by getting the word out and holding a baby frolic!" she exclaimed. "So while the menfolk are setting up the tables for a picnic outside, we gals can have a little hen party for you, Leah—"

"We brought along a big batch of bird's-eye cotton for sewing diapers after dinner!" Cora Miller called out.

"We shared most of our spare baby things last time Jude came asking for them," Rose Wagler remarked, "so we've also brought fabric for onesies and little dresses—"

"Not to mention another surprise we think you'll find useful," Mama chimed in from a couple rows in front of Leah. "But instead of talking about it, let's go out on the porch and take a look!"

"*Jah,* and we'll get out of the men's way while they handle the meal setup," Naomi put in with a laugh.

"Now wait just a minute." The district's deacon, Saul Hartzler, stood up with a scowl on his swarthy face, silencing the excited crowd. "This being Sunday, you women aren't to be doing such work as sewing—especially with a sewing machine."

"Ah, but this is a *frolic,*" Margaret countered quickly. "And my son the bishop gave me permission to organize this hen party, considering the circumstances Leah and Jude face now that Betsy's come back without any clothes or diapers."

Martha Maude Hartzler rose to address her son as well. "This is no different from you men giving feed and water to the livestock on Sunday," she pointed out. "Animals have to eat on the Sabbath, and babies have to dirty their diapers no matter what day of the week it is."

Laughter filled the room. As Leah situated Betsy in her basket, the women all began chattering excitedly as they headed outside. Leah welcomed the breeze as she stepped onto the porch, where Mama and Margaret were already standing with bright smiles lighting their faces. With a flourish they lifted a sheet that had been draped over some large, lumpy items that must've been positioned and covered after Leah had entered the house.

"A new washing machine!" she gasped as her hand flew to her mouth.

"*Jah*, with two wee ones in diapers, you'll be doing a lot of laundry," Mama explained. She was smiling as though she were the one receiving the gifts, probably because she and Margaret had so quickly organized this surprise party without Leah knowing about it.

So much for Mama going to Cedar Creek yesterday for her clothes and such, Leah thought. *She really went to the mercantile—maybe with Margaret and some of these other ladies.*

"We got lots of baby bottles, too, and a new pot for warming them on the stove," Delores Floud said, pointing at the box of items on the floor.

"And diaper pins and ointment and wipes—"

"And a new bassinet—"

"And the pillow and sheets to go with it—"

"And little stuffed toys—"

"And sippy cups and baby bowls—"

"Oh, my word," Leah said as she tried to keep up with the ladies' rapid-fire responses. She set Betsy's basket on the porch floor and approached the huge assortment of gifts these women—truly her friends now rather than just curious neighbors—had accumulated for her on very short notice. "I—I don't know how I can possibly thank you all for helping us yet again."

"It's what friends do, Leah," Anne Hartzler said gently. "Where would any of us be without other hens to cluck with when we need them?"

Leah smiled, unable to argue with that statement. The door banged behind them, and Stevie quickly made his way through the gathered women to stand beside her.

"Wow-ee!" he blurted out as he gawked at the items arranged on the porch. "It's even better than Christmas! We got stuff for Betsy—and we'll be ready for the new baby, too! But don't go sewin' a lot of pink stuff, coz it's gonna be a boy. I just know it."

The women laughed, and when one of them held the door open, the men began carrying long tables outside. Jude caught Leah's eye and came up beside her with two folding chairs in each hand. When he saw the assortment of gifts, he nodded.

"You ladies outdid yourselves—and I'm grateful for all your help on such short notice," he said. "If anybody deserves a party, it's Leah."

"Hear, hear!" Margaret said. "Any woman who can steer my granddaughters back onto the straight and narrow while taking on another girl's child—twice—gets my vote."

Leah gaped. Was this her mother-in-law, the same Margaret Shetler who'd made a cruel joke at the wedding about her inability to cook?

"*Jah*, Leah doesn't just sit around making tiny stitches in a quilt," Naomi put in with a nod. "She's out there *doing* things for people, and getting involved. I had my doubts about her ever getting along with Alice and Adeline, but I'm a believer now."

"My life—my family—would be a hopeless mess if Leah hadn't married me." Jude gazed at her with a wistful sigh. "Happy first Mother's Day, Leah. All these things piled on the porch are nothing compared to the gift of love you give me every day."

Leah was speechless. She saw envy on the faces of other

wives, while the twins and their friends were aglow with romantic wistfulness. Had there ever been another husband as attentive and expressive as Jude? Even Esther and Naomi were nodding their approval of his admission.

Another table came through the door, with Jeremiah carrying one end of it. He looked toward Leah and Jude with a warm smile. "I have a confession," he said to all the friends gathered on his big porch. "I was wrong—and I'm glad."

Folks glanced at one another with questioning expressions, waiting for the bishop to explain his odd admission. Jeremiah set down his end of the table so he could slip his arms around Jude and Leah.

"Remember that tough talk I was giving you the night before you married this woman, little brother?" Jeremiah asked. "I believed you were rushing into marriage with Leah, and I couldn't see any way for her to fit into your family. I stand corrected."

Leah felt her cheeks heating up as the friends around her nodded.

"You weren't the only one, son," Margaret chimed in. "I thought Jude was making the biggest mistake of his life because Leah bore no resemblance to our idea of what a wife should be like. Nobody's happier than I am that Leah has proved us wrong."

Jude began chuckling, and he elbowed his brother. "*Jah,* I recall your lecture the night before our wedding," he teased Jeremiah, "and *I* said that someday we'd look back on it and laugh, because Leah and I would be deliriously happy. Am I a prophet, or what?"

Leah chuckled, because she *was* deliriously happy. "Mama gave me the same sort of talk before we married, Jude—with the best of intentions," she added, smiling at her mother. "Considering all we've come through since that wedding on December first, I can only believe that God has made our life together—our happiness—possible. Without His blessing, we wouldn't be standing here sharing our joy with all these friends, looking forward to more happiness ahead. That's my story, and I'm sticking to it."

Jude's smile made Leah feel like the most beautiful woman on earth. "That's your story, and I wouldn't change a word of it," he murmured. "I'm just grateful that you've written me into it, sweet Leah."

More heartwarming Amish romance from
Charlotte Hubbard, available now!

A Mother's Love

Faith, tenderness, security—there's nothing a mother won't give. Now beloved author Charlotte Hubbard brings you an unforgettable tale of hope, courage, discovery . . . and the most precious gift of all.

For widow Rose Raber, it's been a year of tragic loss and difficult decisions. She thought providing for her young daughter was the greatest challenge she faced. Until her dying mother revealed that Rose was adopted—and her birth mother is someone with much to lose if the secret comes out. As Rose struggles to reconcile the truth with her faith—and her troubling curiosity—outgoing newcomer Matthias Wagler is another surprise she didn't expect. His optimism and easy understanding inspires her. And his prospective partnership with wealthy deacon Saul Hartzler promises a possible new life for them—together. But with this second chance comes yet another revelation for all involved.

When Saul's wife unexpectedly turns up at Rose's new job, their bond as mother and daughter is instant and unmistakable. And it isn't long before an unforgiving Saul discovers the truth, threatening Matthias's livelihood and Rose's future. Now with more than just their happiness at stake, Rose and Matthias must find the strength and courage to stand strong—and trust God's enduring miracles of motherhood, forgiveness, and love.

"An Amish love story with an added twist! This story has secrets, romance, mystery, and memorable characters. The storyline is well-written, and the twist makes it all even more believable. Hubbard writes from her heart, and her light shines in all her novels."

—RT Book Reviews, 4 Stars

"[An] endearing romance . . . By making a space for determined women inside the Amish community and providing a satisfying conclusion to various familial hurts, Hubbard provides readers with a comforting tale of love and forgiveness."

—Publishers Weekly

Chapter 1

Rose Raber looked away so Mamma wouldn't see the tears filling her eyes. As she sat beside her mother's bed, Rose prayed as she had every night for the past week. *Please, Lord, don't take her away from me. . . . I believe You can heal my mother's cancer—work a miracle for us—if You will.*

Tonight felt different, though. Mamma was dozing off more, and her mind was wandering. Rose had a feeling that Mamma might drift off at any moment and not come back.

"Was church today?" Mamma murmured. "I don't . . . recall that you and Gracie . . . went—"

"We stayed here with you, Mamma," Rose reminded her gently. "I didn't want to leave you by yourself."

Her mother sighed. As she reached for Rose's hand, Rose grasped it as though it could be a way to keep Mamma here—to keep her alive. They didn't speak for so long, it seemed Mamma had drifted off to sleep, but then she opened her eyes wide.

"Is Gracie tucked in?" Although Mamma's voice sounded as fragile as dry, rustling leaves, a purpose lurked behind the question.

"*Jah,* she is, but I'll go check on her," Rose replied, eager for the chance to leave the room and pull herself together. "All that fresh air from planting some of the garden today should make her sleep soundly."

"Gracie was . . . excited about doing that. She asked me . . . how long it would be before the lettuce . . . peas, and radishes shot up." Mamma chuckled fondly, remembering. Then she gazed at Rose, with her eyes fiercely bright in a face framed by the gray kerchief that covered her hairless head. "When you come back, dear, there's something we . . . must discuss."

Rose carefully squeezed Mamma's bony hand and strode from the bedroom. Out in the hallway, she leaned against the wall, blotting her face with her apron. Her five-year-old daughter was extremely perceptive. Gracie already sensed her *mammi* was very, very ill, and if she saw how upset Rose had become, there would be no end of painful questions—and Gracie wouldn't get back to sleep.

The three of them had endured a heart-wrenching autumn and winter after a fire had ravaged Dat's sawmill, claiming Rose's father, Myron Fry, and her husband, Nathan Raber, as well. The stress of losing Dat had apparently left Mamma susceptible, because that's when the cancer had returned with a vengeance, after almost thirty years of remission. The first time around, when Mamma was young, she'd survived breast cancer, but this time the disease had stricken her lungs—even though she'd never smoked.

With the family business gone, Rose and Gracie had moved into Mamma's house last September. Rose had sold her and Nathan's little farm so they would have some money to live on—and to pay Mamma's mounting bills for the chemo and radiation, which had kept her cancer manageable. Until now. Rose had a feeling that this date, April third, would be forever emblazoned on her heart, her soul.

Little Gracie has lost so many who loved her, Rose thought, sending the words up as another prayer. She composed herself, took a deep breath, and then climbed the stairs barefoot. She peeked into the small bedroom at the end of the hall.

The sound of steady breathing drew Rose to her daughter's bedside. In the moonlight, Gracie appeared carefree—breathtakingly sweet as she slept. Such a gift from God this daughter was, a balm to Rose's soul and to her mother's as well. For whatever reason, God had granted Rose and Nathan only this single rosebud of a child, so they had cherished her deeply. Rose resisted the temptation to stroke her wee girl's cheek, feasting her eyes on Gracie's perfection instead. She'd seen some religious paintings of plump-cheeked cherubim, but her daughter's innocent beauty outshone the radiance of those curly-haired angels.

Rose quietly left Gracie's room. Standing in her daughter's presence had strengthened her, and she felt more ready to face whatever issue Mamma wanted to discuss. Rose knew of many folks whose parents had passed before they'd had a chance to speak their piece, so she told herself to listen carefully, gratefully, to whatever wisdom Mamma might want to share with her. Instinct was telling her Mamma only had another day or so.

Pausing at the door of the downstairs bedroom, where Mamma was staying now because she could no longer climb the stairs, Rose sighed. Mamma's face and arms were so withered and pale. It was a blessing that her pain relievers kept her fairly comfortable. When Mamma realized Rose had returned, she beckoned with her hand. "Let's talk about this before I lose my nerve," she murmured. "There's a stationery box . . . in my bottom dresser drawer. The letters inside it . . . will explain everything."

Rose's pulse lurched. In all her life, she'd never known Mamma to keep secrets—but the shadows beneath Mamma's eyes and the fading of her voice warned Rose that this was no time to demand an explanation. Rose sat down in the chair beside the bed again, leaning closer to catch Mamma's every faint word.

"I hope you'll understand . . . what I've done," Mamma mumbled. "I probably should have told you long ago, but . . . there just never seemed to be a right time—and I made promises—your *dat* believed we should let sleeping dogs lie."

Rose's heart was beating so hard she wondered if Mamma

could hear it. "Mamma, what do you mean? What are you trying to—"

Mamma suddenly gripped Rose's hands and struggled, as though she wanted to sit up but couldn't. "Do *not* look for her, Rose. I—I promised her you wouldn't."

Rose swallowed hard. Her mother appeared to be sinking in on herself now, drifting in and out of rational thought. "Who, Mamma?" Rose whispered urgently. "Who are you talking about?"

Mamma focused on Rose for one last, lingering moment and then her body went limp. "I'm so tired," she rasped. "We'll talk tomorrow."

Rose bowed her head, praying that they would indeed have another day together. She tucked the sheet and light quilt around Mamma's frail shoulders. It was all she could do. "*Gut* night, Mamma," she whispered. "I love you."

She listened for a reply, but Mamma was already asleep.

Rose was tempted to go to Mamma's dresser and find the mysterious box she'd mentioned, but desperation overrode her curiosity. She couldn't leave her mother's bedside. For several endless minutes, Rose kept track of her mother's breathing, which was growing slower and shallower now, as the doctor had said it would. He had recommended that Mamma stay in the hospital because her lungs were filling with fluid, but Mamma had wanted no part of that. She'd insisted on passing peacefully in her own home.

But please don't go yet, Mamma, Rose pleaded as she gently eased her hands from her mother's. *Stay with me tonight. Just one more night.*

Exhausted from sitting with Mamma for most of the past few days and nights, Rose folded her arms on the edge of the bed and rested her head on them. If Mamma stirred at all, Rose would know—could see to whatever she needed.

In the wee hours, Rose awakened with a jolt from a disturbing dream about two women—one of them was Mamma, as she'd looked years ago, and the other one was a younger woman Rose didn't recognize. They were walking away from her, arm in arm, as though they had no idea she could see them—and didn't care. Rose called and called, but neither woman turned around—

"Oh, Mamma," Rose whispered when she realized she'd been dreaming. Her heart was thumping wildly and she felt exhausted after sleeping in the armchair beside her mother's bed. She lit the oil lamp on the nightstand. "Mamma? Are you awake?"

Her mother's eyes were open, staring straight ahead toward the door, but they didn't blink when Rose gripped her bony shoulder. Mamma's breathing was so much slower than it had been yesterday, and in the stillness of the dim room, the rasping sound of each breath was magnified by Rose's desperation.

Rose stared at her mother for a few more of those labored breaths, trying again to rouse her. Mamma's expression was devoid of emotion or pain. She was unresponsive—as the doctor had warned might happen—and Rose curled in on herself to cry for a few minutes. Then she slipped out to the phone shanty at the road.

"Bishop Vernon, it's Rose Raber," she said after his answering machine had prompted her. "If you could come—well, Mamma's about gone and I . . . I don't know what to do. *Denki* so much."

Rose returned to the house with a million worries running through her mind. Soon Gracie would be awake and wanting her breakfast and—how would Rose explain that her *mammi* couldn't talk to her anymore, didn't see her anymore? How could she manage a frantic, frightened five-year-old who would need her constant reassurances for a while, and at the same time deal with her own feelings of grief and confusion? All the frightened moments Rose had known this past week, when she'd thought Mamma was already gone, were merely rehearsals, it seemed.

"Oh, Nathan, if only you were here," Rose whispered as

she walked through the unlit front room. "You always knew what to do. Always had a clear head and a keen sense of what came next."

Rose paused in the doorway of the room where Mamma lay. Her breathing was still loud and slow, and the breaths seemed to be coming farther apart. Rose hoped it was a comfort to Mamma to die as she'd wanted—even though it was nerve-racking to Rose. There had been no waiting, no doubts, the day she and Mamma had returned from shopping in Morning Star to discover that the sawmill had caught fire from a saw's sparks. The mill, quite a distance from any neighbor, had burned to the ground with her father and husband trapped beneath a beam that had fallen on them. Their men's deaths had been sudden and harsh, but quick. No lingering, no wondering if she could be doing some little thing to bring final comfort.

Once again, Rose sat in the chair beside Mamma's bed, and then rested against the mattress as she'd done before. The clock on Mamma's dresser chimed three times. It would be hours before the bishop checked his phone messages. Rose didn't want to rustle around in the kitchen, for fear she'd waken Gracie, so she placed a hand over her mother's and allowed herself to drift. . . .